new uses
for old
boyfriends

Center Point
Large Print

Also by Beth Kendrick and available from Center Point Large Print:

Cure for the Common Breakup
The Week Before the Wedding
The Lucky Dog Matchmaking Service

**This Large Print Book carries the
Seal of Approval of N.A.V.H.**

new uses for *old* boyfriends

Beth Kendrick

CENTER POINT LARGE PRINT
THORNDIKE, MAINE

This Center Point Large Print edition is published in the
year 2015 by arrangement with NAL Signet,
an imprint of Penguin Publishing Group,
a division of Penguin Random House LLC.

The text of this Large Print edition is unabridged.
In other aspects, this book may vary
from the original edition.
Printed in the United States of America
on permanent paper.
Set in 16-point Times New Roman type.

ISBN: 978-1-62899-522-0

Library of Congress Cataloging-in-Publication Data

Kendrick, Beth.
New uses for old boyfriends / Beth Kendrick. —
    Center Point Large Print edition.
  pages cm
  Summary: "After growing up in privilege and marrying into money,
Lila Alders has gotten used to the good life. But when her happily-ever-
after implodes, Lila Alders returns to Black Dog Bay, the tiny seaside
town where she grew up and struggles to reinvent herself"—Provided
by publisher.
  ISBN 978-1-62899-522-0 (library binding : alk. paper)
  1. Single women—Fiction. 2. Large type books. I. Title.
  PS3611.E535N49 2015b
  813′.6—dc23
                                                    2014049679

For my mother,
who believes that I can do anything . . .
and makes me believe it, too.

Acknowledgments

Thank you to . . .

Robert, Jen, and the "couture curators" at Fashion by Robert Black in Scottsdale, Arizona. Your knowledge and passion for timeless style breathed life into this story.

Marcia Pierce at Sew Creative, who told me all about dress design, repair, and the power of perspective.

Janine and Whitney Yates, who shared wit and wisdom about the realities of real estate.

Barbara Ankrum, Kresley Cole, Marty Etchart, Amy and Jason Serin, and Chandra Years. You are living proof that the world is full of love, magic, and second chances.

new uses for *old* boyfriends

Chapter 1

The last thing Lila did on her way out of town was sell her wedding rings.

When she arrived at the pawnshop, she looked flawless—she'd made sure of that before she left her custom-built brick house for the last time. Her honey blond hair was freshly straightened, her nails impeccably manicured, her blush and mascara tastefully applied. Her blouse matched her skirt, her shoes matched her handbag, and her bra matched her panties because, as her mother had always reminded her, if a terrible accident should ever befall her in a grocery store parking lot, she would be on display to a whole team of paramedics and hospital workers.

But as she pulled her diamond rings out of her purse, all Lila could think about were the things that didn't look right. The dark roots that were starting to show where her hair parted. The visible tension in her face from months of clenching her jaw at night. The pale stripe on her finger where her rings had been. And even worse than the flaws she couldn't hide were the ones she could. Out in the parking lot, her white luxury SUV awaited. Spotless and brand-new and jam-packed with the last remnants of her life she'd managed to salvage from the divorce.

For a solid two minutes, Lila kept her hands in the pockets of her stylish rose pink trench coat and listened to soft jazz on the sound system while the store employee scrutinized every facet of the diamonds. Beneath the glass display case, rows of rings sparkled in the light, each one representing a promise exchanged by two people coming together in trust and faith and hope. Lila tried to imagine the men who had proposed with these rings: rich and poor, old and young, each of them in love with a woman they believed to be as unique and dazzling as these jewels.

And they had all ended up here: the relationship boneyard. An "estate jewelry" storefront sandwiched between a dry cleaner and a pet groomer in a suburban strip mall.

The clerk finally looked up, clicking her tongue. "The setting's very dated, but the stone itself is decent."

Lila blinked. "Dated? Decent? That ring was on the back cover of *Elle* magazine the month I got engaged."

"And how long ago was that?"

"Well. Seven years." Lila squinted to read the employee's name tag and tried a different approach. "Norma. I appreciate that you have a business to run and a family to support, but look at the cut and color of this diamond! The stone was imported from Antwerp, the setting is really quite classic—"

"If I've learned one thing in this business, it's that everything goes out of style eventually." The saleswoman lowered her loupe and tilted her head, her gaze shrewd. "The whole 'timeless classic' line? It's a marketing myth."

"But the cut." Lila cleared her throat. "It's exquisite."

Norma lifted one corner of her mouth. "Do you happen to have the GIA certification papers?"

"Not anymore." Lila knew she was being assessed for weakness. How desperate was she for cash? How much did she value this touch-stone of her past?

What was the bare minimum she would accept?

She should lift her chin and meet the other woman's gaze, but she couldn't. She'd been completely depleted—of confidence, of certainty, of the will to stand up for herself.

"We can sell the diamond, but the setting will have to be melted down and refashioned." Norma put on her glasses, picked up her pen, and wrote a few numbers down on the pad in front of her. "Here's what I can offer you."

Lila glanced down at the figure and swallowed back a sigh.

"I know it's probably not what you were hoping for, but the fact is, diamonds just don't hold their value." Norma's tone was both apologetic and insincere.

"But that's less than a third of what my husband paid for it." Lila hated how tentative and soft she sounded. Then she corrected herself. "My *ex*-husband, I mean." She flattened her palm on the cool glass case and tried to rally as she stared at the number written on the pad.

You can do this.

She knew better than to accept an opening offer. She needed to negotiate.

You have to do this.

But she glanced up at the jeweler through lowered eyelashes, her eyes watering and her lip trembling. All the fight had been drained out of her. The spark inside had flickered out.

"I . . ." Lila trailed off, cleared her throat, forced herself to start again. "I'll take it." The amount wasn't enough to save her, but she needed every bit of cash she could get right now. So she let go of all her old hopes and dreams and prepared to take the money.

Norma half smiled, half sneered. "Let me write you a check."

An electronic chime sounded as the shop's door opened; then a shrill feminine voice rang out. "Holy crap! You're Lila McCune. I love you! I'm your biggest fan. Marilyn Waters." A short, windblown woman in a green turtleneck shook Lila's hand, squeezing tightly.

"I can't believe this! Do you live around here?"

"Until recently." *Like this morning.*

Marilyn turned to the jeweler and demanded, "Did you know she's a celebrity?"

Norma's sneer got a little sneerier. "No."

Lila bowed her head. "Oh, I'm not really—"

"She was the late-night host of my favorite shopping channel for three years." Marilyn turned back to Lila. "You probably don't recognize my voice, but we've spoken on the air. I called in a few times, and you were so nice. You made me feel good about myself when I was fat and hormonal and losing my damn mind."

Lila was beaming as she struggled to reclaim her hand. "It's a pleasure to meet you in person— I love connecting with callers. What were some of your favorite items?"

"Oh, Lord, I bought so many things. When I was up with my first baby, I watched you every single night. I was exhausted and healing from a third-degree tear, but your show was really soothing. This woman can sell anything to anyone," Marilyn informed the jeweler. "Crystal Christmas tree ornaments and fancy French sauté pans and this amazing cream that gets rid of the calluses on your heels. Works like magic. Would it be okay if I take a quick picture with you?"

"Of course." Lila summoned her cheeriest, camera-ready smile.

"One more, just in case." Marilyn clicked her

camera phone three times in rapid succession. "I can't wait to put this up on Instagram! My sisters are going to be so jealous."

While Marilyn fiddled with her phone, Lila sidled over to Norma and murmured, "Make the check out to Lila Alders, please. A-L-D-E-R-S."

Norma raised one finely penciled brow. "I thought you were Lila McCune?"

"I was. Now I'm back to my maiden name."

Marilyn clicked off social media and rejoined the conversation. "So, what happened, Lila? You're not on the air anymore."

"My contract was up, and, um, my agent and I decided it was time to transition." Lila's jaw ached. "I'm exploring some new opportunities."

"Ooh! Like what?"

"Like . . ." Lila had never been so happy to hear her phone ring. "Would you please excuse me for a moment? I have to take this." She pressed the phone to her ear and walked toward the front window. "Hi, Mom."

"Where are you right now?" her mother demanded.

"I'm at the engagement ring boneyard."

"The where?"

"I'm selling my rings."

Her mother made a little sound of disappointment. "So you won't be here for dinner?"

"No. Sorry I'm running late; it took me forever to pack up the car and then I had to drop

16

by my attorney's office to pay off my balance."

"Well, now you can put it all behind you." There was a pause on her mother's end of the line. "Did you get a good price for the rings, at least?"

"No." Lila forced herself to relax as her temple started throbbing.

"How much?" Her mother's voice stayed light and airy, but Lila detected an urgent undertone. "Approximately?"

"Why do you ask?"

"Oh, no reason." Another pause. "We'll talk about it when you get here."

"Talk about what?"

"Nothing. Drive safe, sweet pea. I can't wait to see you." Her mother hung up before Lila could say anything else.

When Lila returned to the glass counter, Marilyn was frowning and nibbling her lower lip while Norma examined a hair comb fashioned of tarnished metal.

Lila stepped closer to Marilyn and asked, "What's that?"

"It's a hair comb," Norma said flatly.

"It belonged to my great-aunt," Marilyn confided. "And her mother before her. It's not really my style, but I thought maybe we could find a buyer who would really appreciate it. Stuff like this should be worn, you know? Doesn't do me any good collecting dust in a drawer."

"It's beautiful." Lila peered over Norma's shoulder. The comb was shaped like a flower atop two thin prongs. "What's it made of?"

"Steel. Dates back to the early eighteen hundreds." Norma sounded disapproving. "Not interested."

Marilyn's whole body folded in a bit. "But it's vintage."

Norma remained impassive. "Worth a hundred bucks, max. Try listing it on eBay."

Marilyn took back her family heirloom with evident shame.

"Well, *I* love it." Lila straightened her shoulders. She ran her fingers along the faceted edges of the flower's petals. The steel had been cut like a gemstone, designed to look dainty despite its strength.

"You do?" Marilyn's voice was barely a whisper.

"Absolutely. Tell you what—I'll give you two hundred dollars for it." Lila opened her wallet, realized her current net worth stood at thirty-seven dollars and three maxed-out credit cards, and closed her wallet. "Let me go cash this check really quick."

The sparkle returned to Marilyn's eyes. "Keep your money. Just give me your autograph and we'll call it even. It will be such a thrill to know that somewhere out there, *Lila McCune* is walking around wearing my great-aunt's comb."

"Oh, I couldn't—"

"I insist." Marilyn gave a little hop of glee.

Lila accepted the metal comb and slid the prongs into her hair. "Thank you, Marilyn. I'll make sure it always has a good home."

"I want it to be with someone who loves it." Marilyn shot a hostile look at Norma. "Someone who understands that everything doesn't have to be made out of platinum to be worth anything."

For the second time in ten minutes, Lila's eyes welled with tears. She hugged Marilyn, said thank you a dozen more times, and hurried back out to the parking lot before she lost her composure.

The woman on TV who kept you sane in the middle of the night isn't supposed to have a nervous breakdown in the middle of the afternoon.

The prongs of the metal comb were biting into her scalp, and she reached up and pulled it out of her hair, then unlocked her car with a click of her key fob.

"Oh, Lila, wait!" Marilyn's voice called. "If I could just trouble you for one more thing before you go."

Lila startled. In her hasty attempt to shove the comb back into her hair, her thumb hit the button to open the SUV's back gate.

A jumble of linens, clothes, shoes, books, file boxes, and a lamp tumbled out onto the asphalt.

Marilyn stopped midstride and looked down at the mess, then back up at Lila with an expression that was equal parts shock and pity.

"I'm transitioning," Lila explained in her perky, late-night shopper voice as she picked up a fragment of the shattered stained-glass lampshade. "I'm considering my options."

Chapter 2

Steady, pounding rain drenched the windshield of Lila's SUV as she made the drive to Black Dog Bay, Delaware. The night sky was starless, the roads were treacherous, and Lila stayed in the right-hand lane of the highway, praying that she wouldn't skid on an oil slick or scrape a guardrail or misjudge her braking speed.

She wanted to turn on the radio and take a sip of coffee from the travel mug resting on the console, but she was too afraid to release her death grip on the steering wheel.

Buying this car had been a mistake; she could admit that. A huge mistake. Almost as huge as the vehicle itself.

Once upon a time, in her heyday of hawking callus cream on late-night cable, she had driven a sporty little black coupe. She'd never given a second thought to issues like braking speed or turning radius.

And then, ten months ago, her father had died. And after the funeral, she'd come home to the news that her producers had opted not to renew her contract. Six weeks later, her husband had explained that, while he would always love her on some level, he was not actually *in* love with her. Because he was in love with someone else.

The morning after Carl broke the news that he was abandoning her for something new, Lila had decided she deserved something new, too. And Carl deserved to pay for it. She'd stalked out of the house, roiling with rage, and driven to the nearest auto dealership.

"I want the biggest car you have on the lot," she told the first salesman she saw. "Fully loaded: leather seats, sunroof, power everything."

The salesman didn't miss a beat. "Backseat DVD player?"

"Sure, why not?" she'd replied, though she had no children. She didn't even have a dog. There'd be nothing in her backseat but baggage after Carl sold the house she'd spent five years decorating with custom flooring and fabric and furniture.

"Do you have a color preference?" the salesman asked as he led her toward a line of shiny new vehicles.

"No." She pulled out her checkbook. "Let's

just get this done before my husband closes the joint accounts."

And that was how she'd ended up with this all-wheel-drive behemoth with an interior large enough to set up a pair of sofas and a coffee table. This sumptuous, super-safe SUV—or, as she privately referred to it, the "FU"-V.

She'd driven back home in a spurt of renewed optimism, feeling invincible.

Then she'd turned into the circular driveway in front of their stately brick home and realized that she had blind spots the size of a small planet and insufficient clearance to maneuver the vehicle into the garage. She'd had to park outside and slink in to face the scorn of the man who'd vowed to love her in sickness and in health, for richer or for poorer.

Except that man hadn't been waiting for her in the house. He'd vanished, taking his laptop and golf clubs with him, leaving a certified letter from his accountant explaining that because his businesses had been "gifted" to him by his father, she wouldn't be entitled to any portion of his company's equity or revenue going forward.

All her outrage and optimism sputtered out after that, followed quickly by her savings, because Carl did indeed freeze the joint accounts.

But she still had this FUV, cocooning her within steel crossbars and countless air bags as she cruised down Coastal Highway 1. She had a world of comforts at her disposal—heated leather seats, climate control, enough cup holders to accommodate a case of cola, and, of course, the backseat DVD player. She'd signed the purchase agreement thinking that she was buying a guarantee of safety and protection.

Ding.

She instinctively tapped the brake as she glanced at the dashboard. An orange alert light in the shape of an exclamation point was blinking. She had no idea what that meant, but she knew it was bad.

Reminding herself to stay calm, she tried to watch the road ahead and maintain her speed.

One hazard light wasn't the end of the world. She could call Triple A. How did the Bluetooth system work, again?

Ding.

Another light illuminated—this time, the engine temperature alert.

Ding.

The oil level alert.

Ding.

The battery life alert.

BEEP BEEP BEEP.

The antitheft alert blared to life at eardrum-shattering decibels.

Lila didn't realize she was yelling until she heard the sound of her own voice in her ears in the split-second pauses between beeps and dings.

Her fingers gripped the steering wheel so tightly her wrists trembled. She tried to focus on the road, but all she could see in front of her was a cluster of red and orange lights, announcing crises she hadn't even imagined.

She glimpsed a gas station on her right and swerved into the parking lot, skidding on the wet pavement and jumping the curb in her haste. For a moment, she worried the enormous hulk of machinery would simply topple and roll over, but it righted itself with a shudder.

The cacophony of beeps and dings continued. She threw the transmission into park and started jabbing at buttons on the dashboard and key fob. Nothing changed—the lights kept blinking, the alarms kept blaring.

She heaved the door open and jumped out, stumbling on the retractable assist steps that automatically unfolded.

"Shit!" She fell into a gasoline-scented puddle. Though she managed to catch herself with her hands, the water splashed onto her cheeks and collar.

The car alarms kept sounding.

She grabbed the edge of the massive metal hood and pulled. Nothing budged. She could barely see at this point; her hair was plastered to her face in the icy downpour.

"Stop." A calm, authoritative male voice filtered through all the honking and dinging. A hand pressed down on her shoulder. "Give me your keys."

Shaking and breathless, she whirled around to face a man wearing a baseball cap and a dark wool jacket. He smiled at her and held out his palm.

Lila hesitated for a moment, worst-case scenarios flashing through her mind. If she handed over her keys, this guy could steal her car. She'd be stranded here, shivering and alone.

Without the three-ton vehicle that she could barely drive.

Good.

She pointed toward the driver's side door. "They're in the ignition."

The man stepped onto the metal ledge, reached into the SUV's cabin, and cut the engine.

Everything stopped at once—the dinging, the honking, the panic and despair.

Lila listened to the raindrops spatter against the pavement during the long, lovely pause.

Then the engine rumbled to life again as the man turned the keys in the other direction.

She started to protest, but the words died on her lips when she realized that she could *hear* the engine now. She could also hear the steady squeak of the windshield wipers. All the alarms had been silenced.

And the guy that had done the silencing was now staring at her.

She took a faltering step back.

He kept right on staring. "Lila?"

She took another step back.

He took off his hat, and suddenly those features fell into place in her memory. The brown eyes and thick hair and the deep, teasing voice. "Lila?"

"Ben?" She clapped a hand to her mouth, suddenly aware of how bedraggled she must look. "Ben!"

Without another word, he opened his arms to her and she ran to him, closing her eyes as she pressed her cheek against his shoulder. It had been years since he had held her, but she suddenly felt sixteen again, hopeful and shy but safe.

"What are you doing here?" Something about the way he asked this made her wonder how much he'd glimpsed of the FUV's contents.

"I promised my mom I'd come stay with her through the summer," she mumbled into his jacket. "She's been having a hard time with everything."

His arms tightened around her. "I heard about your dad. I'm so sorry. He was a great guy."

"Yeah, it's been a tough year. But we're hanging in there." She looked up at him.

He cupped her chin in his hand. "It's so great to see you."

"What about you?" she asked. "I thought you were still in Boston."

"I moved back last month. I'm taking over my dad's company. We're starting some new projects down by Bethany Beach."

She was grinning now, not her camera smile but her real smile. She knew she looked toothy and ridiculous, but she couldn't stop.

Because the first boy she'd promised to love forever was smiling down at her with what could only be described as adoration. "You changed your hair."

She nodded. "I went blond a few years ago."

"It looks great. You always look great, Lila."

"Oh, please." She pulled away, trying to straighten her hair and her shirt and her earrings all at once. "I'm a drowned rat."

Ben shook his head. "You get prettier and prettier. Listen, here's my card. We should get together sometime and catch up."

She forced her lips into a more demure expression as her mother's voice resounded in her head: *Don't be too eager. There's nothing a man likes more than a woman who has other options.* "Thanks. I'd like that."

"You're staying with your mom?"

She nodded.

"Take it easy on the drive into town, and get your car checked out, okay?" He nodded at the SUV. "This model has a lot of electrical problems. Probably a short somewhere."

"How do you know?"

"My foreman used to have the same car. Emphasis on *used to*."

Lila climbed back into the FUV, buckled her seat belt, and just sat for a few minutes. Relishing the heated seats and warm air gusting out of the vents. Watching the dashboard for any more emergency lights.

Reeling from the unexpected gift she'd just been given.

Finally, she put the FUV into gear and started back down the highway to her hometown. And five minutes later, when she passed the quaint clapboard sign adorned with the silhouette of a Labrador retriever—WELCOME TO BLACK DOG BAY—she removed one hand from the wheel, turned on the radio, and scanned through the static until she found a song she could hum along to.

Maybe coming home wouldn't be so bad, after all.

Chapter 3

As if on cue, Cake's "Short Skirt/Long Jacket" came on as Lila piloted the FUV toward Main Street. The bass line brought back a flood of memories: drinking diet soda in the cafeteria, stretching her hamstrings before cheer practice, pinning corsages to the velvet bodices of her formal dresses.

She hadn't heard this song since high school. She'd barely been back to Black Dog Bay in the last ten years, except for the occasional summer weekend and her father's memorial service. Once she left for college, her parents had always been happy to come to her for visits and vacations. Her mother, in particular, had welcomed any opportunity to get out of small-town Delaware and meet her daughter for restaurant Thanksgivings in New York and Philadelphia. They'd had Christmases in Colorado, Easters in West Palm Beach and the Bahamas, August getaways in Maine and Vermont.

But even though she'd barely set foot here in ten years, she knew exactly what to expect. This town was her safety net, her fallback plan, her last resort she could always depend on when the rest of the world failed her. As she drove down Main Street, she recognized the familiar standbys: the candy shop that sold hand-pulled saltwater taffy, the Eat Your Heart Out bakery, the white gazebo and bronze dog statue in the town square. Of course, a few businesses had changed hands since she'd graduated from high school. The old ice cream shop had been replaced by an antique store. The diner where she and her friends had hung out on Friday afternoons had been deposed by a bar called the Whinery. There was a bookstore now, and a boutique called Retail Therapy.

But everything important, the essence of Black Dog Bay, remained unchanged.

And Ben was back.

As the first wisps of fog rolled in from the sea, Lila pulled up in front of the huge white house where she'd grown up. Her father had built this home as a wedding present for her mother, and her mother had spent the past three decades customizing the mansion on the beach. Over the years, the eighties architecture and decor had been remodeled to reflect a more historical sensibility, and now, thanks to endless updates, the house looked as if it had been there for centuries.

A bronze-accented light glowed warm and bright on the wraparound porch. Lila parked the FUV on the gravel driveway, left her belongings in her car, and sprinted through the rain to the house.

Before she could make it up the wooden steps, her mother flung open the front door. Even in a bathrobe, Daphne Alders looked perfectly put together. She had modeled in New York for several years before she got married, and she'd never lost her sense of chic, her smooth complexion, or her lithe physique.

"Sweet pea!" Daphne threw both arms around her daughter. "You're here!"

"I'm here." Lila closed her eyes and breathed in

the faint notes of jasmine from her mother's perfume. "I made it." When she opened her eyes, she glanced around the foyer and living room. Her mother had gone on another redecorating binge. Lila recognized the abstract bronze sculpture on the mantel and the vintage candelabra hanging from the ceiling, but the living room wallpaper—finely woven grass cloth that looked almost like burlap—was definitely new, as was the retro gray settee that looked like it had been stolen from the set of *Mad Men*. But everything somehow worked together, punctuated by green glass vases of white hydrangeas, to create a balanced, beautiful tableau.

"Thank goodness. I've been waiting all night for you." Daphne pulled out of the hug, grabbed a stack of mail from the hall table, and handed the pile to Lila. "Here. You'll know what to do with these."

"I will?" Lila shuffled through the stack, glancing at return addresses from utility companies and banks and health insurance corporations.

"Your father paid all the bills online, and you know I'm hopeless with a computer."

Lila flipped over an envelope. Some of the postmarks were from months ago. "You haven't opened any of these?"

"I just can't bear to. You know the finances were your father's department."

"Yes, but what about the attorney? I thought you had set up a trustee?"

Daphne dabbed at her eyes. "And the registration for his truck is due. I have no idea how to renew it."

"Oh, well, we can just—"

"And the water heater's broken."

"The water heater?" Lila stopped thumbing through the stack of envelopes.

"Yes. The pilot light's out and I need to take a shower and I can't deal with one more thing right now. You'll handle it, won't you? Oh, I'm so glad to see you, sweet pea. Your father was right—he always said you'd take care of me."

Lila pressed her back against the bathroom door, dabbing the sweat off her forehead with a fluffy white hand towel made from the finest Egyptian cotton.

She could hear her mother bustling around the kitchen, making tea and cutting up a single apple, which was Daphne's idea of a decadent late-night snack. The water heater was still inoperable, but Daphne's relief was evident. Because her daughter was here to take care of everything.

Lila rattled off a string of obscenities into the Egyptian cotton and resolved to be the daughter her mother needed her to be. She had been fired from the land of late-night TV shopping and ruthlessly litigated out of her marriage, so helping her mother was her full-time job for now. She would strive to uphold the image her father had always had of her as the gifted golden child. She would use whatever weapons she had in her arsenal.

She would fix this damn pilot light if it was the last thing she did.

After splashing her face with cold water, she emerged from the powder room with what she hoped was an air of calm capability.

"Let's take a look at the water heater."

Daphne offered her an apple slice, then handed over a three-ring binder labeled "House Instructions."

"What's this?" Lila flipped through the laminated papers, which were full of notes and diagrams in her father's blocky handwriting. There were colored dividers marked "bathroom," "kitchen," "furnace," and "A/C system."

"Dad left you a book of instructions?"

Daphne broke into tears. "He put that together years ago, so I could do things like light the pilot lights when he was out of town."

That was typical of her father—always taking care of "his girls." Lila waited for the wave of emotion to pass, then asked, "So you must have dealt with this stuff before, right?"

"No. I always just waited until he came back to fix it or called one of the neighbors."

And this time, her father wasn't coming back.

Lila closed her eyes for a moment, then forced them open and flipped to the page marked "water heater." She found her father's explanation of how to rekindle the pilot light and read it several times. "Okay . . . okay . . . This doesn't look so hard."

Her mother regarded her with a mixture of hope and despair. "So you can do it."

"Yes." Lila took a deep breath. "I think I can do it."

"I can't do this." Fifteen minutes and two singed fingers later, Lila gave up.

"But you're following the instructions."

"I know! Which is why the pilot light should be lit." Lila, crouched on the epoxy-coated cement floor in the garage, shoved her sweat-drenched hair back from her face. "And yet."

Her mother collapsed against the hood of the pickup truck with expired tags and started to sob.

"Don't cry, Mom. Don't cry." In desperation, Lila flicked the cigarette lighter's spark wheel one more time. But she couldn't even get a flicker of flame.

"What are we going to do now?" Daphne choked out.

Lila considered this for a long moment, then resigned herself to the inevitable. "Now we move on to plan B. How late is the hardware store open tonight?"

"How on earth would I know? I've never set foot in the hardware store."

Lila led the way back into the house and checked her watch: quarter to ten. "Well, let's hope they're open till ten, because there might be someone there who can talk me through this." She located her handbag on the kitchen counter. When she pulled out her phone, a white business card fluttered out.

Daphne snatched it up. Her jaw dropped when she spied the name embossed on the card. "Ben Collier?"

Lila's mood lifted at the memory. "Yeah, he's back in town. I just ran into him at the gas station out on Highway One."

Daphne's shock turned to horror. "Looking like that?"

"Well, I wasn't all sweaty, obviously." Lila recounted their reunion, leaving out the part where she had been drenched with rain and reeking of gasoline.

"Why didn't you tell me this earlier?"

"Because I got distracted with the water heater drama. Now let me call the hardware store before—"

"Forget the hardware store." Daphne's dark eyes gleamed. "You're calling Ben Collier."

"Mother. No." Lila grabbed for the business card.

Daphne skittered out of reach, putting the

limestone-topped kitchen island between them. "Yes! Don't you see, Lila? This is a sign. You and Ben, back together after all these years. It's perfect. It's meant to be!"

Lila held up both palms. "No way. I am not calling him to fix the water heater when he had to fix my car two hours ago."

"Fine; *I'll* call him."

At this, Lila planted her hands on her hips. "Don't you have any shame?"

"I don't need shame. I need hot water." Daphne picked up the landline and started dialing. "Now stop talking back and go clean yourself up. Your hair's a mess, your fingernails are filthy, and you need to change your shirt. That shade of pink is too pale for you."

Chapter 4

In the twenty minutes it took Ben Collier to arrive at the Alderses' front door, Daphne managed to comb out Lila's hair, shape her eyebrows, apply fresh foundation and mascara, and outfit her in a low-cut red top.

"This is overkill," Lila protested. "I look like Scarlett O'Hara about to throw herself at Ashley Wilkes."

"Stop talking and hold still so I can put on your lipstick." Daphne hummed a little tune while she selected a shade from her vast array of lip color options. The master bedroom featured a makeup alcove separate from the bathroom, and mirrors and lighting had been strategically located around the vanity table.

"I thought you always said I shouldn't call boys." Lila tried to talk without moving her lips. "That it makes me look desperate."

"If *you* called Ben, it would look desperate. But when *I* call him, I'm just a helpless widow in need of rescue." Daphne exchanged her bathrobe for a cream georgette tunic and black leggings. "And he's such a nice boy, he couldn't have been sweeter about it."

"Appalling." Lila stuck out her tongue at her relentlessly well-lit reflection. "Do you really not see how embarrassing this is? For me to fall over my high school boyfriend the second I get back to town?"

"Don't worry." Daphne slipped a chunky gold statement necklace over her head. "I'll do the talking. You just make a cameo when I tell you, then make yourself scarce. Always leave him wanting more." Daphne stopped humming. "Are you aware that your roots need a touch-up?"

"I'm aware," Lila said. "I'm also aware that I look like a hussy in your shirt."

"Don't blame me for that. You're the one who

shoved all your clothes in a wrinkly heap in the back of your car."

The doorbell rang and Daphne flitted downstairs. As instructed, Lila remained up in the master suite, waiting for her cue.

"Ben Collier!" Daphne's voice soared up to the handmade French chandelier hanging above the open foyer. "Come in, honey! It's so great to see you again and you're just as handsome as ever. How *are* you?"

Ben's reply was lost in a flurry of Daphne's high-pitched exclamations.

"I can't tell you how happy I was to hear you're back in town. How's your sister? Where are you staying?" Without even pausing for breath, Daphne half turned and called up the grand, curving staircase. "Lila, baby, look who's here!"

Lila made her appearance at the top of the stairway, waving and smiling down. Ben looked up, so much taller and stronger and stubblier than she remembered, and smiled back.

And the old feelings came rushing back. The giddy anticipation of dates on Friday nights. The thrill of breaking curfew. The warmth and pride of knowing that she was young and beautiful and worthy of adoration.

And yes, she had been a cheerleader and Ben had played varsity football. Yes, they had been elected prom queen and king their senior year. Yes, they embodied every cheesy high school stereotype. So what? That hadn't detracted from the sincerity of their feelings. Their love had been pure and strong and steadfast.

Maybe her mother was right. Maybe feelings like that never really went away.

Lila tucked her hair behind her ear and mouthed, "Thanks" at this stranger she had once gone parking with in her mother's Mercedes.

He threw her a charming, heart-melting smile, and winked. Then he turned his attention back to Daphne, who chattered all the way into the garage.

"Our Lila's a celebrity now, you know. A *very* popular shopping channel host on a *very* popular station. Doesn't she look stunning as a blonde?"

Four minutes later, the water heater was working and Daphne's dossier on Ben Collier was up-to-date.

Mrs. Alders sent him off into the night with a kiss on the cheek and a promise that he'd let her bake him cookies in gratitude. The moment the door closed behind him, she beckoned Lila down to the foyer. "He's single, he's taking over his father's property management company, and he's renting a house by the golf course for the summer. Never married, no kids. His manners are still excellent, he's got a good sense of humor, and he knows his way around a toolbox. You officially have my blessing."

Lila blinked. "For what?"

"For living happily ever after." Daphne dusted off her hands and headed back to the kitchen. "Now, I know second weddings are supposed to be subdued, but we could host the whole thing here at the house. You could wear my ecru Alexander McQueen coatdress, very tasteful."

Lila laughed. "Easy on the marriage talk. I just finished paying off my divorce lawyer, remember?"

Daphne's smooth forehead wrinkled with worry. "You didn't say that to him, did you?"

"No, but I'm not going to lie about it. I'm divorced. It's a fact. I know you don't like to think about or talk about it, but it's the truth."

"Sweet pea, I just don't want you to dwell on it." Daphne's brow furrows deepened. "And divorce, well, it's so unpleasant. It makes people uncomfortable. Part of being a good conversationalist is putting people at ease."

"I know, I know." Lila had heard that phrase repeated a thousand times since childhood. "But before you call the florist and the caterers, keep in mind that he hasn't even asked me out."

"Only because your mother was standing right here."

Lila opened the refrigerator and scanned the shelves for a snack. "Promising to bake him cookies. Yes, I heard that. You are shameless. Not to mention a liar."

"How dare you! I'm a wonderful baker."

"Really. You know what I see in your refrigerator? Bottled water, eight kinds of lettuce, coconut oil, and yams. You know what I don't see? Butter, eggs, anything with refined sugar or white flour."

"Fine, so I won't bake cookies. But I'll let him marry my daughter. He's coming out ahead."

Lila grimaced as she dug through stacks of spelt bread in search of a bagel. "I'm done with this conversation."

"Just promise me one thing. If he does ask you out, promise me you'll say yes."

Lila gave up foraging and decided to choke down a slice of spelt bread. "I don't have to promise that."

"Now you're being contrary. Why wouldn't you go out with him? Don't try to tell me the old flame isn't still burning."

Lila kept her head hidden behind the refrigerator door so her mother wouldn't see her grin.

"Wait and see." Daphne opened the cabinet doors and handed Lila a plate. "I'll try not to say I told you so. But we both know you loved him."

"I did love him." Lila paused, trying to sort through all the nostalgia and trepidation. "When I was sixteen. But it's been like thirteen years. He's probably a totally different person."

"Haven't you learned by now?" Daphne turned her eyes to heaven. "Men don't change."

"I'm going to bed." Lila managed two bites of spelt bread, then decided she'd rather go hungry. "But before I do, why did you ask about how much I got for my rings?"

Daphne was suddenly consumed with the need to empty the dishwasher. "Oh, just curious."

Lila moved closer. "Are you having cash flow problems?"

"Don't be ridiculous." Daphne hunched lower, fiddling with the silverware rack. "I merely happened to be thinking about money this afternoon because I was looking over my property tax bill, and—"

"I thought you didn't open the mail."

Daphne practically climbed into the top-of-the-line, stainless steel Bosch. "Let's talk about all this tomorrow. I'm desperately tired, and I need a hot shower and a good night's sleep."

"But—"

"See you in the morning." Daphne kissed her cheek and fled up the stairs.

"Tomorrow," Lila said. "We're going to talk. Summit meeting. State of the Union."

"Sweet dreams!" Her mother's voice echoed down the hall.

Lila cupped both hands around her mouth and called, "What time for the summit meeting?"

All she heard in response was the slam of a bedroom door and the hiss of the shower water.

Chapter 5

After spending the night in her childhood bedroom (her mother had replaced the girlish white furniture and bulletin boards with an elegant four-poster bed, custom pink and white linens, and a series of black-and-white lithographs), Lila felt more disoriented than ever. Clad in pink pajama pants and a T-shirt emblazoned with the logo from her high school cheerleading squad, she padded down the stairs to grind and brew strong black coffee for her mother, a task her father used to perform without fail.

Everything was the same, yet undeniably different—this house, her mother, the entire town of Black Dog Bay. Everywhere she looked, she saw framed photos of the girl she used to be, so self-assured in her tutus and tiaras, blessedly unaware that her lifelong winning streak would come to an end and her future would turn out nothing like what she envisioned.

While she sat in the huge white kitchen listening to the steady drip of coffee, Lila closed her eyes and *felt* the presence of her father. The foundation he'd laid and the load-bearing beams he'd installed were still here beneath all the imported limestone and woven wall coverings. He'd been the bedrock of the family, always steady and determined to stay the course. Though the house had been his grandest labor of love, he'd also demonstrated his devotion in smaller, more mundane ways. Bringing coffee to Daphne every morning before he left for work. The time he'd indulged eight-year-old Lila's request to decorate a rental house's bathroom in pink and purple polka dots.

That house had become famous with vacationers over the years. Families who made annual pilgrimages to the shore would ask the rental agent for the house with the pink and purple bathroom. Her father had bragged about this, declaring his daughter a brilliant businesswoman.

She'd been in crisis mode for the past few months, so consumed by the divorce and the loss of her job that she hadn't really had time to grieve her dad. But here in the kitchen, where she'd shared so many meals with him, her heart finally caught up with her head.

She sat motionless in the cold, pale dawn, trying to absorb the enormity of her loss, until she smelled the coffee starting to burn. Then she pulled herself together, tamped down her sorrow and despair, and got busy with pouring and planning and preparing for everything still to come.

• • •

"I can't go," Daphne declared when Lila knocked on the door and announced she had sweet-talked her way into the first available appointment with the financial trustee. "I have nothing to wear."

Lila put the coffee mug on the nightstand, sat on the edge of the bed, and gazed up at the white-washed oak ceiling beams of the guest room. The view from this side of the house wasn't nearly as impressive as the oceanfront vista of the master suite, but Daphne said she couldn't bear sleeping alone in the bedroom she'd shared with her husband for decades.

"Now, Mom," she said pleasantly, the very voice of reason, "I'm sure that if we go through your closet together, we can find something perfect for a day of financial planning. Maybe a power blazer? A few pinstripes? What do you say?"

Daphne pressed her hand against the varnished walnut headboard and closed her eyes against the sunlight filtering in through the curtains. "I have nothing, Lila. Nothing."

Lila picked up the mug and took a sip of coffee. "Let's just look."

Big, breathy sigh. *"Nothing."*

Lila nodded, her molars grinding as she maintained her chipper facade. "Tell you what. You stay here. I'll go peek in your bedroom closet and find a few options."

"Don't treat me like a child and don't you dare paw through my closet." Daphne went from indolent to incensed in the blink of an eye. She pushed off the headboard, hopped out of bed, and hurried down the hall toward the master bedroom. "I'm perfectly capable of putting together an outfit."

Lila trailed behind her, trying to figure out where she'd gone wrong.

"And I don't need fashion tips from someone wearing baggy flannel pants, thank you very much."

"I was trying to help." Lila remained doggedly cheerful as she crossed over to the closet. "Sometimes it's fun to pick out stuff together. Remember that time we—"

"Don't!" Daphne cried before Lila could grasp the doorknob.

Lila froze, stricken by the panic in her mother's voice. "Don't what?"

"Don't open that door."

Lila pulled her hand back, her eyes huge. "Why not?"

Daphne's whole face tightened. "Because I told you not to, and I'm your mother."

"But—"

"Don't argue with me." Daphne pointed to the door. "Step away from the closet."

Lila kept her hands up as she slowly moved aside.

"Must I remind you that I am a grieving widow?" Daphne fluffed her sleek brunette bob, which looked camera-ready right out of bed. Must be an ex-model thing. "You have to mollycoddle me and let me have my way."

But her mother didn't sound grief-stricken at the moment. She sounded bossy and sharp and a little bit fearful.

Lila raised one eyebrow.

Daphne took her daughter's elbow and hustled her back toward the mirrored vanity table. "Bea good girl and change the subject, won't you?"

Lila narrowed her eyes but complied. "Fine. What do you want to talk about? And don't say Ben."

"Fine. Let's talk about your other friends."

It took Lila a few moments to admit the truth: She didn't have a lot of girlfriends. Not anymore. Over the past ten years, she'd given up her single social life to be part of the perfect power couple. She and Carl had couple friends, and when Carl left her, many of the wives patted her hand sympathetically but said they didn't want to choose sides. She'd told them that of course she understood. She didn't want anyone to feel awkward or uncomfortable. Even in the court-ordered mediation sessions, she'd smiled and spoken softly and comported herself like a lady . . . and then gone home and sobbed in the shower. "I haven't really stayed in touch with anybody from high school."

"But you were the most popular girl in your class." Daphne seemed a bit anxious at the thought that this might no longer be the case. "Stacie and Christa and Valerie still live nearby. You should call them and have lunch."

"I haven't seen Val since her wedding, and Stacie gave up on me a few years ago. I didn't even get a Christmas card from her last December. It would be weird, calling them out of the blue after all this time."

"They'd be delighted to hear from you," Daphne said. "Remember how much fun the four of you used to have together?"

Lila glanced down at her cheerleading shirt and softened. "I'll think about it."

"Good." Daphne cleared her throat. "Because you're having cocktails with them at the country club at four."

"What?"

"I made some calls last night." Daphne picked up a tiny bottle of oil and started ministering to her cuticles. "Valerie still lives right here in town, Stacie moved to Rehoboth Beach, and Christa works up by Dover, but she said she'd be happy to take the afternoon off and come catch up."

Lila sat down on the edge of the bed. *"What?"*

"Don't take that tone with me, young lady. I

spent two hours on the phone with their mothers arranging all this." Daphne looked offended. "A simple 'thank you' might be in order."

"I am a grown woman. I do not need you to arrange *playdates* for me."

"Of course you don't. I'm just trying to help." Daphne's mood was improving by the moment. "Getting out and about will do wonders for your confidence. Although you really should try to get your highlights touched up before you go." She glided over to Lila and peered down with concern. "What's the matter, pumpkin?"

Lila literally bit her tongue and forced herself to count to twenty before she replied. "I cannot believe you did that."

Daphne's enthusiasm ebbed away. "I didn't mean to . . . I just wanted to surprise you. I thought you'd be thrilled."

Lila started back at zero, counted to twenty again, and then kept right on counting.

"I only wanted to make you happy." Her mother was wilting before her very eyes. "They're your friends. I thought you might want to have some fun and chat with someone who isn't your mother."

Thirty-eight, thirty-nine . . . "I'll go," Lila ground out. "Thank you for thinking of me. I'll go. But no deal on the highlights. I'm in a bit of a cash crunch; I don't have the budget to constantly go to the salon anymore."

Daphne scoffed. "There's always enough money for highlights."

"There's actually not." Lila glanced out the side window toward the driveway. "My net worth consists of a heap of wrinkly clothes and a car that's trying to kill me."

"Look at the time." Daphne glanced at the clock and got to her feet. "No more putting it off—we've got to get ready. Run along and get changed."

Lila lingered in the doorway.

Daphne took the coffee mug back. "Yes? May I help you with something?"

"What's in your closet?"

"None of your business."

"Come on. Just tell me!"

"No."

"Why not?"

"Because." Daphne dabbed eye cream onto her face. "You don't get to know every single thing about me, that's why. Believe it or not, there's more to me than just being your mother."

As soon as she glimpsed the receptionist's face, Lila braced herself for bad news.

The interior of the estate attorney's office was tasteful and subdued with lots of dark wood, tufted leather furniture, potted plants, and a woman with pearl earrings and a chignon stationed at a desk. She glanced up when Lila opened the door, and Lila recognized the emotions flickering across the woman's face. Pity. Condolence. The urge to soften the blow.

Lila had seen the same look in Carl's eyes in the weeks before he announced that their marriage was over. It took all of her self-control not to turn around and walk back out of the office.

But her mother sat down on a long, low leather sofa against the wall, so Lila forced herself to approach the receptionist.

"Hi. We're here to see Mr. Walther." She nodded over at her mother, who was listlessly flipping through a magazine. "Daphne Alders."

"Of course." The woman focused on her computer keyboard and avoided direct eye contact. "He'll be with you in a moment."

The sky had been dark and gloomy all morning, and the first few droplets of rain splashed onto the windows. Her mother flipped through an old issue of *Architectural Digest*. "What do you think of this wallpaper? For the upstairs hallway?"

Lila glanced at the nubby, oyster-colored swatch. "Didn't you just redecorate the upstairs?"

"The bedrooms, not the hallway," Daphne replied. "And that was eighteen months ago. The wallpaper, sweet pea. What do you think?"

"I think I'd rather spend my imaginary money on highlights."

"Don't be a spoilsport." Daphne's smile didn't

reach her eyes. "Maybe after this, we can go to that home decor shop in Rehoboth Beach and look at upholstery fabric and rugs. Go crazy and buy some drawer pulls."

"Let's worry about the property tax bill first, okay?"

"Let's not worry at all." Daphne turned to the next page. "Money matters always work themselves out in the end."

Lila half coughed, half laughed. "Um."

"Remember what your father always used to say: 'If you can solve the problem with money, it's not a real problem.' "

"Mr. Walther is ready for you." The receptionist stood up and motioned for Lila and Daphne to follow her through a doorway. "Go right in."

"We have a real problem here and it's time to address it," the estate attorney said as he shuffled a stack of papers. "This isn't going to be an easy conversation. Mrs. Alders—"

"Oh, Richard, stop with the 'Mrs. Alders.' " Daphne smoothed the crisp folds of her skirt. "I'd say we're well beyond that by now, wouldn't you?"

"Daphne." Mr. Walther's smile was sad and sympathetic. "Your estate is . . . well, it's in the red."

Lila froze, her posture perfect. "Excuse me?"

She stared at her mother. Her mother stared at

the lawyer. The office was so quiet that she could hear the faint whoosh of air circulating through the ceiling vents.

Richard cleared his throat and consulted the paperwork. "May I speak frankly?"

Daphne settled back in her chair and sighed.

"Please do," Lila said.

"When your father died, he left behind substantial debts. Most of the business loans can be discharged, but the personal loans have to be repaid and your mother and I have had several conversations about downsizing her lifestyle and reconfiguring her budget."

"Wait, how much debt are we talking about here?" Lila turned to her mother. "I thought everything was going great. Dad's business made it through the recession—he never said a word about loans. And I know you've never said a word about downsizing."

"Because I'm fine." Daphne's voice was high and thin. "I'm the parent and you're the child. I don't need a guilt trip from you right now."

Lila threw up her hands. "I'm not giving you a guilt trip. I'm just trying to figure out—"

"Let's look at the portfolio." Richard pushed a folder across the desktop. "Let's focus on the numbers."

Lila set her jaw and inched forward in her seat.

"Bill's construction business never recovered

after the recession, and he took on a lot of secured debt trying to salvage the company."

"He did?" Lila glanced at the contracts and spreadsheets in the portfolio.

"He did."

"And you knew about this?" she asked her mother.

Daphne shrugged one shoulder. "Your father didn't like to talk about money."

Lila gripped the chair's carved wooden armrests and addressed the attorney. "So there were business problems."

"Add that to the outstanding credit card debt, the maintenance and taxes on the primary residence, the line of credit leveraged on the house, and the liquidated investments, and it's . . ." The lawyer cleared his throat. "It's not very promising, from a financial standpoint."

Lila looked back at her mother. Her mother gazed out the window. "You did know about this."

She nodded.

"And it's been going on for a year now."

"You had just lost your father, and then you lost your job, and then that nasty legal battle with Carl . . ." A single tear slid down Daphne's cheek. "I didn't want to worry you."

"Since when did you take out a home equity loan?" Lila asked. "And credit card debt! Weren't you the one who gave me a big lecture about the dangers of high interest payments when I left for college?"

"Stop yelling at me! I already feel terrible!" Daphne broke into sobs.

Richard raised his index finger, calling for calm. "Your mother and I have had several discussions about her current cash flow and the need for economy."

"I see." Lila folded her arms. "And how is that going?"

Daphne kept crying.

Lila took a deep breath. "So where are we right now?"

"There are no remaining assets to speak of," the attorney said. "And very little investment income."

Lila glanced over at her mother. "But what about all the rental houses?" Lila examined one of the financial documents, but couldn't make sense of what she was looking at. "The retirement accounts?"

"Your father liquidated everything trying to salvage his business," Mr. Walther said. "I did advise him at the time that he'd be better off declaring professional bankruptcy and safe-guarding his personal property, but I believe it was a point of honor. He very much valued his reputa-tion in the community."

"Of course he did," Daphne snapped. "He was the best builder in Black Dog Bay."

"Bill and I had several meetings about the state of his financial affairs before he died." Richard handed a tissue to Daphne. "He kept hoping things would turn around once the real estate market recovered."

"But they didn't." Lila flinched as she heard her jaw joint click. "So now what?" She released her death grip on the chair, reeling at the implications of this. She was shocked, of course, and angry that her father had hidden this from his family, but she also tried to imagine the crushing sense of responsibility he must have felt, charged with taking care of his daughter and wife. His success had become a matter of routine and expectation. He had always been the bedrock, the hero, the provider. "We have a property tax bill to pay. Among a lot of other things, apparently."

"You're in a financial state of emergency," the attorney declared.

"Okay." Lila kept studying the legal documents as if the answers to all of life's problems were buried in the tiny rows of text. "What's the first thing we have to do to turn this around?"

"To be blunt, turning things around isn't an option. Daphne, you're going to have to sell the house—"

"Never." Daphne jumped back into the conversation. "Absolutely not. I'm not selling the house."

"He's saying we don't have a choice," Lila pointed out.

"I spent thirty years pouring my heart and soul into that house. I just updated the living room this fall. Selling it is out of the question, and I won't hear another word on the subject."

Lila made eye contact with the attorney. "No way to save the house?"

He raised an eyebrow at her. "I assume you're not in a position to assist your mother financially at this time?"

Lila felt her cheeks flush. "That would be a correct assumption."

"Well, there's no need to call a real estate agent today." He shot a sidelong glance at Daphne, who was blithely ignoring them. "I do think, though, that action should be taken sooner rather than later. Because, given the monthly expenses and the debts your mother is already responsible for—"

"We're screwed." Lila shot to her feet. "Got it."

"This is obviously an emotional time." The lawyer adjusted the knot in his tie. "Why don't the two of you take a day to collect your thoughts, come to a decision about the house, and—"

"The decision is made," Daphne said. "I'm not selling the house."

Richard gave Lila a look and handed her a stack of folders.

Lila accepted the paperwork and gathered up her coat and handbag. "Mom? We're going."

Daphne waited for the attorney to stand up,

walk around the desk, and help her put on her sable-trimmed black coat. Then mother and daughter walked back through the waiting room and out of the office.

Finally, once they'd pushed through the building's glass doors to the wind and cold rain, Lila trusted herself to speak. "I need a few minutes alone."

Daphne dabbed at her eyes with the wadded tissue. "I think that's a good idea. Take some time to process everything before you meet the girls at the country club."

Lila pivoted on her heel and rounded on her mother. "Are you insane? I'm not going to the country club to have cocktails right now."

Daphne held her ground. "You have to. Canceling would be rude; everyone will be so disappointed. What will people think?"

"Sorry; I got my priorities screwed up for a second there." Lila let out a dry little laugh. "Who cares what's really going on? All that matters is what people will *think*."

Daphne drew herself up to her full, formidable height. "Lila Jane Alders—"

"I know, I know." And Lila did know, before her mother could say the words, what she should focus on. The fact that her friends, whom she hadn't seen in over ten years, had taken time off work to drive to Black Dog Bay to see her. They deserved to be greeted by the warm and bubbly girl they remembered, not a bitter and penniless divorcée. Lila would meet everyone's expectations of her; she always did.

After all, she had learned from the best.

She turned back to the FUV and offered her hand to her mother. "Watch your step. I'll drop you off at home."

"Thank you." Despite her imposing stature, Daphne looked smaller than Lila had ever seen her. "And I'm sorry. For everything."

Lila kept her gaze on the asphalt. "I know."

"I don't know how I ended up here."

"Me, neither."

Daphne settled into the passenger seat with her handbag in her lap. "But don't let this ruin your day. Go to the club. Have fun." She leaned forward and rubbed her index finger against Lila's cheek. "There. Your blush wasn't quite blended."

"Thanks."

"Oh, and you've got the tiniest little blemish on your chin." Daphne rummaged through her purse. "Not to worry—I've got the most amazing concealer. By the time I'm done with you, you'll look flawless."

Chapter 6

Lila sauntered into the Gull's Point Country Club at four o'clock sharp, selected a seat at the bar, and waited for her friends to show up.

Ten minutes later, she was still waiting.

When the bartender asked what she'd like to drink, Lila had a stroke of brilliance. "Yes, I'll have four"—she had to look away to finish the sentence—"sex on the beaches, please."

"Oh, you're here!" A familiar voice rang out behind Lila. "Sorry I'm late; traffic was a nightmare."

"You guys better not have started without me!" another voice cried. "My son was a beast when he woke up from his nap, and the sitter had to pull him off me like a barnacle from a battleship."

"I'm here, I'm here!" chimed a third voice. "It's not like I could ever be on time in high school, so why should real life be any different?"

Lila turned around and threw herself into a giggly, weepy, four-way hug. The first few minutes of the reunion was a blur of squealing and exclaiming over how fantastic everybody looked. Christa's long, wavy hair had been cropped into a sassy shag; Stacie's trademark red lipstick had been replaced by a more subdued shade of rose; Val had let two of the four holes in her earlobe close up. They all looked a bit more buttoned-up and a lot more tired than they had twelve years ago. But they were still friends. They could pick up right where they left off.

The bartender approached, bearing a tray with four peachy pink cocktails. "Here you go, ma'am."

"What is that?" Christa stared at the frosty glasses.

"I'm surprised you don't recognize our signature drink from high school." Lila wagged her finger at them. "Shame on you."

Val burst out laughing. "Sex on the beach? Oh my God!"

"How could I have forgotten?" Stacie groaned at the memories. "We thought we were sooo sophisticated."

Christa picked up one of the drinks and sniffed it suspiciously. "What's in these things, anyway?"

"Vodka and juice and, like, peach schnapps."

"I thought it'd be fun." Lila raised her glass. "For old times' sake."

"I actually can't drink." Val made a face. "Still breast-feeding."

Christa nibbled her lower lip. "I have to drive all the way back to Dover, and I'm such a light-weight."

"I have to leave early so I can finish up a presentation for work." Stacie shook her head ruefully. "Kids and jobs have ruined our social lives."

"Let's have iced tea and talk fast." Val signaled the bartender, then gave Lila a quick kiss on the cheek. "So, how long are you going to be in town, lady?"

"I'm not sure." Lila folded a paper napkin into little triangles. "I'll be here through the summer, helping my mom."

"And then?" Stacie prompted. "Doesn't your viewing public need you back?"

"We'll see. My agent's been lining up a few auditions." Lila's agent had been lining up auditions for months now, for increasingly smaller and more obscure jobs. Lila had shown up early, schmoozed with the casting directors, networked like mad, but the feedback had been increasingly negative:

She's too generic.

She's too short.

She's too old.

"Do you have your own fan club?" Christa grinned. "I always knew if any of us ended up famous, it would be you."

"Lila Alders, living the dream."

Lila laughed weakly. "Not really."

"Oh, please." Stacie looked wistful as she sipped her iced tea. "You did just what you always said you would—moved to the big city and broke into show business."

"Our lives are so boring by comparison." Val dipped her napkin in her water glass and patted a blobby stain on her cardigan. "You're wearing silk and I'm wearing spit-up stains."

Stacie smiled sympathetically. "Chase still has reflux?"

"We don't know what it is." Val frowned. "Now the pediatrician is saying it might be an allergy or maybe dairy intolerance."

"I'll keep my fingers crossed it's not an allergy," Christa said. "Those are so hard to deal with once the kids start school. Although my niece has a serious tree nut allergy, and they've done a great job managing it at her preschool."

Lila sat back, sipped her iced tea, and tried to contribute to the conversation, which bounced from teething to elementary school districts to corporate benefit packages to upcoming wedding anniversaries.

"Eight years!" Val gushed. "Can you believe it's been that long?"

"What are you and Troy going to do to celebrate?" Lila asked.

"Well, at first we wanted to go to the Caribbean. But that's so expensive, and it's hard to be away from the kids so long, so then we thought maybe Florida. And then Troy's boss left and he's up for promotion, so we'll be lucky to squeeze in a weekend in North Carolina."

"Make the time," Stacie advised. "I know it's hard when your babies are little, but if you don't . . ." She trailed off as everyone's gazes slid toward Lila. "Oh. Sorry, Lila, I didn't mean . . ."

"Of course not!" Lila waved this away with manic energy. "It's fine."

"You're just lucky you didn't have kids with your ex," Stacie opined. "That makes divorce so much harder."

"And it makes you a much better dating prospect," Christa said. "A lot of guys don't want to date a woman with kids. But you're so pretty and fun, you'll be remarried in a hot minute."

"Here's to that!" Val trilled. They all clinked glasses.

"Speaking of which . . ." Stacie motioned everybody in. "What's going on with you and Ben Collier?"

Lila glanced away from the trio of inquisitive faces. "Um . . ."

"Don't play coy. Word's all over town that he's back and you're back and the epic love story of our time is going to have a second chapter."

Christa gasped. "I didn't hear this part! Damn work getting in the way of my gossip. Why is Ben in town?"

"Oh, I think we all know why." Everyone nudged one another and giggled and looked at Lila.

"Remember how you guys used to go to the bonfires on the beach after every football game?"

"Remember when Ben sent all those roses to you in homeroom on Valentine's Day?"

"Remember how devastated you were when you guys decided to break up?"

"Even your breakup was better than everybody else's," Christa marveled. "The perfect breakup for the perfect couple."

"And now, the perfect reunion."

"You guys." Lila felt herself blushing. "He's just here to oversee some retail construction."

"Oversee, nothing. He's inheriting a real estate empire," Val informed everybody. "His dad's company does residential and commercial development, and they've done very well." She shot Lila a meaningful look. "*Very* well. You should snap that man up while the snapping's good."

"Have you talked to him yet?" Stacie demanded.

Lila nodded. "Just for a few minutes."

"And . . . ?"

"And he said he was going to call me."

More squealing and hand clasping.

"But he hasn't actually called," she hastened to add.

"Oh, he'll call."

"Absolutely."

"How many kids do you think you'll have? He's going to be such a great dad."

Lila rolled her eyes. "You guys are worse than my mom."

"You know who else I heard is back?" Christa said. "Malcolm Toth."

Lila tried to place the name. "Who?"

"Malcolm Toth," Christa repeated. "He was in our class."

"Oh, that quiet guy?" Stacie nodded. "Yeah, I think he joined the army or something after graduation."

Lila shook her head. "Don't remember him."

"Yeah, you do. Didn't you go out with him once sophomore year? Before you and Ben got together?"

Lila shook her head. "No."

"Well, his sister lives here, too. Her baby goes to the Montessori center my cousin just opened down by the elementary school."

Which sparked a spirited debate on the merits of Montessori versus Reggio Emilia. After another thirty minutes, everyone started making noises about work deadlines and sitters and Lila picked up the check, just as she always had in high school. No one else even reached for it.

"We should do this again," Christa said.

"Definitely." Val tapped away at her cell phone.

Stacie started hugging everyone again. "We should do this every month."

But after five minutes of poring over their schedules, they couldn't manage to find a free evening for the next cocktail hour. So the old friends disbanded, making vague promises to text one another and keep in touch.

"No one wants to stay here and have a real drink with me?" Lila cajoled as everyone gathered up their briefcases and diaper bags.

Everyone shook their heads and headed back to their busy lives, leaving Lila alone with the bill and four watery sex on the beaches.

"I haven't had one of these since high school." She smiled at the bartender and took a sip, then almost gagged at the sweetness. "And now I remember why." She surveyed the sedate, elderly clientele seated in the dining room. "Listen, is there someplace to get a margarita around here where I won't run into anybody who knows me and/or my mother?"

"There's a new wine bar on Main Street." The bartender wrinkled her nose in distaste. "Very touristy, very pink. Ben Collier wouldn't be caught dead there."

Lila blinked. "You know about me and . . . ?"

The bartender nodded. "Everyone knows. You're the talk of the town."

"The Whinery, you say? Full of booze, devoid of ex-boyfriends?" Lila handed over her credit card and prayed that the transaction would go through. "Then that's my next stop."

Chapter 7

The first person Lila saw when she walked into the Whinery was Tyler Russo, whom she had dated throughout the fall semester of her freshman year of high school. His linebacker physique looked even bulkier now, and she could glimpse the beginnings of a bald patch at the crown of his floppy brown hair, but his face was still boyish and his baggy jeans appeared to be the exact same ones he'd worn to Black Dog Bay High School fifteen years ago.

He put down the cardboard crate he was carrying when he saw her. "Lila Alders, is that you?"

"It's me." She forced herself to smile and wave, even though she wanted to duck and cover.

Tyler looked her up and down, and for a moment, his eyes flickered with longing and admiration. "I heard you were back in town."

"Yep, here I am." She held up her arms.

"Huh. You look different."

Her whole body screamed for a margarita. "It's the hair. I went blond."

"No, it's more than that. You look a little . . . tired."

"That, Tyler, is an understatement." Lila glanced around at the decor, which was so pink and frilly, it would make a sorority house seem butch by comparison. A sparkling crystal chandelier hung just inside the entrance, little silver candy dishes brimming with chocolates lined the glossy black bar top, the sound system was playing "Walking After Midnight" by Patsy Cline, and a chalkboard advertised a drink special called "Cure for the Common Breakup" in curlicued script.

"You work here?" she asked Tyler, thinking back to the days when he wouldn't even wear red because it was "too girly."

"Nah, I'm a wine distributor." He handed her a business card.

"Second Star Spirits and Wines," she read. "Nice."

"Yeah. My cousin owns it, but I'm going to buy in as a partner next year." He pulled a bottle out of the box. "Here. You like Cabernet? This is a great Napa blend."

"Thank you." She resisted the urge to pull the cork out with her teeth and guzzle the contents on the spot, opting instead to tuck the bottle into her oversize leather satchel. "So you're doing well?"

"Can't complain." Nor could he hide the boastful note in his voice. "Went to college in Wilmington; wife's an accountant. We've got a three-year-old daughter who just started pre-school." He pulled up a picture on his phone, and Lila oohed and aahed and counted the minutes until she could politely excuse herself and go have a nervous breakdown in the ladies' room.

"What about you?" Tyler asked. "I heard you were a famous talk show host in New York City?"

Lila leaned over and grabbed a miniature Reese's peanut butter cup from the nearest silver candy dish. "Not exactly. It was a home shopping cable affiliate in Philadelphia."

"Still, you were on TV. You must be pretty rich, huh?"

Lila didn't even finish the first peanut butter cup before she unwrapped the second one. "Yeah, not so much."

"Really? But last time I saw your mom, she said—"

The last vestige of Lila's perky politeness disintegrated. "You want to know what I've been doing since high school? I've been marrying the wrong man, selling people overpriced crap they don't need in the middle of the night, and using all the money I earn to buy Botox and personal training sessions and fancy furniture for the humongous house I lost in the divorce."

Tyler backed away, holding up the box of wine as if to shield himself. "Well, I've got some cases of wine to unload—"

"And now I'm broke and moving back in with

my mother so I don't have to live in the SUV that I bought for spite, and the highest hope anybody has for me is that I might get back together with the guy I dated when I was sixteen." Lila shoved the second peanut butter cup into her mouth and leaned forward to show him her dark roots. "Look at my hair, Tyler. Let this hair be a cautionary tale."

Glass bottles clinked as he shifted the case of wine. "Uh . . ."

"Remember when we read *Walden* in Mrs. Turner's English class?"

He took another step backward. All the longing and admiration had vanished from his eyes. "Yeah."

"Remember how Thoreau went on and on about quiet desperation? *That's* what I've been doing since high school. Living a life of quiet desperation."

She heard rustling on the other side of the bar, and then a female voice said, "Sounds like someone needs a drink."

Lila looked up to find a tall, willowy woman with choppy platinum hair, sparkling blue eyes, and an unmistakable *joie de vivre.*

"Lila Alders, this is Summer Benson. Summer, this is Lila. Bye." Tyler escaped out the door.

Lila saluted him as he went. "There goes one ex-boyfriend I'll never hear from again."

"Nice to meet you, Lila." Summer strolled

around to the other side of the bar. "Let me mix you up a glass of something delicious and highly alcoholic."

"Beat it, Benson." A petite brunette with curly hair emerged from the back room. "Stop pretending you work here."

"I do work here," Summer shot back. "Sooner or later, you'll come to accept that."

"You know, it's funny, but I don't seem to remember ever paying you a dime. Get out from behind my bar or I'm telling Dutch you violated health code regulations."

"Go right ahead." Summer offered up her cell phone. "I violate health code regulations with Dutch every day."

The bartender laughed and shooed Summer away. Then she offered a handshake to Lila. "Hi, I'm Jenna. I actually own this place, despite what Summer here would have you believe."

"Hi." Lila cleaned her chocolate-stained fingers with a pink cocktail napkin before shaking hands. "Sorry, I'm not usually this . . . disheveled."

"Have some M&M's," Summer advised as she sat down next to Lila. "You look like I felt when I first showed up in town."

"Don't exaggerate. No one looks as bad as you did when you first got here." Jenna addressed Lila. "Think translucent zombie with dead eyes and poor driving skills. Although, you both had the blond-hair-dark-roots thing happening."

"Rebound Salon, two blocks thataway." Summer pointed down the street. "Cori and Alyssa will fix you right up. Tell them I sent you."

Lila nodded, deciding to spare them the whole *Walden* spiel.

"Is this your first visit to Black Dog Bay?" Summer popped a Hershey's Kiss into her mouth. "We'd be happy to show you around."

"Oh, I'm not a tourist. I grew up here."

The Whinery's front door opened and a tall, coltish teenager with unruly russet hair poked her head in. "Hey. Stop socializing, you guys. Summer's got to be home at six thirty. Family dinner."

"That's Ingrid Jansen," Jenna explained to Lila. "Summer's sister-in-law-slash-stepdaughter. Sort of. It's complicated."

"It's only complicated because she and my brother insist on living in sin instead of getting married like regular people," Ingrid informed the room at large. "They're setting a bad example."

"We're doing family dinner tonight?" Summer checked the calendar on her phone. "Is Dutch home from that conference already?"

"No, but *I'm* home. And I'm making spaghetti squash with marinara sauce, so you'd better be there." Ingrid gave Summer a stern look.

"Fine. But if this turns out anything like your coconut creamed kale, I'm getting pizza."

Jenna waved to Ingrid. "Can I get you something, honey? Iced tea? Fresh orange juice?"

"No, thank you. I'm on my way to the bookstore. It's Tuesday, and you know what that means—new release day. Hollis said she has some recommendations for me." Ingrid leveled her index finger at Summer. "See you at six thirty . . . or else."

As soon as the door closed behind Ingrid, Summer turned to Jenna. "Break out a new bag of candy. I need to fill up before six thirty."

"Do you know Hollis?" Jenna asked Lila. "Runs the bookstore down the street?"

Lila shook her head. "Doesn't sound familiar."

"She's only lived here for two or three years. She used to be in show business, too. You guys should talk."

"Yeah, she has some deep, dark secrets and scandals." Summer tapped her fingernails on the bar. "She hasn't told us everything yet, but we're working on her."

"Yeah, we'll break her code of silence eventually," Jenna agreed. "You know how girlfriends are."

And to her horror, Lila felt the sting of tears in her eyes. She folded her arms on the bar top, laid her face in the cradle of her hands, and cried. Loud, broken, uncontrollable sobs that shook her entire body and drenched her face and forearms. An outpouring of emotion that felt as though it would never relent. She couldn't even compose herself enough to apologize.

But no one seemed perturbed. She heard a slight rustle and felt the brush of a tissue on her wrist.

"Have some ice water," Jenna advised. "You're going to be dehydrated from all that crying."

"Drink at least a gallon of water every day," Summer chimed in. "We're very big on water around here—you'll see."

"I'm sorry," Lila choked, lifting her head up for a moment. "I'm sorry, I'm sorry. I can't stop."

"Don't be sorry." Jenna squeezed her shoulder. "We see this kind of thing on a daily basis."

"But I must look so . . . so . . ."

"You're healing," Summer said. "It's not a pretty process."

"Take your time," Jenna said. "Let it out."

"Thank you," Lila said as Summer offered her another tissue. "I don't have a lot of girlfriends anymore."

"You do now."

Two hours later, Lila drove home with a stomach full of chocolate and a slightly soothed soul.

The evening was shrouded in thick, wet fog, but she could hear the ocean as she parked the FUV in the driveway and jogged up the porch steps.

She had to grope for the hall light when she stepped through the front door—the house was silent and dark, and at first, she wasn't sure anybody was home.

"Mom?" she called, wincing as her handbag nearly knocked over an antique crystal vase. "Hello?"

"I'm in here." Daphne's voice drifted down from the second floor.

Lila went upstairs and found her mother, still dressed in her smart black suit from the appointment with the attorney, in her father's study.

Daphne had overhauled this room at least three times since Lila left for college. The white built-in bookshelves and crown molding contrasted with dark wood chairs and natural planks of wood paneling the walls. Floral-patterned navy and white curtains offset the rustic masculinity, as did a green, live tree in one corner.

Behind the glass-topped desk, Daphne was tapping away at the computer keyboard, pausing every few moments to spoon up what appeared to be ice cream from a dainty china teacup. Lila had to do a double take, because she'd never seen her mother eat ice cream. Ever.

"Mom?" She stepped onto the Prussian blue rug as Daphne took another bite. "Are you okay?"

Instead of answering the question, Daphne put down the cup and turned the computer screen around so that Lila could see the images on the monitor. "Look at this: Sophie Thibodoux just launched her own skin care line."

"Who's Sophie Thibodoux?" Lila asked.

"She was a model at my agency back in the eighties. Pretty face, okay body. But she married some Russian oligarch, and now Sephora is stocking her moisturizers and self-tanners. Her clothing line is set to debut this fall at Dillard's."

"What's an oligarch?" Lila asked, still squinting at the ice cream.

"A filthy rich sugar daddy who makes your father look like a pauper in comparison." Daphne paused for a bitter laugh and a scoop of ice cream. "Well, you know, before he actually *was* a pauper."

"Mom—"

Daphne held up her hand and typed in another name. "Gemma Jones, who I beat out for a shoe ad campaign, just opened a spa in Beverly Hills. Cepucine Benoit, who walked with me in my first New York show, married some venture capitalist; now she's on the board of about ten high-profile charities."

Lila couldn't take her gaze off the little pink smear on her mother's sweater. "Is that ice cream?"

"Yes. It's peppermint, my favorite."

"I had no idea you liked peppermint ice cream."

"That's because I haven't eaten it since I was twelve. Empty calories, you know. But after that meeting with the lawyer today, who really gives a damn, right?" Daphne poised her fingers over the keyboard.

Lila lunged to intercept her mother before she could Google again. "No, no. Don't go down this rabbit hole right now. It's a portal to misery and low self-esteem."

Daphne swatted Lila's hands away. "Leave me alone; I'm on a roll. Let's see . . . Callum Fox, who I broke up with because he was too short, is now heading up a hedge fund in Manhattan. My former booking agent now owns her own agencies in Los Angeles, London, and New York."

Lila rested her hip against one edge of the desk. "So . . . good for them?"

"Good for them?" Daphne straightened up, her eyes glinting with angry tears. "Really? That's what you're going to say to me right now?"

"It's not like they started their skin care lines to rub it in your face," Lila pointed out. "Besides, haven't you heard that saying 'A high tide floats all boats'?"

"No one is floating my boat," Daphne snapped. "My ship has sailed. Never mind, you wouldn't understand. You have no idea what it's like to have hopes and dreams and a vision for your future and to end up with nothing."

"Is that so?" Lila snatched up the china cup and shoved a scoop of peppermint ice cream into her mouth. "You think I don't understand? Step aside, Mother. Step aside."

"Look, here's Becky Young's Facebook profile." Lila clicked on a photo of the girl who had once co-captained the cheer squad with her. "She's married, she's got two sons, and she teaches kindergarten."

Daphne glanced at the profile picture, which featured a beaming family in matching green polo shirts. "Her husband's very handsome."

"Yeah. Apparently, in addition to being the middle school principal, he also coaches the kids' soccer team." Lila commandeered the last of her mother's ice cream and scanned through the other search results. "Oh, remember Alex Heath? He was my very first boyfriend in seventh grade?"

"Alex Heath." Daphne drummed her fingers on the desk. "Was he the baseball player? Or the basketball player?"

"He was the tennis player," Lila corrected. "Anyway, he's an orthodontist now. Has his own practice in Lewes."

"Is he single?"

Lila gave up on the spoon and licked the rim of the cup. "Greta Czerzny, who I used to go shopping with every weekend, is now a NICU nurse. Tim Wallace is vice president of an accounting firm, and Jason Shermer, who asked me to homecoming sophomore year but I turned him down because he wore the wrong brand of sneakers, founded an environmental charity to help preserve wildlife near the bay. All of these people are winning at life. They're getting married and having kids and saving newborns and getting promoted and, like, distributing wine. Oh, that reminds me—I have wine."

Daphne jumped to her feet and grabbed two highball glasses from the wet bar next to the bookshelf. "What are you waiting for? Open it up!"

Lila did as she was told, pouring out two generous servings of the red blend Tyler Russo had given to her.

She raised her glass to the computer screen. "Here's to sucking at life."

"But remember, sweet pea, *you* got to be on TV. You got to see the world. All your classmates stayed right here in Delaware."

"Not Amy Greenbank." Lila pulled up a LinkedIn profile.

Daphne sipped her wine. "I don't remember anyone named Amy Greenbank in your class."

"Probably because she was always studying. And look—now she has her MD from Yale. She just joined an oncology research team at some fancy hospital in Chicago."

"Yes, but you . . . well, I'm sure you're much prettier than her." Daphne nodded at the keyboard. "Look up Ben Collier."

"No way."

"Why not?"

"Because I don't have any crack cocaine, and that's what I need to handle Ben Collier's LinkedIn page right now, okay?"

Daphne twisted her diamond earring. "Has he called you yet?"

"No." Lila pushed back from the desk in despair. "Ben hasn't called me, Amy Greenbank is literally curing cancer, and what do I have to show for the last ten years?" She took another gulp of wine and made a face. "This wine does not go with peppermint ice cream."

Daphne put down her glass. "Hang on; I bought fudge ripple, too. It's in the freezer downstairs."

"You got two kinds of ice cream?" Lila nearly fell off her chair. "Who are you and what have you done with my mother?"

"I have no idea," Daphne yelled back as she headed down to the kitchen. "No idea who I am and no idea what I'm going to do with the rest of my life."

Lila grabbed the wine bottle and followed her mother. They both ended up in the kitchen, hunched over the countertop and eating fudge ripple ice cream directly out of the carton.

"What am I going to do?" Daphne demanded, spattering drops of melted chocolate on the gleaming white limestone. "What am I supposed to do for money? I could live another forty years!"

"Um . . ." Lila gazed out at the black sky.

"We'll figure something out." She didn't sound at all convincing, even to herself.

"Like what?" Daphne demanded. "I've been out of the workforce for thirty years, and there's not much demand for over-the-hill models in Black Dog Bay, Delaware. What on earth would I put on my résumé? I can wear the hell out of a laser-cut Yohji Yamamoto gown? I can walk a runway in Milan after four days of no sleep and no food?"

Lila's eyes widened. "Did you really go four days at a time with no food?"

"Oh, pumpkin, there's a reason I never wanted you to be a model." Daphne patted her daughter's hand. "But your dad took me away from all that. He promised me that I would never have to worry and I would always have the best." She grabbed a paper towel off the roll as her eyes filled with fresh tears. "And he literally worked himself to death trying to keep that promise."

"I remember that," Lila murmured. "I remember him telling the story of how you guys met."

The tale had become legend in the Alders household. Every anniversary, after presenting her mother with flowers and jewelry, Lila's dad would recount the tale of their romance, starting with their first encounter in a crowded Manhattan ballroom.

"The moment I saw your mother," her father would say, "I knew. I knew she was the one."

And her mother would laugh. "But I took a little more convincing."

"Six months," her father said. "That's how long it took me to get your mama to go out to dinner with me. But I finally wore her down." He winked at his wife. "Lucky for her."

"How did you know?" Lila asked her father. Even as a small child, she'd been desperate to understand the power and parameters of yearning and desire. "How did you know you were in love?"

"Your mother used to be a model, you know."

"I know." Lila had seen the leather-bound portfolio her mother kept in the master bedroom. Page after page of her mother pouting at the camera in swimsuits and gowns and skintight pants. Some of the photos were in color, some were black-and-white. All of them were beautiful.

"Well, on the day I first saw your mom, I was visiting my old roommate in New York. We were at a big, fancy party. It was right after your mom was on the stage—"

"The runway," Daphne corrected. She turned to Lila, her eyes sparkling at the memory. "It was Fashion Week."

"I spotted her from all the way across the room, as soon as she walked in," Bill said. "I grabbed a glass of champagne and went straight over to her."

Lila wanted every last detail. "What did you say to each other?"

Daphne and Bill looked at each other again and burst out laughing. "You know, I don't remember."

"It was too loud to talk, anyway. We just danced and looked at each other."

"And then I asked her out. Again and again."

"I had a lot of boyfriends," Daphne interjected.

"But I was persistent. And finally she said yes." Her father turned to her mother, his eyes shining with pride. "And the night we went out to dinner, you wore a red dress—"

"Red vinyl, Paco Rabanne," Daphne reported to Lila. "Very edgy. It had gold rings through the shoulder straps and a hemline up to *here*." She indicated the top of her thigh.

"—and I almost had a heart attack right there."

"So you fell in love with Mama because she was beautiful," Lila said.

"Is, was, always will be." Bill beamed at his wife. "Inside and out."

She turned to her mother. "Why did you fall in love?"

"Well, I didn't have much choice! Your father is right when he says he's persistent. But once I got to know him, I couldn't help myself. I loved him so much, I left New York and moved here to be with him."

"And you'll love each other forever?" Lila prompted.

"Forever," her parents answered in unison. They kissed, and Lila gave herself a hug, feeling lucky to be part of such a special family. She knew she would have boyfriends one day, too. She hoped that her destiny was a life like her mother's—she would be special and beautiful and the center of a strong, handsome man's world.

Lila squeezed her eyes shut, wishing that she could be back in this kitchen twenty years ago. Before her father died. Before she knew that everything she had taken for granted was going to be taken away.

But when she opened her eyes, she saw only her mother staring back. Their eyes reflected a shared sense of terror and despair, two grown women who had no idea how to take care of themselves.

"I still have that red Paco Rabanne mini-dress," Daphne said softly. "Up in the attic somewhere." She set her spoon down on the counter with a hard, cold clink. "He promised. He promised to take care of me."

Lila collected the spoons, got to her feet, and started rinsing off the dishes in the sink. "We need to call a real estate agent tomorrow. We have to sell the house. It's time."

"I'm not selling the house. Don't be ridiculous."

"We have to. You heard the estate guy. The

money I got from selling my rings will cover the property taxes, but we still have to deal with the loan payments, all the utilities, lawn care, groceries. . . ." Lila paused, waiting for her mother to agree. "Hello?"

"I heard him." Daphne examined her impeccable manicure. "But he's only looking at the worst-case scenario. He's very conservative, that's what your father always said."

"Our current scenario *is* the worst-case scenario," Lila told her. "It's time to face reality."

"I can't." Her mother covered her eyes with her hands. "I just can't."

"Well, I can." Lila paused. "Or at least, I can try."

Chapter 8

The next morning, Lila drove to Main Street to set up a meeting at Black Dog Bay Brokers.

She stood on the sidewalk for a few minutes, scanning the real estate listings taped to the office's front window and trying to envision her family home among them. Decades of life and love and hard work would be reduced to a few well-lit photos and two paragraphs of descriptive text highlighting the new roof and the septic system. And then the house her father built would be gone, sold to another family who would start fresh with new memories and traditions.

And Lila and her mother would move on to . . . where?

When she finally worked up the nerve to go in, the receptionist greeted her with a cheery hello, an offer of a latte, and an invitation to "Go right back—Whitney's free and she'd be happy to chat with you."

A smartly dressed blonde who looked barely out of high school met Lila at her office doorway. "You're Lila Alders? *The* Lila Alders?"

Lila pulled back a fraction of an inch. "I guess so. Have we met?"

"I'm Whitney Sosin, but my maiden name is Toth." Whitney shot her a knowing look. "My brother is Malcolm Toth."

"Oh?" Lila tried to keep her smile in place as she racked her brain. She had just heard that name recently.

"So I've heard *allll* about you."

"I see." *Malcolm Toth, Malcolm Toth . . . oh right, the guy Christa mentioned at the country club.* "So, um, what's Malcolm been up to?"

"He went into the Marines after college. Did all kinds of super-secret stuff I'm not allowed to ask about. But he moved back a few months ago. I found him a great house over by the nature preserve. It's like something out of *Walden*." Whitney opened her door wider and ushered Lila into a small office furnished with a pair of utilitarian IKEA-style chairs that would make Daphne weep. "What about you, Lila? What brings you to our office today?"

"You know, the usual." Lila perched on the edge of her seat and crossed her ankles. "Death. Divorce. Impending financial disaster."

"I'm sorry to hear that." Whitney paused delicately. "And you're in need of a real estate agent?"

"Yes. My mother's alone now, and it's just too much house for her." *In so many ways.* "We'd like to sell it as soon as possible, but I don't want to undervalue it. We need the best price we can get."

"Don't worry; the market is on an upswing right now, especially for beachfront lots." Whitney paused again, still standing and looking down at Lila. "Sorry, I'm being a total fangirl, but I can't believe *the* Lila Alders is in my office!"

Lila had to smile. "Me, neither."

"Everyone from high school still talks about you. You're famous. You're on TV!"

"Uh-huh." Lila pretended to search for something in her handbag. "So how do we get the ball rolling? Do you come look at the house?"

"Yes, I'll do a walk-through with you and then we'll schedule an appraisal. How's tomorrow morning?" Whitney asked. "Around nine thirty?"

"Nine thirty works for me." Lila slid on a pair

of big, dark sunglasses. "Go down to the end of Shoreside Drive. It's the big—"

"I know exactly where it is," Whitney assured her.

"Right. I forgot everyone knows everyone around here."

Whitney grinned. "No such thing as privacy in Black Dog Bay. See you tomorrow." She leaned in conspiratorially. "Should I tell Malcolm you say hi?"

"Um . . ." Lila was saved from having to reply by the arrival of a uniformed police officer in the reception area.

"I'm looking for the owner of that white SUV?" the officer called.

Lila squeezed past Whitney and hurried down the hall. "That's me."

"Lila Alders?" The officer jerked his thumb toward the sidewalk. "That's your vehicle out there? You're going to have to move it immediately. You're blocking a fire hydrant."

"I am?" She peered out the plate glass window. "But I pulled up into the parking space."

"Not far enough." The officer pointed out the placement of her rear bumper. "The back end's still in the red zone." He followed her gaze. "And you're technically taking up two parking spaces with the front end. I'm supposed to ticket you for that, but if you move right now, I'll let it go."

Lila ran for the door. "Thank you."

As she left, the officer called out, "That's a really big car you have there."

"I know." She clicked the button on her key fob to unlock the FUV and winced as the running boards folded down and banged her shins. "I know."

It took her several minutes and a dinged hubcap to maneuver out of the parking spot, and when she finally merged into the lunch-hour traffic, Lila understood why the police officer had been peeved about the FUV taking up more than one spot. Main Street was unseasonably crowded today, with lots of drivers waiting for spaces. But right before she passed the town square, another car pulled away from the curb, leaving a vast expanse of prime parking territory.

Right in front of the Rebound Salon.

She took it as a sign and hit the brakes.

Two hours later, Lila glanced at her reflection in the windowpane of the front door, trying to reconcile her image of herself with this pale-faced brunette. As Summer Benson had promised, the salon stylists were very talented, their rates were dirt cheap compared with her colorist in Philadelphia, and they'd assured her that her natural shade of brown made her look younger and more chic.

They were probably right. But even so, no one wanted to be a brunette due to austerity measures.

She unlocked the door and strode past the entryway mirror as quickly as possible. "We have to talk, Mom. Strike that—we need to *stop* talking. The time has come to take action."

Daphne had hunkered down in the den with a soft wool blanket and a thick sheaf of papers, which she shoved under a throw pillow when Lila walked in. Even at midday, this room was shaded by the sloping porch overhang, and Daphne squinted up as though she couldn't believe what she was seeing.

"You changed your hair."

"Yes, I did. Because I can no longer afford to be a blonde. See? Taking action." Lila lifted her chin to indicate the throw pillow. "What are you hiding under there?"

"Hiding?" Daphne shifted her body and tucked the pillow behind her. "Nothing."

Lila held out her palm. "Let's have it."

Her mother straightened her shirt collar, her eyes wide and her expression guilt-stricken.

"Come on," Lila coaxed. "Whatever it is, just tell me. It's not like our situation can get any worse at this point."

Daphne hesitated for another moment, then pulled the stack of papers out from behind the cushion and handed them over with the air of a child who'd been caught sneaking a cookie between meals.

Lila glanced at the credit card logo on the

top sheet, then checked the total amount due.

"Oh my God." Her knees literally went weak, and she had to sit down on the coffee table. "Mother!"

"Don't yell at me!" Daphne covered her face with both hands. "I can't take it."

"How long have you been running up this bill?" Lila flipped through the itemized statement, which was at least five pages long.

"I didn't run up the bill!" Daphne cried. "Your father paid the full balance every month." She cleared her throat. "Well, he did on *this* card, anyway."

"He did?" Lila peered closer at the bill to check the purchase dates. "Then what . . . Holy crap, you bought all this stuff in the last few months?"

"I was bereaved, okay? And you of all people should understand that shopping sometimes helps when you're lonely. Wasn't that the whole point of your job? To sell people things they didn't need when they were feeling vulnerable in the middle of the night?"

Lila gasped. "First of all, don't try to turn this around on me. Second of all, everybody needs breathable, high-quality percale sheets for a one-time-only clearance price at two a.m. Third of all, what the hell did you *buy?*" Lila scanned the retailers listed. "What's this huge charge at Bloomingdale's?"

Daphne shrank into the sofa cushions. "New

breakfast dishes. They're casual and bright, but they're still fine china. And they're dishwasher safe. I was trying to be practical."

"Pottery Barn, Sephora, Bergdorf Goodman, Tiffany . . ." Lila dropped the bill and regarded her mother with confusion. "Did you go to New York?"

"Don't be ridiculous." Daphne sniffed. "I haven't left this tiny little backwater town in years."

"So this was all online shopping?"

Daphne nodded.

"But if you never leave this tiny little backwater town, why do you need expensive shoes and fancy jewelry?"

Daphne started crying, but these weren't her dainty, ladylike, get-out-of-jail-free tears. She was genuinely upset, shaking and red-nosed in her sorrow. "I don't know."

"Well, where is this stuff?" Lila demanded. "Where do you even keep it all?"

"The closet."

"You mean the master bedroom closet that I'm not allowed to open?"

"Well. Yes." Daphne twisted her hands together. "And the guest room closets. The attic. The storage space over the garage."

Lila opened and closed her mouth several times before demanding, "Show me."

Her mother led the way up the elegant staircase with the hand-carved banister, past the family portraits hanging in the upstairs hallway, across the restored antique rugs, and through the master bedroom.

Lila threw open the closet door and discovered . . .

"So basically, your closet is the women's department at Nordstrom. Look, this dress still has the tags on." Lila pointed at a plum-colored silk gown. "So does this one. So does this one."

Daphne hung her head.

The floor of the closet was obscured by dozens of cardboard shipping boxes and shopping bags, all of them stuffed with tissue paper and plastic wrap and receipts.

"I'm sorry," Daphne said softly. And in her mother's voice, Lila heard layers of remorse, years of regret, untold stories of frustration and loneliness and longing. So she stopped arguing and asking questions. Instead, she fell back on her new mantra: *Take action.*

"The good news is, we can return a lot of the stuff that still has receipts," Lila said. "Let's go through all the boxes. You start over there, and I'll start over here."

"No, no." Daphne clutched the plum-colored gown with both hands. "We're not returning anything!"

"Yeah, we are." Lila glanced inside a bright blue box from Tiffany & Co. "Everything's going back."

"Have you no heart?" Daphne demanded.

"Mom, come on." Lila held up a sequined evening gown with a plunging neckline. "Where are you going to wear this in Black Dog Bay?"

"Just because I've been stuck here for thirty years doesn't mean I have to give up and be frumpy forever, does it? I'll always love fashion, no matter where I live or how old I am."

"You can love fashion without spending tens of thousands of dollars on it." Lila gasped as she opened the flaps of a carton from Bergdorf Goodman. "Hold the phone—is this what I think it is?" She lifted out a caramel-colored Chloé bag made from buttery soft leather. "I tried to find this last spring and it was sold out everywhere! How did you get this?"

Daphne shrugged. "I have my ways. You have to know how to shop, sweet pea."

"And it's still in the box? You just left it here to rot?" Lila shook her head at her mother. "*You're* the one who has no heart!"

"What difference does it make, since everything is going back to the store?"

"Everything *is* going back to the store." Lila ran her fingers along the cool gold hardware and the smooth leather. "Everything, that is, except this bag."

The real estate agent showed up at nine twenty-five the next morning with a box from the Eat Your Heart Out bakery.

"I hope you like orange cranberry scones," Whitney said as she climbed the porch stairs.

"We love orange cranberry," Lila assured her, positioning her body just outside the front door. "But there's been a slight change of plans."

Whitney's smile flickered. "Is this not a good time?"

Lila glanced back at the closed door and lowered her voice. "I'm thinking maybe we should wait to do a walk-through of the house until my mom's not here."

Whitney lowered her voice, too. "She's the homeowner, correct?"

"Correct."

"Doesn't she want to be part of the process?"

"That's the problem." Lila opened the white box and grabbed a scone. "She doesn't want there to *be* a process. Don't get me wrong—we're definitely selling. But she's still, you know, warming up to the idea."

"Got it." Whitney nodded. She couldn't have been more than twenty-four, but she exuded a degree of confidence and capability that Lila could only dream of. "And I hope you'll trust me to handle it. Most of my business really comes down to dealing with people. Buying or selling a home can be very emotional."

" 'Emotional' is one word for it." Lila paused for a bite of the zesty, buttery scone. "Have you met my mother?"

"We haven't been formally introduced, but I've seen her around town." Whitney's dimples were back in full force. "She seems lovely. Very stylish."

"She is both lovely and stylish," Lila conceded. "But she's also recently widowed, and she's had more than her fair share of bad news over the last few days."

The door opened and Daphne emerged, crisp and coiffed and perfectly put together. She wore her asymmetric-shouldered tunic, double-wrapped belt, and tight black leggings with an almost aggressive hauteur. "Lila? Who are you talking to?"

Whitney stepped forward, offering a handshake. "Hi, Mrs. Alders, I'm Whitney Sosin. I'm here to—"

Lila threw herself between the real estate agent and her mother and tried to do some preemptive damage control. "I asked her to come, remember? Since we're thinking about putting the house on the market?"

Daphne rounded on Lila with the most ferocious frown her Botoxed face could muster. "I already told you, we are not selling the house."

Whitney retreated toward the porch steps. "Maybe I should give you two a moment."

"Good idea," Daphne agreed. "Lila, I told you: I'm not ready for this."

"And that's fine, because we're not really doing

anything," Lila assured her. "We're just walking." She brushed past her mother, held open the door, and whispered to Whitney, "Hurry."

Whitney gushed over the interior design, the high ceilings, and the ocean views. Daphne looked mollified and for a moment, Lila relaxed. Then they headed upstairs where, upon seeing the home office, Whitney remarked, "You might want to consider replacing the carpet in here."

Daphne stiffened. "I picked out this color specifically. It's my husband's favorite."

"And it's lovely," Whitney said heartily. "But prospective buyers don't always share the aesthetic vision of the homeowner."

"Well, I would never sell to someone who would rip out my flooring," Daphne declared.

"It's just carpet," Lila said. "Maybe we could replace it with some neutral shade like beige?"

"Death first."

Whitney kept moving. "Let's look at the bedrooms, shall we? You also might want to take down some of the photos and pictures. It helps buyers to focus on the layout and the size of the rooms instead of the decor."

"The layout?" Daphne scoffed. "If a buyer is too stupid to see what a gem this house is, they have no business buying it."

"We'll revisit the decor issues later." Whitney led the way back down to the kitchen, placed her leather folder on the center island, and extracted a few papers. "I ran the comps on this neighborhood and I think, if we price it right, we should be able to sell quickly. I'll put the For Sale sign up as soon as you sign the papers."

"Oh, no." Daphne blanched. "No For Sale sign."

Lila held up her hand. "Now, Mom—"

"No sign! I don't want the neighbors to know I'm moving. People gossip enough around here as it is."

Lila turned to Whitney. "How fast can we close the sale once we get a buyer?"

"We can ask for a short escrow, but of course we'll have to allow time for a home inspection and appraisal."

Daphne stopped wringing her hands and snapped to attention. "I'm sorry, a what?"

"Home inspection and appraisal," Whitney repeated.

"There's nothing wrong with this house. This house is in perfect condition. *Immaculate* condition."

The Realtor exchanged glances with Lila. "I can see you've taken good care of it, but this is a standard part of the process. The buyers are going to hire somebody whose job it is to find something wrong with the house." She cleared her throat. "You're also going to need to empty the closets. We want buyers to appreciate how much storage space is available, and the best way to do that is to clear out the clutter."

"Clutter?" Daphne gasped. "Do you have any idea what's in those boxes? Couture pieces from my modeling days. Timeless works of art."

Aka neon jumpsuits and leather blazers from the eighties. Lila mentally scheduled multiple trips to Goodwill.

"I used to be a model, you know. In New York." Daphne paused so Whitney could ooh and aah. "And beauty runs in the family, as you can see. Lila is a celebrity in her own right."

Lila cringed. "Mom, please don't." She turned to Whitney. "We'll start clearing out the closets tomorrow."

"Great." Whitney glanced out the window at the overgrown yard. "Just one more thing. We want to make sure the exterior of the house is in tip-top shape. Curb appeal is one of the most important factors in selling a house."

Lila sat down, overwhelmed. "So mow the lawn?"

Whitney nodded. "And trim the trees, prune the bushes, make sure the sand on the beachfront is groomed."

Lila rubbed her forehead and nodded. "No problem; we'll get everything taken care of. Thank you so much for taking the time to come over."

"Give me a call when you're ready and we'll take it from there!"

Lila walked the real estate agent out to the

porch, waved as Whitney drove away, and then tried to keep the smile on her face as she opened the garage door.

"What are you doing?" Her mother stepped out on the porch.

"Finding the lawn mower." Lila rolled up the sleeves of her white linen shirt. "You heard the woman. Someone's got to cut this grass."

"Someone, yes. But not *you.*"

Lila glanced around the garage until she located her father's spotless red lawn mower on the far side of her FUV. "Who else do we have left?"

Daphne's eyes lit up. "Well, there's always—"

"Do not say Ben Collier."

"Why not? I'm sure he'd be happy to help us out."

"No. He hasn't called me for a date," Lila said. "I'm not calling him for lawn care."

"You mean he hasn't called you *yet,*" Daphne corrected. "He will. The man's running a real estate empire. Give him a few more days. And if you won't let me call Ben, then let me call the lawn service. We have a quarterly account with them. I'll just put it on my credit card."

Lila pulled her hair back into a ponytail, her determination growing with every passing second. "Nope."

Daphne looked at the rolled-up shirtsleeves and sloppy ponytail with alarm. "Sweet pea, be reasonable!"

Lila shook her head. "You go wait by the phone if you want. I'll be out here, taking action."

"Do you even know how to start that thing?" her mother asked.

Lila stared at the mower with steely resolve. "No. But I'm guessing it has something to do with this cord right here. Have faith, Mom. I have opposable thumbs and YouTube. Victory will be mine."

Chapter 9

"Welcome back! You look . . . a bit flushed." Jenna poured a tumbler full of ice water as soon as Lila entered the Whinery.

Lila grabbed the glass, downed the contents in thirty seconds flat, and passed it back to Jenna for a refill.

"What happened to you? Should I even ask?"

"Lawn insurgency." After five minutes of yanking the pull cord and swearing, she'd managed to get the mower started. While Daphne had dis-appeared back into the house, Lila tried to crush the grassroots rebellion. And she'd broken eight out of ten fingernails in her struggle.

For the next few hours, as the sun sank in the sky and the stars came out, Lila worked as hard as she could. She started at the back corner of the yard, where the grass was longest and densest. The Alders house was situated on a gentle slope; she had never realized this before. But now she was keenly aware of every tilt in the earth, every hill that made her job harder.

She'd kept pushing. She'd sweated enough for three Bikram yoga sessions. And finally, her senses inundated with the roar of the engine and the scent of gasoline and the dull ache in her arms and shoulders, she'd admitted defeat. The lawn still looked like crap. She was too overheated and grimy to even think about eating dinner— but her mood was surprisingly good. So she showered off the errant blades of grass, put on a demure pink sweater and pearls, and did her hair and makeup to Daphne's specifications before heading out for a celebratory glass of (the cheapest available) wine.

"I like your hair," Jenna said. "The color looks good on you. Snickers?" She offered up a silver dish of candy.

Lila waved it away. "No, thanks. Just keep the ice water coming, please."

"You know we're fans of hydration here." Jenna poured two more glasses of water and set them down in front of Lila. "Knock yourself out."

As the lilting piano notes of Fiona Apple's "Get Gone" started playing on the sound system, an Amazonian redhead stalked into the bar with a fistful of T-shirts and a murderous expression on her face. "I heard you guys set up an Ex Box?"

"Right over there." Jenna pointed out a tall cardboard box in the corner. The brown corrugated carton had been adorned with ribbon and a glittery pink label: *The Ex Box*.

"What's an Ex Box?" Lila asked.

"Oh, that's where heartbreak tourists can drop off their breakup baggage," Jenna explained. "T-shirts, baseball caps, wedding dresses, whatever. Marla—she runs the Better Off Bed-and-Breakfast down the street—has bonfires a few times a week, but it seemed like a waste to burn perfectly good clothes. So now visitors can pitch their karmically tainted hand-me-downs in here and we donate everything to charity."

"Good to know." Still guzzling water, Lila hopped off her barstool and examined the box. "I'm forcing my mother to clean out her closets and I'm guessing we'll have a lot to donate."

As she started back to her barstool, the door swung open and Ben Collier walked in.

Instinctively, she froze and conducted a quick mental inventory. Hair, face, wardrobe, jewelry, footwear? Washed, powdered, pressed, sparkly, and on trend.

Oh, and her bra and panties matched. Baby blue La Perla, purchased back when she still thought three hundred dollars was a reasonable price to pay for underwear.

When she glanced up, Ben was watching her with that slow, sweet smile that had always made her melt.

"Hey, Lila." He strode over and gave her a hug. She thought she felt him brush his lips across the top of her head, but she couldn't be sure.

"What are you doing here?" she asked. "I thought . . ." *I thought the bartender at the country club said you wouldn't be caught dead here.* No. That was not an acceptable conversation opener.

"I called your house, and your mother said you'd be here."

"Oh." She gazed up at him through lowered lashes. "You called the house?"

He nodded, put one arm around her shoulder, and led her back toward the bar. "Let's have a drink and catch up."

"Okay." As she eased onto the wrought iron stool, every muscle in her legs protested.

"Your hair." He rubbed a lock between his fingertips. "It looks just like it used to."

She redoubled the fluttery-eyelashes routine. "Do you like it?"

"Yeah. It reminds me of—" He broke off, frowning with concern. "Are you okay?"

"I'm fine, why?"

"Nothing. You looked like you had something stuck in your eye."

She stopped flirting and scanned the specialty

drinks listed on the chalkboard over the bar. "Let's order."

Right on cue, Jenna appeared with the wine list. "I have a great new Sauv Blanc."

Lila nodded. "Sounds good."

Jenna turned to Ben. "Two?"

He nodded. "Sure."

Lila settled back in her seat. "Look at us. Drinking wine out of real glasses instead of warm beer out of red plastic cups. We're all grown up." When Jenna returned with two delicate stemmed glasses, they toasted with exaggerated solemnity.

"To old times and new beginnings." Ben took a sip of the chilled white wine, then made a face. "There's something to be said for warm beer in plastic cups."

"Go ahead and get your beer." Lila swept her hair back off one shoulder. "You know you want to."

Ben nodded at Jenna, who grabbed a bottle of Dogfish Head ale from the refrigerator. "So did you get your car checked yet?" he asked Lila.

"Not yet. We've had a lot going on."

He chuckled. "I bet. I know how your mom gets."

Lila finally started to relax. "You have no idea. She's gotten like ten times squirrellier with age."

"She's lucky to have you."

"Thanks." She nudged his elbow with hers.

"Your mom must be thrilled to have you back home, too."

He shrugged. "I guess."

"What do you mean, you guess?"

"She's glad to have more time with my dad, now that he's retiring, but he makes her go fishing with him."

Lila laughed at the mental image of Ben's chatty, extroverted mother confined to a rowboat for hours on end.

"And, you know. She thought she'd have grandchildren by now." He poured his beer into a glass. "She brings it up about five times a day."

"Let me guess—if you ask her to stop, she gives you the Bambi eyes and says she does it out of *looove*."

"The Bambi eyes are a killer." He scrubbed his cleanly shaven jawline with his palm. "So you're divorced?"

She tried not to flinch. "Yep."

"What happened?" He moved in closer. She could smell the fresh, lingering scents of laundry detergent and shaving cream. "If I'm allowed to ask. You don't have to talk about it."

"No, no, it's fine." She turned the base of her wineglass clockwise, then counterclockwise. "His name was Carl; we were married for almost seven years." She tried to figure out what to reveal and what to leave out. How to avoid making him feel awkward or making herself look pathetic. "We were just different people. We grew apart."

He reached over and rested his hand on hers. "You grew apart?"

She laughed and confessed, "Okay, the truth is, it was every horrible cliché you can think of. He cheated on me, he lied about it, he left me for another woman, and then he screwed me over in the divorce. It was a total Lifetime movie."

"With a very beautiful leading lady." His hand was still holding hers.

"Well, thank you."

He let go and took a contemplative sip of beer. "Your ex is an idiot."

"I agree."

"Why'd you marry him?"

Lila drank her wine and tried to remember. "He wasn't like that in the beginning. Or maybe he was, but I just didn't see it. I was only twenty when I met him, and he was older and already established, and he came from this important family and he seemed so sure about everything, and I thought . . ." This had never occurred to her until now, but she realized it was the truth. "I thought our marriage would be just like my parents'."

Ben nodded knowingly. "Your mom could do no wrong."

"Exactly. My dad just adored her, no matter

what. And she adored him. And I assumed that that's how it always was."

He nodded again. He'd known her parents for decades; he understood her history and her family's little quirks. It was so nice not to have to explain everything.

"What about you?" she asked. "I'm kind of surprised you haven't settled down yet. I always figured you for the white-picket-fence lifestyle. Wife, kids, golden retriever, Subaru . . ."

Ben grinned, and she caught a glimmer of the charming, confident football star she'd fallen so hard for. "Me, too. That was always my goal: married by thirty, two kids by thirty-five."

"You and your goals."

"What can I say? All of Coach's lectures stuck with me." He looked down at the bar top. "I turned thirty last month."

"I know."

"I had a serious girlfriend last fall. Allison. And I thought that was it. I thought she was the one."

"Uh-oh. I'm guessing this story doesn't end well."

"I picked out a ring, I was all set to propose, but as soon as I mentioned the word 'marriage,' she freaked out." Now it was Ben's turn to study the specials on the chalkboard. "Then my dad called and asked me to consider coming back and taking over the family business, so here I am."

"And you haven't talked to her since . . . ?"

"Fifty-three days ago." He shook his head. "What is there to say?"

"I don't know." Lila gave his shoulder a little squeeze. "But I do know that girl's crazy. She's never going to find another guy like you."

"She said she wasn't sure if she could move down here. She said she needed more time."

"More time? How long had you guys been together?"

"Six months."

"Oh." Lila frowned. "Well, actually, that's . . ." She trailed off when she saw the obstinate expression on his face. Ben had never been one for long, detailed discussions about feelings. He'd always been decisive and direct, and she'd always liked that about him.

"Thirty," he said.

She left a little lull in the conversation. Then she said, "Maybe you just haven't found the right woman."

There was a long silence between them. Sugarland's "Already Gone" started playing.

Finally, he spoke. "I always figured you and I would settle down someday."

"Is that why you broke up with me when you left for Tufts?" She smiled to soften the words. "My tender eighteen-year-old heart was shattered."

"Come on, Lila. We both knew that the 'hometown honey' thing never lasts when you're in college. We were so young. But I always knew

110

that we'd come back together someday." He brushed his fingers against hers. "And here we are."

"Here we are."

There was another long pause, and then he shifted in his seat. "I'll be right back."

As he headed for the restroom, Jenna paused the music and held up her hand.

"What?" a woman at the other end of the bar asked.

Jenna cocked her head. "Do you hear that?"

Everyone froze, listening. "No."

"It sounds like a car alarm out in the parking lot," Jenna said.

And then Lila did hear it: the insistent, electronic bleating muffled by the thick brick walls.

"Any idea whose car that is?" Jenna asked.

"I can't be sure." Lila got to her feet and grabbed her car keys out of her bag. "But I have a guess. I'll be right back."

She dashed out the door and around the corner. Sure enough, the FUV was staging a full revolt. The headlights were blinking in time to the deafening blasts of the horn. Lila twisted up her face and hit her key fob.

After a little beep of protest, the FUV went silent.

Lila stepped closer and glared at the vehicle. "Don't stand there and pretend to be normal," she hissed at the shiny white door. "You're not fooling me. *This isn't over.*"

She heard rustling behind her, and turned to find a man who had apparently interrupted his evening run to assist her. She deduced the running part from the fact that he had sneakers and earbuds . . . and the fact that sweat was literally dripping from his face. His gray cotton T-shirt was saturated, clinging to what she couldn't help noticing were very nice abs.

"Everything okay?" He was tall, broad shouldered, square jawed, and oh so very sweaty.

She watched a trickle of perspiration make its way down his forehead. "Everything's fine, thank you. My car alarm went off, but it does that all the time. Randomly. Just to keep me on my toes."

Darkness had fallen and the nearest streetlight was half a block away, but she could see his expression flicker as he looked at her.

"Lila." His voice was deep and low and one hundred percent unfamiliar.

"Yes!" She tried to cover her confusion with near-manic enthusiasm. "Hi! You must be . . ."

"Malcolm."

She felt her expression change, too. "Malcolm Toth?"

He looked surprised. "You remember me."

"Of course!" She waved one hand around. "We went to high school together, right?"

His face went all stony again. "That's what you remember?"

"Well, that and, of course, the time we . . ." She waited for him to fill in the blank.

He stared down at her.

She forced a breathy little laugh. "Listen, I've been drinking all night. My memory's kind of fuzzy."

He nodded.

"And I'd better be getting back inside." She jerked her thumb over her shoulder. "Ben's waiting for me."

He betrayed no hint of surprise. "That figures."

"Hey!" She took a step toward him. "What's that supposed to mean?"

"Nothing." He clapped one hand against her upper arm. "Welcome back to Black Dog Bay." When he took his hand away, he left a faint trace of sweat on her cardigan.

She tried to hide her dismay. She failed. "My sweater!"

"Sorry." He put his earbuds back in and prepared to resume running.

"You should be. This is dry-clean only, I'll have you know. I can't go back in there with . . . with *sweat* on my sweater."

"Take it off." He looked her straight in the eye, then turned his back and left her, his stride long and steady.

She stood there in the dark for a moment, trying

to come up with a cutting retort. She could still feel the warm pressure where his hand had been.

Take it off. Who the hell did he think he was?

No wonder she couldn't remember him from high school. The man had more sweat glands than social skills.

She slipped off her cardigan and returned to the bar in her camisole, flustered and flushed.

Ben clearly noticed the newly bared expanse of neck and arms and shoulders, but he didn't mention it. Because, unlike some people, *he* had manners.

He was paying the check and chatting with Jenna. "Lila, I'm so sorry, but I have to run. My mother just called. My dad's out of town, and apparently there's some sort of bat-related emergency in the garage."

Lila smiled. "No need to explain. I know the drill."

"It's great to see you." He leaned in. "We should do this again sometime."

"Absolutely." She tipped her face up, parted her lips, and closed her eyes. For this brief, beautiful moment, she felt young and carefree again.

He wrapped his arms around her, pulled her against him, and kissed her. On the cheek.

"What was that all about?" Summer had joined Jenna at the bar by the time Lila had said good-bye to Ben and regained her sensibilities.

Lila flipped her hair and tried to sound casual. "Oh, that was just me reuniting with my long-lost love. We were the 'it' couple in high school." She paused to help herself to a mini Milky Way. "And yes, I realize exactly how that sounds. But whatever—we were passionately devoted."

Jenna looked dubious. "Devoted, maybe. But passion? I don't see it."

"You don't? Really?"

Jenna shook her head.

"Look again. We're perfect for each other! He was a football player, I was a cheerleader. He used to send me flowers and make me CDs full of sappy songs. Even our parents were friends. Our dads used to do business together all the time."

"Maybe so." Jenna scrunched up her nose. "But I'm not seeing a lot of chemistry."

"Oh, we have chemistry," Lila assured them, draining the last of her wine. "Lots of chemistry. Entire meth labs' worth of chemistry."

Summer and Jenna exchanged a look. "If you say so."

"I do say so! Back in the day, we used to make out for hours on end. He's a great kisser, for your information."

"But you never had sex," Summer said.

"We might have." Lila's voice rose. "We might have had sex all over this town."

Summer laughed and rolled her eyes. "Try to keep your clothes on. I dare you."

"Go ahead and mock me. But you don't know our history. What we had was special, and it still is. Ben and I are meant to be."

Summer scoffed. "Meant to be *friends* who kiss like brother and sister."

"We don't kiss like brother and sister." Lila was outraged. "It's been like thirteen years and we're in public! He was being a gentleman!"

"And you're into that sort of thing?"

"Absolutely." Lila pounded the bar top. "When we finally do get together, it's going to be hot. Scorching. The heat of our passion will burn this whole town to the ground."

"So we should be on the lookout for random acts of spontaneous combustion, is what you're saying?"

"That's right," Lila retorted. "But there won't be anything random about it. Because it's *meant to be.*"

Chapter 10

The next morning, Lila put on jeans and a threadbare T-shirt from high school, pulled her hair up into a ponytail, and prepared to brave the attic. She grabbed a mug of coffee and an ancient portable radio as she passed through the kitchen, where her mother was slumped at the table in a yellow silk robe.

"Mom? You okay?"

"I'm fine." Daphne stirred her tea with a dainty silver spoon. "Just tired. Overwhelmed. Missing your father."

Lila put one hand on the refrigerator door. "Can I get you anything?"

"No, I just need to sit for a while." Daphne kept stirring, her hand on autopilot, and Lila suspected that the tea had gone cold. "Where are you going looking so grubby?"

"Time to tackle the attic. You heard what the Realtor said. What's in all the boxes up there, anyway?"

Daphne stared into her cup.

"Want to come with me and find out?"

"No." Daphne sighed and stirred, sighed and stirred. "I can't face all the memories."

Lila paused, then said very gently, "Maybe this will end up being a blessing. A new house, a new start."

Daphne snapped out of her daze and released the spoon with a clink. "Your father dying is not a blessing."

"Mom, no, I didn't mean—"

"I already told you: I'm not moving. This house is my life's work, Lila. I chose every shutter, every rug, every quilt. This house is your birth-right."

Lila touched her mother's shoulder. "I know this is hard, but unless we win the lottery, we don't have a choice."

"People are already talking, you know. Someone in that law office must have a big mouth, because everyone in this petty, provincial town is *looking* at me. They feel sorry for me now." Daphne's eyes flashed. "Me! Can you imagine? Ever since your father died, they won't make eye contact when they see me in the store and they keep bringing over these"—she wrinkled her nose in disgust and gestured toward the freezer—"these casseroles. I ask you, Lila. Do I strike you as someone who might enjoy casseroles?"

"No."

"Someone actually gave me a carton of wine over the holidays. It would be laughable if it weren't so appalling. What on earth am I going to do with wine in a box?"

"Drink it?" Lila suggested.

Daphne shuddered.

"Well, if you aren't going to drink it, can I?"

Daphne pointed at the doorway. "Get out of my sight."

Lila didn't argue. She tucked the radio under her arm and headed upstairs.

Twenty minutes later, while singing along at the top of her lungs to "Fancy" by Reba McEntire, she discovered the first Dior.

She'd slit open an unlabeled carton, expecting to find moldering 1980s blouses with massive shoulder pads, but when she folded back the crisp layers of tissue, she discovered a pale pink shirtdress, along with a matching jacket and hat. The style looked like something from the 1960s.

The surrounding boxes held similar pieces of vintage couture: brilliantly cut black cocktail dresses, a coffee-and-cream-colored spectator suit, and a showstopping gold Halston evening gown.

She carried the gold gown down to her mother, who was still in the kitchen.

"Is this yours?" Lila held up the Halston with both hands.

Daphne reached out and embraced the dress. "Oh! I had no idea this was up there."

Lila pointed toward the ceiling. "There are boxes stacked to the rafters."

"This is one of my collector's pieces from New

York." Her mother smiled a secret, faraway smile. "I thought it was in the storage unit."

"Storage unit?" Lila's eyebrows shot up. "You mean there's more?"

"Pieces like this need to be kept away from moisture, sunlight, and extreme temperatures," Daphne explained. "You wouldn't catch the Louvre taping the *Mona Lisa* up on somebody's kitchen refrigerator, would you?"

Lila crossed her arms. "How many storage units?"

"What?" Daphne, clearly stalling, pretended not to hear.

Lila gave her a bad-cop stare. "How. Many."

"One. Okay, two."

"And what's the monthly rental fee for the units?"

"You can't put a price on art, pumpkin."

"Where did you even get all this?" Lila asked. "A lot of it looks like it's from the fifties and sixties."

"Well, I found some of it at vintage boutiques and flea markets in Paris and Milan." Her mother's smile turned mischievous. "And I might have liberated a few pieces from the runway and designer showrooms."

"You *stole* this stuff? I had no idea you were such a criminal."

"I was all kinds of things before I met your father." Daphne suddenly looked about twenty years younger. "Before I got married and moved here and had you, I used to . . ."

"You used to what?" Lila took a seat next to her mother, fascinated.

Daphne caught herself and shook her head. "Nothing. It was a different time in my life, that's all." Her expression had gone carefully neutral.

"Well, what do you think we should do with these clothes?" Lila thought about what the estate jeweler had suggested to the woman trying to sell the antique hair comb. She tried to figure out how to word this delicately, then decided it was best to be blunt. "We could put a few up for sale on eBay."

Daphne shook her head. "Pack everything up and put it back where you found it."

"But we need to—"

"I said no, Lila." Her mother's tone sharpened. "It's my *life* packed away up there, not some archaeological fashion dig. We're not selling my heart and soul on eBay."

"Okay, okay." Lila nodded, then pushed her chair away from the table. "Actually, you know what? It's not okay."

Daphne gasped. "Excuse me?"

"You can't keep going like this." Lila took a deep breath. "*We* can't keep going like this."

"Speak for yourself, Lila Jane."

"Fine, I will. *I,* Lila Jane Alders, am broke. I'm

scared. I have no idea what I'm going to do with the rest of my life. But the one thing I do know is that waiting for someone else to come along and bail me out isn't working."

"Our situations are different." Daphne pulled the lapels of her robe tighter. "Your husband left you. Mine died."

Lila paused to absorb the sting of this. She kept her voice low and calm. "Yes, Mom. He died. And now you have no money."

"I have money." Daphne ducked her head. "It's just a temporary cash flow problem—"

"No money," Lila repeated. "Wake up and smell the red ink."

At this, her mother's bravado vanished.

Lila leaned over, both hugging and shielding her mother. "I know you have no idea what to do next. Neither do I. But we have to help each other. We have to try."

Daphne relaxed into her daughter for a moment, then pulled away, sighing. "Designers used to make dresses with me in mind. There was a famous designer in the eighties named Cedric Jameson. You've heard of him, of course."

Lila had no clue who Cedric Jameson was, but she nodded anyway.

"Cedric loved me. He adored me. He used to beg me to go to the Maldives for a week with him. He called me his muse. I was a muse, do you hear me?"

"Your ex-boyfriends are way cooler than mine," Lila admitted.

"I used to date designers and artists and musicians—two or three at a time. And now I'm old and anonymous and stuck in *Delaware*. I didn't mind it when I was with your father; he loved this town so much. But now . . ." A few drops of tea sloshed out of Daphne's mug as she gestured at the overcast gray horizon beyond the bay window. "Put yourself in my shoes, Lila. What would you do if you were me?"

Lila saw her opening. "*I* would put my old clothes up for auction on eBay. There's got to be some demand for vintage Halston in perfect condition."

"Here." Daphne handed Lila the silver spoon with a dramatic flourish. "You might as well just use that to carve my heart out."

"Let's not be hasty. No point in carving your heart out unless someone meets the reserve price."

"How can you joke about this? How can you *laugh* about selling my Halston?"

"Fine, then pick something else. We could probably get a week's worth of groceries for some old Gucci."

Daphne turned up her nose. "I'd rather go hungry."

"Spoken like a true model." Lila hurried back up to the attic and returned to the kitchen with a cloth garment bag, out of which she pulled a gauzy white floor-length gown with a cluster of peach roses at the waist. "The label says Christian Dior. Is this authentic?"

"Well, of course." Daphne looked offended. "Do you think I'd pollute my wardrobe with knockoffs?"

"When was this made?"

"I'm not sure." Daphne glanced at the silk roses. "Sometime in the mideighties. That was never one of my favorite pieces. It's a little too sweet and froufrou for my tastes."

Lila smiled. "Great. Then you won't care if I sell it."

Daphne's complexion went ashen. "What? No!"

"You just said it wasn't one of your favorites."

"But it's still special. It's in perfect condition. It's one of a kind!"

"Great. Hopefully, it'll fetch a nice price." Lila zippered the gown back up. "Let me sell this one, as an experiment. Just to see what the market's like. *Take action,* Mom. That's our new motto."

Daphne stammered for a few seconds, then breathed a sigh of relief as a thought occurred. "But you can't. Neither one of us has any idea how to use eBay."

"Maybe not currently. But if I can vanquish the lawn, I can figure out eBay. Talking people into impulse buys is what I do best, remember?"

• • •

The next day, Lila dropped by the real estate office on her way into Black Dog Bay's blink-and-you'll-miss-it downtown. Whitney finished up a phone call and waved her into an office.

"Hey. I just wanted to give you an update," Lila said. "We're still planning to sell the house. I have to work on my mom a little, but eventually, she'll break down and sign the broker contract. I just don't want you to feel like we're wasting your time."

Whitney sat back in her desk chair, and Lila noticed framed photos of a baby girl next to the computer. "You're not wasting my time. Your mom's been in that house for years, and she cares about what happens to it. That's normal."

Lila peered more closely at the photographs. The baby was wearing a darling seersucker sailor dress. "Is that your daughter?"

Whitney nodded and beamed with maternal pride. "Kyrie Rose. That picture's a few months old. She just started walking—scratch that, she skipped walking and went straight to running."

Lila gazed at the photo with a physical pang of longing and regret for the marriage she'd lost and the children she'd planned to have. "I love that dress. I didn't know they even made those little sailor suits for girls anymore."

"Isn't it cute? It's actually mine from when I

was little. My mom kept some of my baby stuff and gave it to me when I got pregnant."

"That is so sweet. And she really took care of it—it looks brand-new."

"Well, actually, my—" Whitney broke off and clapped her hand over her mouth.

"What?" Lila tilted her head, waiting.

"Nothing. It's just . . ." Whitney's eyes darted from side to side and then she whispered, "My brother redid some of the stitching on the neckline and the sleeves."

Lila blinked, remembering the encounter she'd had with Malcolm outside the Whinery—*that* brute had hand-smocked a cute little nautical dress for his niece? With his strong, calloused, sweaty hands?

"*Please* don't tell him I told you. He'd die if anyone knew. He only did this for Kyrie's birthday because I begged him." Whitney gave Lila a little nudge. "He's good, though, right?"

"He's amazing." Lila picked up the photo and examined the ruffles and pin tucks. "But I thought you said he was off in the Marines doing super-secret, badass stuff?"

"He was. Which is why you can never say one word about any of this to anyone. Seriously, I'll disappear in the night and no one will ever find my body."

Lila continued to marvel over the craftsman-ship. "Where did he learn to sew like that?"

"Oh, well, our mom was a seamstress, you know."

"I didn't know."

"Yeah, before she married our stepdad. Anyway, the community theater hired her to make all their costumes. And she and my grandma would force Malcolm to help as soon as he was old enough to thread a needle." Whitney smiled. "I'm not surprised he never told you. I'm sure he was very concerned with impressing you with his seventeen-year-old manliness. Once he started running track, he didn't even look at a spool of thread for like twenty years."

Lila glanced up from the photo. "And you're *sure* I went out with him?"

"According to him." Whitney paused, an impish grin on her face. "He only sews now if I guilt-trip the heck out of him. We'll both be in trouble if he finds out that I blabbed." She became pensive. "He probably could kill both of us with just his pinkie finger and a paper clip. He did do all that badass, super-secret Marine stuff."

"I'm the soul of discretion." Lila exclaimed a few more times over how cute Kyrie was, then said good-bye to the Realtor and got back to her busy schedule of *taking action*—with maybe one little detour along the way.

The Ramones' "I Wanna Be Sedated" was blasting on the Whinery's sound system while

Jenna wiped down the bar. Summer was sitting front and center, tapping away on her laptop.

"Hey." Summer lifted her glass of lemonade in greeting. "Working from my satellite office today."

"You look troubled." Jenna poured a glass of ice water and slid it across the bar to Lila, Old West saloon–style. "Sit down and spill your guts."

"I need tech support." Lila took a seat and positioned her stool so she wouldn't be blinded by the afternoon sunlight reflecting off the crystal chandelier. "I want to sell one of my mother's Diors on eBay, but my computer skills are pretty much limited to looking up my old classmates on Facebook and weeping bitter tears."

"I've been there." Jenna blew out her breath. "Existential angst, red wine, and Facebook do *not* mix."

"Hold up." Summer tapped her fingernail on the bar. "So these Diors—your mother has more than one?"

"Her attic is crammed full of couture," Lila said. "Plus the guest room, most of the closets, and at least two storage units that she'll admit to."

"That's a lot of fancy old clothes."

"Yes, it is. And everything must go, because she needs to downsize, like, yesterday."

Summer kept tapping her nail. "Know what you

should do? You should rent out a storefront for the summer season."

Lila seized on this idea and got all excited—for about three seconds, after which reality set in. "We don't have the cash flow to open a business right now. In that we have no cash at all. That's why we're selling the Dior gown in the first place."

"You have to spend money to make money," Summer declared with supreme authority. "Go big or go home—words to live by."

"I can't even figure out how to put together an eBay listing," Lila protested. "How am I supposed to open a retail business?"

"You just do it," Summer assured her. "It's amazing how much shit you can get done when you don't stop to think about the consequences."

"Everyone comes to Black Dog Bay for a reason," Jenna said. "Maybe this is your reason."

Lila considered this for a moment, then shook her head. "You have to remember, I grew up here. This is the opposite of a fresh start. I'm up to my eyeballs in old mistakes and ex-boyfriends and unfinished business." She paused to laugh. "That would be a good name for the vintage boutique: Unfinished Business. Appropriate on so many levels."

"That boutique is going to happen," Summer predicted. "Mark my words."

"But how?" Lila turned up her palms. "I don't

have any money or business experience, and my mother will fight me on every single sale."

"Put it out to the universe and wait for a sign," Jenna advised.

"I'd need a pretty clear sign," Lila said. "Like, flashing neon right in my face."

"Then throw that out there and see what comes back. In the meantime, let's get you up and running on eBay." Summer made a little moue with her lips as she reviewed their tech support options. "Let's see, Dutch is in meetings all day; Ingrid could probably help, but she has science Olympiad after school. We need someone smart and reasonably computer literate, with too much free time on their hands." She snapped her fingers and grabbed her cell phone. "I know just the guy." She dialed the phone and held it to her ear. Instead of greeting the other party with "Hello," she yelled, "Proof of life, Sorensen! Where the hell have you been? Did you *die?*"

Jenna clapped both hands to her heart. Lila glanced around in confusion.

Summer turned her back on them and walked outside to finish her conversation. Two minutes later, she was back on her barstool. "We're all set," she told Lila. "Jake Sorensen's on it."

"Who's Jake Sorensen?" Lila asked.

"The hottest guy to ever walk the streets of Black Dog Bay." Jenna twisted up a pink dish towel. "Everybody's dream man."

Summer rolled her eyes at this. "He's pretty hot. He's also emotionally crippled, too rich for his own good, and suffering from a terminal case of ennui."

"Like I said." Jenna nodded. "Everybody's dream man." She looked longingly at the cell phone. "Did you tell him I love him?"

"I don't have to, honey. He knows. Ooh, I love this song." Summer did a little chair dance as Dierks Bentley's "Drunk on a Plane" came on.

"Jake Sorensen," Lila repeated. "Never heard of him. He must have moved here after I left."

"He only lives here part-time," Summer said. "No one knows what he does for the rest of the year. He's very inscrutable. It adds to the whole Jake Sorensen mystique."

"As do the bedroom eyes and the bone structure of a Michelangelo sculpture," Jenna added.

"Mark my words: One of these days Mr. Inscrutable is going to meet his match, and all his money and mystique won't mean jack. But until then, he might as well make himself useful." Summer, still chair dancing, put her hands in the air and waved them like she just didn't care. "E-mail some pictures of the dress to me. I'll forward them to him, and he'll take care of everything."

Chapter 11

"Holy crap." Five days later, Lila sat at her father's desk, staring at the winning bid for the white Dior dress. "Mom, check it out!"

Daphne peered over Lila's shoulder at the computer screen. "Did someone buy my gown?"

"Yeah—for about ten times what I expected." Lila skimmed the message from the winning bidder. "The buyer wants to know if we have any more pieces similar to this one."

"No."

Lila kept reading the buyer's note. "She says the seam construction and appliqué work look meticulous. And check out her signature—she's a member of some online vintage clothing forum."

"Stop clicking!" Daphne cried as Lila started to investigate the forum. "No good can come of this."

"Are you kidding me? Cash money can come of this, Mom! We're sitting on a gold mine full of silk and cashmere and Chantilly lace." Lila bookmarked the online discussion board.

"I don't care for that look in your eyes," Daphne said.

"Look how many bidders we had." Lila pored over the analytics that eBay provided. "Look how many page views we got for this one item! There's a real market here."

"For the last time, it's not merely an 'item'; it is a one-of-a-kind couture original. It has a history. It was designed and created by artisans. And you sold it to the highest bidder like a soulless mercenary."

"You say 'soulless mercenary'; I say 'financially solvent.'" Lila mulled over her options. "You mentioned you were friends with Cedric Jameson back in the day?"

Daphne's expression flitted between brassy and bashful. "Oh, we were a bit more than friends, sweet pea. I was his muse. His obsession."

"I remember you saying that." Lila cleared her throat and pulled up some bio information. "But Cedric Jameson is gay, according to Wikipedia."

Daphne waved one hand. "Who are you going to believe, me or Wikipedia? Besides, the relationship between artist and muse can't be reduced to base sexuality."

"Whatever. Wikipedia also says he has a cult following in the fashion world and his older pieces are extremely rare and valuable. Do you still have anything of his?"

"I have hand-sewn, made-to-measure originals. They're not even dresses; they're labors of love." Daphne narrowed her eyes. "And you may not lay a finger on them, so don't even think about it."

"Too late." Lila jumped to her feet. "People will pay for old clothes. And hats and handbags and luggage. Anything with the right label."

"Stop right there!" Daphne threw up her palm. "No one touches my Louis Vuitton luggage. Not now, not ever. And the fact that you think this is about labels shows how ignorant you are. The labels aren't what matter to a real collector. What matters is the stitching, the fabric, the style."

"My mistake. So back to the original question: Any chance you're still in touch with your old buddy Cedric?"

Daphne gazed out the window. "He's been a recluse in Brussels for the last twenty years. One of those tortured artistic geniuses."

Something in her mother's tone stirred Lila's suspicions. "I didn't ask if he was a recluse, Mom. I asked if you're still in touch with him."

Daphne hesitated for a long moment. "We exchange letters every few years."

"Uh-huh. And what does he do when he's not wasting away in a garret somewhere in Brussels?"

"I'm not entirely sure." Daphne gestured vaguely. "I believe he travels."

"Interesting." Lila loomed over her mother. "And where do these travels take him?"

Hemming, hawing, and throat-clearing ensued. "I couldn't really say."

"I see." Lila nodded. "Well, get out your pen and your fancy engraved stationery, because we're inviting your tortured genius of an ex-boyfriend to come do a special appearance for his die-hard fans at the fanciest vintage couture shop on the eastern seaboard."

Daphne stopped feigning confusion and focused on Lila with laser-like intensity. "What are you talking about?"

Lila grinned as excitement coursed through her. She couldn't remember the last time she'd felt so energized. "The boutique we're going to open this summer."

"We don't have a boutique," Daphne pointed out.

"You mean we don't have a boutique . . . *yet*," Lila corrected.

Daphne's laugh gave way to an expression of horror as she realized Lila was serious. "We're *never* having a boutique. We can't afford it, for one thing."

"A few more eBay sales like that and we'll have enough for a deposit on a short-term lease." Lila left out the part where they'd be raiding her mother's climate- and moisture-controlled storage units for inventory.

Daphne wasn't going to give up without a fight. "And for another thing, we're targeting a very specialized market. Your average tourist is not just going to walk in off the street and drop a thousand dollars on a cocktail dress."

"Excuse me? You've been to the boardwalk in July. Plenty of those tourists are filthy rich, not to mention the summer residents." Lila tapped her temple, feigning confusion. "Now why are they summer residents, again? Oh, that's right—it's because they have enough money to buy *summer homes* on the beach."

"Just because they have money doesn't mean they have taste," Daphne argued. "Civilians want brand-new, mass-produced 'style' from the mall, not a Louis Féraud maxidress from 1965."

Lila laughed. "Civilians?"

"The general public," Daphne clarified. "Tragic, banal *non*visionaries who wear whatever the magazines tell them to."

"We'll just see about that."

"No, we won't! There's nothing to see!"

"Maybe, maybe not." Lila squared her shoulders and looked out the window at the overcast sky. "I'm waiting for a sign."

Twenty minutes later, as Lila parked the FUV between two vacant spots at the very back of the grocery store parking lot (she'd given up hoping that her spatial skills would improve with practice), the clouds literally parted and golden rays of sun broke through the fog.

She stumbled over the folding metal running boards *again* while trying to get out of the driver's seat. Her purse went flying and her keys, sunglasses, wallet, and phone scattered across the pavement.

Lila snatched up her phone and hit the power button. "Live, damn it, live!"

While she stared down at the screen, a manicured hand offered up her sterling silver key ring.

"You okay?" asked a warm-eyed, middle-aged woman with a burnished copper bob and a slight Boston accent.

"Yes, thank you." Lila sighed with relief as her cell phone screen lit up and demanded her password. "This car and I are battling to the death, and I let down my guard for a second."

"You're going up against three tons of metal and glass and you're wearing those heels? Good luck, girl."

While Lila scooped up her sunglasses, wallet, and lipstick, the other woman located a travel pack of tissue, a tin of breath mints, and a tube of tinted sunscreen.

"I think that's everything." Lila frowned down at the fresh scratch on her sunglasses lens.

"Wait, is this yours?" The woman dashed two parking spaces over and picked up a scrap of silver.

Lila recognized the metal flower comb her biggest fan had given her at the engagement ring boneyard. "Yes, thank you."

The woman handed over the mints and the sunscreen, but held on to the hair comb. "This is beautiful. Is it vintage?"

Lila nodded. "Almost two hundred years old."

"I love it. Where'd you get it?"

Lila summarized her encounter with Marilyn at the estate jeweler. "It's one of a kind." A little stab of guilt shot through her. She'd promised to love this little piece of steel as it deserved to be loved. And here she'd been schlepping it around at the bottom of her bag amid loose change and lint, nearly abandoning it in a grocery store parking lot.

The woman held the metal prongs up in the sunlight, examining the comb from different angles. "Is it silver?"

"Steel," Lila corrected.

"That is so cool." There was a note of wistful longing in the woman's voice. She saw something in this little metal flower that Lila could not.

"Keep it," Lila said.

"Oh, I couldn't—"

"Please. I insist. The original owner wanted it to be worn and appreciated."

"Are you sure?"

Lila nodded. "I'd forgotten it was in my bag, to be honest. And you just saved it from getting run over by a minivan. You and this comb are meant to be together."

"Thank you." The woman fixed the comb in her hair, checking her reflection in the FUV's windshield. "This is exactly what I needed— something beautiful and brand-new. Well, it's technically old, but you know what I mean. I'm staying at the Better Off Bed-and-Breakfast, and I burned half my wardrobe last night in a bonfire." She lifted one eyebrow. "Including my Birkin."

Lila recoiled, clutching her chest as if shot. She finally understood how her mother must have felt, listing the eighties Dior on eBay. "You . . . you *burned* a Birkin bag?"

"It had to be done," the woman said, her expression grim. "Frankly, a lot of unpleasant things have had to be done lately. The Birkin was the least of it. And now, I want to start over with accessories that *aren't* tainted with lies and guilt and deception."

"I know how you feel." Lila put her hand on the woman's cashmere coat sleeve. "I just got divorced, myself. It's like your soul has been strip-mined."

"Yes. Thank you. You get it."

"But just so you know, there's a bar called the Whinery right down the street from your hotel. They have a box where you can drop off any other unwanted Birkin bags. Or you could just call me, and I'll take them off your hands."

"I'll bear that in mind." The woman touched the facets of the little steel flower, looking happy. Looking victorious.

Lila remembered how she herself used to feel, back when she still had the means to shop her way through emotional crises. That sudden surge of yearning, the sense of *having* to have something. She didn't feel that way anymore—not about clothes or furniture or cars, at least.

But she did feel that way about her new idea for a summer storefront. Maybe this whole thing with the hair comb was her sign. Maybe not.

Either way, she decided to take action.

She leaned back against the FUV, pulled out the real estate agency's business card, and dialed the office number. "Hey, Whitney, it's Lila. . . . No, I'm actually not calling about the house today. I'm wondering if you deal with commercial real estate at all? . . . Great, because I may be in the market to lease a storefront for the next few months. Do you happen to know if there's anything available near the boardwalk? . . . Oh, really? And it just came on the market today? Well, what a coincidence."

Chapter 12

"Guess what, Mom?" Lila strode into the big white house by the beach and headed straight for the kitchen. "You'll never guess."

"Well, then, you'd better just tell me."

"Remember how I said that we should open a

boutique? That I'd get a sign and everything would fall into place?"

Daphne nodded.

Lila rocked back on her heels. "This is the part where you guess."

"I'd rather not." Daphne sat down and folded her hands on the counter.

"Mom. Guess."

Daphne took her time fetching a glass from the cabinet, filling it with ice, and pouring in some water.

Lila gave up on waiting for her mother to share her enthusiasm. "I made a phone call to our real estate agent."

"Hmmm." Her mother sounded a bit inquisitive, but mostly bored.

"She said a new commercial space just became available this morning. Prime location—a block from the boardwalk, ocean views, lots of foot traffic. She said, and I quote, 'space like this almost never opens up.' "

"My, my. That's certainly something."

Lila sat down next her mother. "Can't you at least pretend to be a little bit excited?"

"No, because I don't think I like where this conversation is going."

"Well, you'll like this part," Lila predicted. "Guess who owns that retail space?"

Her mother turned up her hands in surrender. "Who?"

"Ben Collier."

Daphne finally started to smile. "Ooh, maybe you're right. Maybe we *are* meant to open a boutique."

Lila slapped her palms down on the counter. "Are you serious?"

"Why are you mad? I'm agreeing with you!"

"I can't believe this," Lila fumed. "For days, you've been going on about how much you love your couture and how could I betray you and over your dead body. And then, the *minute* I say Ben Collier is involved, you're on board and ready to open up shop?"

"You have your signs from the universe; I have mine." Daphne sipped her water. "What did I tell you? You and Ben are meant to be. If selling off some of my couture is what it's going to take to get you two back together, then I'm willing to make the sacrifice."

"So me getting back together with Ben means more to you than hanging on to your Halstons?"

Daphne nodded. "Sweet pea, I just want you to be taken care of."

Lila tried to put aside her outrage and focus on the business aspects. "The problem is, we can't afford to pay what he's asking. We're not even in the ballpark."

"Well, then, you'll have to, ahem, negotiate." Daphne gave her a conspiratorial wink. "I'm sure he'll be willing to make an exception for you."

Lila leveled her gaze. "Mom."

"What? Persuade him."

"*Persuade* him?" Lila tsk-tsked. "That's exploitative and manipulative. You should be ashamed of yourself."

"How is it manipulative? You were going to get friendly with him, anyway. You just went out for drinks with him."

"Yes, because you sent him over to the Whinery. Which reminds me, I've been meaning to have a stern talk with you about these play-dates."

"We'll talk about the playdates later. Right now, we need to keep our eyes on the prize, and that's retail space with an ocean view."

"Yeah, but . . ."

"But what?"

Lila furrowed her brow. "I don't know."

"Then stop bickering with me and hop to." Daphne sent Lila off with a little shake of her ice-filled glass. "Retail space by the boardwalk isn't going to last."

"That's what Whitney said."

"And she's the expert. Is Ben working in his dad's old office? Go talk to him." Daphne's tone took on a note of urgency. "Today. Now. Hurry!"

"But isn't this a conflict of interest?"

"No, it's a *combination* of interests. It's fate! Destiny! Get going!"

"All right, all right." Lila grabbed her car keys and headed for the door. "I'll see what I can do."

"I'm so proud of you! My little girl's a woman of action. You're going to save this house for me. Your father would be proud, too."

"Let's not get ahead of ourselves. He hasn't said yes yet."

"He will. Ben Collier could never refuse you." Daphne grabbed her daughter's wrist as Lila headed for the kitchen door. "Especially once you change your lipstick and spritz on some perfume. Here, come upstairs and let me find you the perfect outfit."

Forty minutes later, Lila arrived at Ben's office looking coiffed, coordinated, and ready for her close-up. She had glossy pink lips and a soft cashmere sweater and high-heeled black boots that imbued her with confidence.

She did not, however, have an appointment. Details, details.

But she climbed the wooden steps to the building's second floor and opened the glass door marked COLLIER PROPERTIES. She swept into the reception area with what she hoped was great aplomb and announced, "I'm here to see Ben Collier."

A placid-faced assistant looked up with a smile. "Is he expecting you?"

"No, but I'm his . . ." She faltered. "He and I go

144

back to high school. I know I should have called ahead, but I was hoping I could just pop in and say hi."

The smile flickered. "He's on a conference call right now. Why don't you leave your name and I'll have him—"

Before Lila could respond, she heard another door open, and then Ben's voice. "Great to see you, sweetie! Come on back."

"Wow." Lila glanced around the office, taking in the massive mahogany desk, the matching leather club chairs, and the varnished hickory flooring. "You're a big deal."

Ben laughed. "I'm getting there. Wrestling control away from my dad inch by inch. You know how he is about the business."

"Little bit of a control freak?"

"Little bit. He drops by every morning to make sure I haven't run the place into the ground."

"I'm sure you're doing great." She gave him a flirty hair toss. "Look at you, with your desk and your blueprints. Very authoritative."

"I'm glad someone's impressed."

"You sound surprised."

"I shouldn't be," he admitted. "You always had confidence in me."

She started to relax and enjoy herself. "And you should trust my judgment."

He gestured to one of the leather chairs and

she sat down, crossing her legs and swinging her ankle.

"I'm actually handling my first solo project," he said. "One of our boardwalk properties is up for lease."

"I heard."

"The last tenant had a five-year contract, and now that they're moving, I can finally ask for what the property's worth."

She stopped swinging her ankle. "Yes. About that . . ."

"I put it on the market this morning," Ben confided. "When I told my dad what I was listing it for, he about had a heart attack. He said I was overshooting and I'd never find a tenant."

Lila straightened her back. "You know, it's funny you should bring that up."

"But we had an offer by lunch. I just got off the phone with the new tenant."

She sank back into her seat. "Oh."

"It's some funnel cake franchise. They agreed to all the terms. Didn't even try to negotiate."

How could she take action now? What could she even *say?* "Oh."

"It's a big corporation, so I guess they don't need to nickel-and-dime their landlords." Ben looked inordinately proud, but she had to ask:

"Have you signed the contracts yet?"

"No, but their agent is sending over the documents by Monday. If all goes well, it'll be signed and settled by the end of next week." His smile faded as he noticed her reaction. "What's wrong? You look upset."

"What? No. I was just listening. I had no idea real estate deals came together so quickly."

"They usually don't."

"I mean, four hours from listing to writing up a contract?"

He nodded. "Crazy."

"But I know space by the boardwalk is hard to come by." She cleared her throat. "You don't happen to have any other properties coming onto the market soon, do you?"

"Nope." He dusted off his hands. "This is it for the foreseeable future. My dad will finally have to back off and admit that I know what I'm doing."

She knew that this was the moment to "persuade" him, to lower her voice to a husky whisper and "negotiate," but she just couldn't do it. He had so much to prove and he deserved his success. So she did what she'd always done— supported him. "That's great, Ben. I'm thrilled for you."

"We should have dinner," he said. "To cele-brate."

"That sounds lovely."

"Friday night?" he suggested. "My place?"

She stood up and collected her handbag and coat with a sinking heart. "It's a date."

He walked her to the door and kissed her. On the lips.

For a moment, she was too startled to process what was happening. Then she registered the warm pressure of his lips against hers, the pressure of his arms around her waist.

She could hear the phone ringing out in the reception area and a car rumbling in the alley below. This was what she'd been waiting for. A moment thirteen years in the making. The kiss that would rekindle the love that was meant to be.

And it felt . . . fine.

Chapter 13

"Well?" The next day, Jenna and Summer demanded Lila report to the Whinery for happy hour. "What happened with you and Ben yesterday? We heard you went to his office wearing some very sexy shoes."

"Um . . ." Lila took a sip of lemonade and stalled for time. "Where'd you hear that?"

"Beryl—she owns the Retail Therapy boutique —saw you while she was taking out the trash." Summer glanced down at Lila's fashionably shod feet. "She said you had Catwoman boots on and your hair looked like a shampoo commercial."

Lila nibbled the end of her straw. "So?"

"So then you came out a few minutes later looking all glowy." Summer turned to Jenna. "Those were Beryl's words, right?"

"Glowy," Jenna confirmed. "We need all the juicy details."

"I don't want to talk about it," Lila murmured.

Jenna smiled. "Sadly, no one here cares what you want. We demand answers."

"Whatever happened to privacy?" Lila went back to gnawing her straw. "Whatever happened to ladylike discretion?"

"Oh, you forfeited your right to privacy and ladylike discretion when you crossed the town border," Summer informed her. "Check the municipal code."

Lila looked at the inquisitive faces staring back at her and gave up on playing innocent.

"It was actually supposed to be a business meeting." She pushed her stool back from the bar. "It turns out his family's company has a storefront up for lease in a prime location."

"Perfect timing!"

"Not really." Lila explained that the space had already been spoken for. "Stupid funnel cakes. And you know I can't afford to get into a bidding war. So much for the Unfinished Business vintage clothing boutique."

Summer looked offended. "You need more real estate options? Why didn't you come to me?"

"Because you're not a real estate tycoon?"

"Ye of little faith."

Lila turned to Jenna. "Does she run this whole town?"

Jenna nodded. "Pretty much."

"Don't lose hope, chickadee." Summer pressed her palms together. "We're not out of options yet."

Lila glanced at the rows of bottles behind the bar. "You're not going to tell me to put on something lacy and low-cut and go back to Ben to 'persuade' him, are you? Because my mother already covered that."

"Nope. I'm going to tell you to put on something high-necked and long-sleeved and prepare to have fun—but not *too* much fun." Summer produced her phone and started dialing. "I've got a drinking buddy with some commercial property investments."

The next morning, Summer met Lila at the Jilted Café and made the introductions beneath the red and white striped awning.

"Jake Sorensen, this is Lila Alders," Summer said. "She grew up here, she's been out in the real world for a bit, and now she's back and needs a place to set up shop for the summer."

Lila shook the hand of the hottest guy to ever walk the streets of Black Dog Bay.

He smiled down at her, all dark eyes and white teeth and Michelangelo bone structure. Lila could see why he had women swooning over him.

Summer snapped her fingers to regain everyone's attention. "Jake here is our designated rebound guy, man of international intrigue, eBay pinch hitter, and all-around man-whore."

Lila broke out her sweetest smile. "*Enchantée.*"

"Behave yourself," Summer warned. "*Both* of you."

"We will," Jake promised, in a tone that promised everything but.

Summer gave him a stern look. "Do I need to ride shotgun and chaperone you?"

Lila and Jake shared a laugh. "No."

"Stop worrying about us," Jake told Summer, "and start worrying about your wedding."

Summer gasped. "Oh my God, have you been talking to Ingrid?"

Lila whirled around to hug Summer. "You and Dutch are getting married?"

Summer sidestepped the hug. "No. Well, not officially. Wedding stuff gives me hives. And don't try to change the subject." She leveled her index finger and pointed it first at Lila, then at Jake. "I'll see you back here in no more than one hour. The clock starts now." She walked toward the historical building, throwing a few threatening looks over her shoulder as she went.

As soon as Summer was out of view, Jake laughed again and turned off the smolder and sensuality. Lila felt completely comfortable with him as they walked toward their cars. (Jake took one look at the FUV and announced, "I'll drive.")

"So the storefront's over in Bethany Beach?" Lila asked.

"Yeah. I'll be honest—the location's not ideal. It's a few blocks west of the boardwalk, but it's all I have available right now. Season's starting in a few weeks. I'll give you a great deal on the lease terms, though."

"Because Summer is your drinking buddy?"

"More like my drill sergeant."

While they made the short trip to Bethany Beach, Lila wondered what it would be like to have a male friend who truly was just a friend. To be able to appreciate masculine energy and perspective without getting all tangled up in sexual attraction and expectations. To have a conversation without feeling it was a mere prelude to physical contact.

In thirty years, she'd never had a mutually supportive, platonic friendship with a member of the opposite sex. And obviously Jake hadn't, either—on the two-block walk from their parking spot in Bethany Beach to the vacant storefront, no fewer than five women approached him:

"Hi, Jake."

"When did you get back into town?"

"I'm Sarah, and I'm staying at the Better Off Bed-and-Breakfast. Room ten. Why don't you drop by tonight?"

One of the women acknowledged Lila with a death glare, but the others ignored her completely. They had eyes (and pouting lips and exaggerated hair flips) only for Jake. He deflected them with his sexy smile and easy charm, never pausing in his stride or committing to any of the indecent proposals.

"You really are famous," Lila marveled as he led her around the corner. "In Black Dog Bay *and* Bethany Beach."

"Yeah." His tone was sardonic. "Some guys do brain surgery. Some guys pull people out of burning buildings. I'm the designated rebound guy. It's my calling."

Lila laughed. "No wonder you and Summer get along. She must be like a breath of fresh air. Or a slap in the face."

He shrugged. "I don't get metaphorical about it. I just answer her calls and do what she says."

"Hey, speaking of which, thank you so much for helping us out with the eBay listing."

"No worries."

"I really appreciate it. I know I should be able to handle a simple Internet auction, but I've been on a very steep learning curve lately."

"I'll deny this if you tell Summer," he confided, "but I made my company tech guy take care of it. So don't be too grateful."

Jake had been right about the location being less than ideal. Although the space was light and airy, the storefront was situated on a side street with limited parking and very little foot traffic.

Lila turned around, taking in the room's dimensions and view of a brick wall. Jake watched her, and then, not even two minutes after he'd unlocked the front door, ushered her back out.

"We're done here."

"But I didn't even say anything!" she exclaimed.

"You didn't have to. I'm good at reading people. Goes with the whole 'man-whore' territory."

"Yeah, about that." Lila waited for him to lock the door behind them. "You don't seem all that man-whorish to me."

"Summer told me to behave myself, and when the drill sergeant gives an order, I obey," he said. "Besides, you're a waste of time right now."

Lila stopped in her tracks. "Excuse me?"

"You're thinking about somebody else."

"That is . . ." Lila geared up for a vehement denial, then decided there was no point in lying to herself or anyone else. ". . . amazing. You really are good at reading people."

He drove back to Black Dog Bay and dropped her off next to her hulking white FUV, which was taking up a parking space and a half across from the café. Lila thanked him, dashed across the street, fished through her purse for her car keys, and then dashed back to Jake.

He didn't seem at all surprised when she

154

knocked on his window. If anything, he looked amused. "Yes?"

She forced the words out. "You're good at reading people?"

He turned off the ignition and settled back in his seat. "That's what they tell me."

"And you obviously know a few things about dating and romance, right?"

His expression and voice went completely neutral. "What's your question?"

"Well, there's this guy. . . ." She gave him the bullet points on Ben, the storefront, and the kissing. "So I'm having dinner with him on Friday, and I know he's going to kiss me again."

He paused for a moment, sizing her up. "You don't seem very excited about that."

"No, I am, it's just . . . should I even bring up the retail space again?"

"Yes." There was no hesitation this time.

"But I don't want to muddy the waters." She nibbled her lip. "I don't want him to feel pressured or manipulated."

Jake launched into a mini-lecture with the authority of a tenured professor. "When a man likes you, he wants to help you. He wants to make you happy and impress you with his power and resources. It makes him feel good and induces you to take your clothes off. Everybody wins."

Lila stuck out her tongue. "That's lovely."

"You asked for the truth; I'm giving it to you."

"But how do I frame it? What can possibly compete with funnel cakes and free-flowing corporate money?"

He mulled this over for a moment. "A red dress and good scotch."

"Hmm."

"You like this guy? You want to seduce him?"

"I want to be seduced by him," she corrected. "I want us to go back to being the way we were."

"Then show up at his door with a bottle of scotch from the year you guys dated."

"Ooh, that's good."

"I know." He didn't bother trying to fake modesty.

"And I happen to have a connection at a liquor distributor." She made a mental note to contact Tyler Russo.

"There you go."

"Okay, so I show up at his door with my bottle of nostalgic scotch." Lila closed her eyes, envisioning the scene. "Then what? I fan the flames of passion with my red dress?"

"Right." Jake was starting to sound the teeniest bit impatient. "But that's only if there's a spark to begin with."

"There is," Lila assured him. "I'm the woman he always imagined himself ending up with. He said so himself."

"Then how could a few funnel cakes possibly compete?"

Chapter 14

In a futile attempt to distract herself from thinking about Ben, Lila spent the rest of the afternoon taking inventory of the guest room closet, where she discovered a gorgeous leopard-print car coat. The lapel consisted of a series of gently ruffled panels of black wool, the nipped-in waistline featured artfully stitched darting, and the bottom half flared out in a dramatic A-line. When she held the garment up for inspection, she noticed that a few of the buttons had fallen off and been stored in a small paper envelope in the pocket.

She had no idea who had made the coat or how old it was, but she had a feeling it would go fast—and for a high price—on eBay. So she folded the garment over one arm and headed downstairs in search of a needle and thread.

As she prepared to reattach the buttons, Daphne's voice rang out from the hallway.

"Stop right there! What do you think you're doing?"

Lila glanced down at the fabric, then back at her mother. "Sewing on a button?"

"Unhand that coat immediately, young lady.

You're not qualified to do any repair work."

"Relax, Mom. It's just a button."

"Just a button." Daphne laughed in disbelief. "Allow me to enlighten you: When it comes to couture, there's no such thing as 'just a button.' Every seam, every sleeve, every zipper, is expertly placed and stitched."

"But—"

Daphne shushed her. "You sewing a button onto that Valentino is like me taking a Sharpie to the *Mona Lisa*."

"Enough with the *Mona Lisa* analogies. There are other paintings, you know."

"Fine. You sewing a button onto that Valentino is like me taking a Sharpie to the *Birth of Venus*."

Lila held up the coat. "Are you sure this is Valentino?"

"Yes."

"How can you tell? There's no label."

"It's Valentino," Daphne said. "I'm positive. I'm also positive that you're about to defile a masterpiece, not to mention bring down the resale value considerably. Put that needle down."

Lila put the needle down.

Daphne paced the perimeter of the rug, thinking. "You know, this is going to be a problem. If we're going to sell vintage pieces, we'll need someone to handle repairs and alterations."

Lila was so happy that her mother had finally reconciled herself to the idea of selling off her collection that she didn't dare interrupt.

"Where are we going to find a Valentino-worthy seamstress in this godforsaken backwater?" Daphne grabbed the coat and examined the loose bits of thread on the lapels. "Maybe we can find someone in Dover or Wilmington who can come in every few weeks."

"No need to outsource to Dover." Lila headed up to her room, taking the steps two at a time. "We've got the perfect solution right here in Black Dog Bay."

Another day, another ex-boyfriend.

As late afternoon faded into dusk, Lila knocked on the door of the charming Craftsman-style cottage and waited on the welcome mat with what she hoped was an air of casual confidence. She'd taken great care with her hair and makeup, striving for a balance of pretty and approachable with jeans, a feminine green blouse, and her hair in loose waves. No sweaters tonight. Or sweat. Or thinking about sweat-drenched shirts and the abs underneath them . . .

No one answered the door, so she knocked again.

Still no response.

She listened to the rustle of the wind blowing through the towering pine trees. Whitney hadn't been exaggerating when she'd compared this place to *Walden*. The wooded enclave obstructed the views of the road and neighboring houses, and the atmosphere was peaceful but remote, in total contrast to the close-knit community of the beach properties.

Lila was deliberating whether she should sit down on the stoop to wait when she glimpsed a man jogging along a winding dirt trail. He was tall, imposing, muscular, and, yes, saturated in sweat again.

And just like that, she was thinking about everything she had resolved not to think about.

Malcolm took out his earbuds and slowed to a walk when he noticed her. "Lila Alders."

"Hi." She smiled and studied his face, trying to remember any specifics about him. "I'm back."

"I see that." He came closer. Despite the perspiration soaking his T-shirt, all she could smell was the faint trace of laundry detergent.

"We didn't really get to catch up the other night." She leaned back against the sturdy wooden porch railing, keeping the canvas bag containing the Valentino coat behind her legs. "How've you been?"

He shrugged, leaning over to retie his shoe-lace. "Fine."

She shoved the bag back with her heel. "You look very serious and grown-up. I heard you joined the military."

He straightened up. "The Marines."

"Were you in the Middle East?"

"Okinawa, Japan. I was in the military police force. SRT."

"What's SRT?" she asked.

"Special Reaction Team. It's like the military SWAT."

She blinked a few times. "That sounds pretty intense."

He finally smiled. "It had its moments. And then I got recruited for one of the intelligence teams in D.C."

"Which I'm guessing you can't talk about."

"It sounds more exciting than it is. We mostly sat around talking and using computers."

"And now you're back in Delaware?"

His smile turned wry. "I guess none of us can stay away, huh?"

"I guess not. I'm here trying to help my mom get back on her feet." She toyed with the pendant at the hollow of her throat. "So what else are you up to these days?"

"Doing some consulting work."

"Oh?" She waited for him to elaborate, but he just stood there. "Like what kind of consulting?"

He started stretching his calf muscles. "Cyber-security, mostly."

"Oh. And, um, what does that entail?"

"Patching digital holes." He moved on to stretching his quads.

161

"Well, if you have a few spare minutes, I could really use your help." She opened the bag at her feet and pulled out the leopard-print coat.

He took a step back. "What's that?"

"It's a Valentino coat from the early sixties. Isn't it beautiful?"

He lifted his water bottle to his mouth, took a swig, and spit into the bushes.

Lila kept her TV-host smile fixed on her lips. "I'm hoping you can help me out with it."

His eyes narrowed. "Help you out with what?"

She pulled the missing buttons out of the pocket. "I need someone to reattach these. Someone who knows what they're doing."

He regarded her with a mix of silent horror and outrage, so she just kept talking. "Can you work with materials of this quality?"

He set the water bottle down on the ground, crossed his arms, and gave her a stare that made her shiver. "I have no idea what you're talking about."

She lowered her voice and whispered, "It's okay. I know everything. I know about . . ." She waited a beat. "The seersucker."

Malcolm visibly paled. "I am going to *kill* Whitney."

"Now, now, let's not go killing anyone just yet." Lila pushed the coat into his arms. "Let's focus on the topic at hand. Can you fix this?"

He picked up one of the buttons and examined it in the fading twilight. "Yeah."

"Are you sure?"

The big, burly former marine looked insulted. "Yes, I'm sure. It's a basic button technique with black upholstery thread."

"I have no idea what that means."

He gave her a derisive smirk. "Not surprised. It's not like you ever had to clean up after yourself."

"You know what? You're absolutely right." She stepped back and held her arms away from her body. "I was spoiled and superficial and apparently cursed with a very spotty memory. Go ahead—take your shots. All I ask is that, when you're done, you give me the best button technique you have."

He mulled this over for a moment. "Why should I help you?"

"Because I'll pay you?" Even as she said this, she realized she had no idea what she should offer. "You just said that your job is patching holes, right? So this is basically the same thing! It's just cloth instead of digital code or whatever!"

He muttered something she didn't quite catch, then asked, "Do you even remember what happened in high school?"

"Um." She crinkled her nose. "Yes?"

"Stop lying. You have no idea what I'm talking

about. I called you at least five times after we hung out. And you never called me back."

"Well, I would have if I'd known you were so good with a needle and thread!" She threw up her hands. "I was young! I was foolish! I'm paying the price now, if that makes you feel any better."

He rolled his eyes in disgust. "Just give me that. I have to fix it now, or you'll tell everyone about me."

"Okay, A, I'm not going to tell anyone anything about you, and B, stop talking about sewing like it's some dirty secret."

He got a haunted look in his eyes. "It is a dirty secret."

"Are you even listening to yourself? You're a former SWAT-military-police-whatever who can baste and backstitch. It's the ultimate woman bait. You should be down at the Whinery right now, talking really loudly about how you can bench-press a Volkswagen and then whip up a darling little sailor suit for your niece." She nodded, considering the implications. "You could put your sweaty hands all over every cardigan in this town."

At this, his expression went from defensive to confused. And then his gaze intensified with unmistakable, almost predatory interest.

She straightened the neckline of her blouse. *"Anyway . . ."*

He folded up the coat and tucked it under his arm.

"Ooh." She winced. "Try not to get sweat on it."

He ignored that. "I'll reattach these buttons on one condition, and that condition is, you keep your mouth shut and we both forget this ever happened."

"Fine." Lila shrugged one shoulder. "I'll keep this quiet if you want me to, but I have to tell you, you're making a major tactical error here. Do you know how many women would love to find a hot, hunky guy who can sew?"

He spit in the bushes again.

Lila took this as her opportunity to open negotiations. "Look, I'm going to need a lot more repairs and alterations over the next few weeks, so I'd love to officially hire you. Can I put you on retainer or something?"

"No. No more repairs. No retainers. I fix this button and then we go our separate ways."

"We don't have to agree to any set terms right now." She set her voice to "soothing three a.m. sales pitch." "Let's just see how this button goes."

"I already know how this button is going to go. It's going to go awesome, because I kick ass." He glanced around to make sure there were no witnesses hiding in the woods. "But you can't come back for more. This is a one-time-only deal."

Lila crossed her arms. "But what if I need more?"

"You can't have it."

She tilted her head, noted the stubborn set of his jaw, and decided she'd pushed him far enough for one day.

"And you can't tell *anybody* about this," he repeated. "I mean ever."

She crossed her heart and hoped to die. "Don't worry."

"Ever."

"It's on lockdown," she assured him.

"It better be."

Lila remembered what his sister had said. "Or I'll disappear in the middle of the night and no one will ever find my body?"

His eyebrows shot up. "What exactly am I going to do with your body in the middle of the night?"

The evening was so humid, she could barely breathe. Everywhere she looked, there was sweat and skin and abs and more skin.

"I'm trusting you, Lila." He glanced down at the Marine Corps insignia on his T-shirt. "*Semper fi.*"

She repressed the urge to give an "Oorah!" in response and settled for a bone-crushing hand-shake. "*Semper fi.*"

Chapter 15

"Sit down, Lila. Stop prowling around like a panther." Daphne spent Friday morning curled up on the back porch with a book and a thick woolen blanket. Her cheeks were pink from the brisk spring wind blowing in from the ocean.

"I'm not prowling." Lila forced herself to stand still and look out at the waves.

"What are you so worked up about, anyway?"

"I need your fashion expertise." Lila started pacing again, thinking about her dinner plans. "And the most, um, *persuasive* dress you have."

"Ooh, you talked to Ben." Daphne threw her book aside. "Is there still hope for our retail space?"

"I'm not sure," Lila admitted. "But I'm going to his house for dinner tonight."

"You are?" Daphne leaped out of her chair and led the way into the house. "And you're standing around with tangles in your hair and dark circles under your eyes? Get it together, pumpkin; we have work to do. Why didn't you tell me this earlier?"

"Because I didn't want you to react the way you're reacting right now."

"Chop-chop." Daphne bounded up the steps to the master suite. "You'll need to shower and shape your brows and touch up your nails. And we'll have to do something to brighten up your complexion—I have a sea salt scrub that works wonders." She gave Lila a look of reproach. "You know I've been telling you to go for a deep conditioning treatment. And if I may ask, have you waxed recently?"

"You may not ask."

"But—"

"Next question."

Daphne sighed but relented. "What are you thinking wardrobe-wise?"

Lila remembered Jake Sorensen's advice about a red dress. "Something that will turn me into Marilyn Monroe, basically. I don't suppose you have anything like that?"

"I've got just the thing." Her mother snapped her fingers and bustled across the room. "Quick, to the closet!"

"This dress should come with a warning label and a waiver." Daphne pulled a cherry red cocktail dress from between layers of acid-free tissue. "It's Ceil Chapman from the fifties, and let me tell you, that woman knew how to cut."

Lila looked at the shapeless swoops of red fabric. "I don't know; it looks a little—"

"Silence." Daphne pressed the dress into Lila's

arms and shooed her toward the bathroom. "I don't want to hear another word out of you until you try it on."

Two minutes later, Lila couldn't stop staring at her own reflection. Ceil Chapman, whoever she was, did indeed know how to cut a dress. The scarlet silk crepe skimmed her body without squeezing, and the fabric had been artfully gathered and draped to accentuate her curves.

"Forget Marilyn Monroe." She opened the door to show her mother. "I could be a double-crossing Bond girl in this thing."

"I told you." Daphne handed over some peep-toe nude pumps and tiny sapphire drop earrings. "Now put these on and never doubt me again."

"Seriously, I don't even know if I can walk down the street in this." Lila stepped into the shoes. "This dress is ridiculous. It's practically winking and blowing a kiss all by itself."

"It's not the dress, sweet pea; it's you. My girl's a beauty."

Lila adjusted the neckline, which started at the outer edge of her shoulders and dipped just low enough to show a hint of cleavage. "What kind of bra am I supposed to wear with this?"

"Well, that depends. Are you going to be leaving it on or taking it off at the end of your evening?"

"Mom!"

"It's a reasonable question! What you wear underneath the dress depends on who will be seeing it."

Lila hesitated, lacing her fingers together. "And you're not going to judge me?"

"Baby, I modeled in New York City in the eighties. I've got no room to judge anybody. Think of this dress as symbolic of your new beginning. It's . . . oh." Daphne knelt down and examined the back of the dress. "Uh-oh."

Lila tried to peer over her shoulder. "What now?"

"Your new beginning needs a new zipper. The old one's literally hanging by a thread." Daphne collapsed on the floor, deflated. "I guess we'll have to find something else for you to wear. There's no way we can get this repair done before dinnertime."

Lila held still while her mother helped her disrobe, then pulled her shirt on and said, "Let me make a call."

"To whom?"

"I cannot reveal my sources." Lila opened the door and pointed to the hallway. "Clear the room."

"I demand to know who you're contacting."

"Demand all you want. I'm not telling."

"Why not?"

"Remember when you said that I don't get to know every single thing about you? That there's

170

more to you than just being my mother?" Lila opened the door even wider. "Well, that goes both ways. Meet you in the kitchen in a few minutes. Let's make waffles for lunch."

"Oh, you can't have waffles today." Daphne looked scandalized. "You're off carbs until you're done with that dress."

"Bye." Lila waited until she heard her mother retreating down the stairs, then spent a moment brainstorming her sales pitch before dialing the phone. "Hi, Malcolm, it's Lila. You know that gas station on Highway One, out by the Black Dog Bay sign? I need you to meet me there in half an hour. Park on the north side of the building by the Dumpster, bring duct tape, and tell no one. It's an emergency."

"This better be good." Malcolm was waiting at the designated rendezvous point in exactly thirty minutes. For once, he wasn't in the middle of some long-distance run. He wore jeans and a soft plaid button-down shirt, the cuffs of which he'd rolled up over his strong, tan, nonsweaty forearms.

Lila stepped out of her white FUV clad in the black Catwoman boots, black skinny jeans, a black leather jacket, and black aviator sunglasses. "Did you come alone?"

He rolled his eyes, but nodded. "Nice outfit."

"You, too." She lowered her voice to a clandestine whisper. "Were you working when I called?"

"Yeah."

"Sorry."

"It's fine. I work from home."

"That's right." She arched one eyebrow. "And who did you say you work for, again?"

"I didn't." He glanced at his watch. "You've got five minutes and the clock starts now. Start talking, Alders."

"Okay." She paused for dramatic effect, then pulled a brown paper bag from the passenger seat.

He accepted the bag from her, took one look at the contents, and tossed it back. "No way."

Lila caught the bag in both hands. "I wouldn't ask if the situation weren't desperate."

He crossed his arms. "No."

"Please?"

"No."

"Come on! It's just a zipper. Can't you even look at it?"

"We had a deal." His blue eyes went all steely. "The coat button was a one-time thing. You agreed to those terms."

"I know, but I'm supposed to wear this dress in a few hours and there's no one else who can fix it." She took off her sunglasses and moved on to plan B: shameless begging. "Please? *Please!* It's Ceil Chapman."

"I don't know what that means, and I don't want to know."

She lifted out the layers of fabric, which were surprisingly heavy. "It's a collector's piece in pristine condition. Or at least, it was until the zipper fell out."

"Let me see that." He took the dress from her and ran his fingers over the ruched red silk. "Here's your problem—the edges of the zipper yoke rotted out. It happens sometimes with old fabric."

"Well, can you fix it?"

"I can. But I won't."

"Listen, I know we said that last night was the last time. But this is different. This is urgent." She put the sunglasses back on. "This is literally a matter of life and death."

His lips twitched. "Literally? You're telling me that if this zipper yoke doesn't get repaired, a human life hangs in the balance?"

"Fine, it's *figuratively* a matter of life and death. I'm supposed to wear this at eighteen hundred hours." She paused. "That's six o'clock in military time, right?"

Suddenly, his whole demeanor changed. He stopped acting irritated and became very—almost suspiciously—chatty. "What's the occasion?"

"Um . . . pardon?"

He glanced down at the red dress. "What's the occasion?"

She shoved her hands into her jacket pockets. "I'm just, uh, wearing it to dinner."

He nodded and leaned back against the FUV. "Tonight?"

"Yeah." It took every ounce of willpower she had not to fidget. "My mother picked it out."

His posture relaxed, but his tone was cagey. "Where are you going?"

"Nowhere special." She shifted her weight, repositioning her boots on the asphalt. "Just, you know, a house."

He let the silence drag on for a few seconds. "This is a pretty fancy dress."

"It's a dinner." She knew she was babbling now. "With friends. A friendly dinner."

"Male or female friends?" He draped one arm along the hood. So casual, so breezy. "Singular or plural?"

She took a step back. "Are you using psy-ops on me? Is this some Marine Corps mind game?"

He turned up his palms. "We're just having a conversation."

"Then why do I feel like I'm handcuffed to a chair in a room with one-way mirrors?" She patted her hair and tugged on her turtleneck, aware that she was now officially fidgeting.

"This dress is going to be smoking hot on you," he announced matter-of-factly. "You shouldn't waste it on a friendly dinner."

She didn't know where to look. She did know,

however, that she had started to sweat. She could feel moisture trickling down her back.

He straightened up and loomed over her. "Did you bring a needle and thread?"

"Yes." She lunged for the sewing supplies in the driver's seat. "Thank you. Thank you. I owe you, big-time."

"Where am I supposed to work?"

She walked around to the back of the FUV and opened the rear liftgate.

"God, there's enough room for a whole sweatshop back here."

"I know. Make yourself at home."

He unspooled a length of red thread and examined it in the sunlight. "This is the wrong kind of thread."

"That was all they had at the drugstore," she said. "Can you make it work?"

"Yeah. But I don't like it." He glanced back at her. "Why did you tell me to bring duct tape?"

"Oh, I just thought it set the right tone." She grinned. "Plus, I figured if you couldn't get the zipper in with thread, we'd need a fallback."

He looked stunned. "You'd stick duct tape on sixty-year-old silk?"

"No, *you* would. But only because it's a matter of life and death. Figuratively," she hastened to add. "Just do what you can with my substandard thread. It only has to hold for a couple of hours; you can repair it properly later."

"Wrong. This is the last time we're doing this." All pretense of breeziness had vanished, replaced with what could only be described as menace. "And Lila?"

"Yeah?"

"This never happened."

Chapter 16

Ben lived in a boxy, contemporary white house bordering the golf club's fairway, far from the boardwalk and Black Dog Bay's "downtown." Lila took a deep breath and rang the doorbell before she could lose her nerve.

The door opened and Ben peered out at her. "Lila?"

She didn't say anything at first, just struck a pose and let him take in the curves and the cleavage and the hair that she'd arranged in a throwback to her high school style. She forced herself to wait for him to speak, but she was suddenly self-conscious of how she looked in the red dress—so obvious, so overdone, so . . .

"You look . . ." He cleared his throat. "Nice."

He was wearing khaki cargo shorts, a faded navy T-shirt, and sneakers. One of them was ready for a cookout, the other for the Oscars.

She held the liquor bottle out in front of her like

a shield. "I brought scotch. It's from the year we graduated high school."

He thanked her and invited her in. The doorframe was narrow, and her body brushed against his as she passed. The house had been decorated in soothing shades of gray, taupe, and white. Soaring ceilings and walls of windows showcased the view of the rolling green lawns, with the result that the interior felt almost sparse. Everywhere she turned, she saw white walls and clean lines and polished silver metal, accented by dark wood and black leather and sharp right angles.

While she looked at the house, Ben was looking at her with her vampy red dress and her sparkling earrings and her long, dark hair. She couldn't think of a single syllable to say to the guy she used to be able to say anything to. All her calculated coquetry and charming bon mots fell away as she gazed out at the moonlight filtering through the clouds.

"Let's do shots," she suggested.

He seemed taken aback, cradling the bottle of scotch protectively. "It's kind of a waste to do shots with good scotch. You're supposed to savor it."

"Okay, then, let's get to savoring."

He led the way to the kitchen and she followed, her high heels impossibly loud against the polished concrete floor.

"This place is beautiful." She twisted her hands together. "And you know how interior designers are always talking about having a point of view? You definitely have a point of view."

Ben opened a cabinet, pulled out two glasses, and confessed, "The house came like this. It's a furnished rental. I'm staying here for the next few months until I have more time to house hunt. My mom keeps hinting that I should move back in with her and my dad, but I'd rather die than live at home in my thirties." Too late, he realized his gaffe. "Lila, I'm sorry. I didn't mean . . ."

"No, it's okay." She waved one hand. "I would have said the same thing about living with my mom, but it's actually been interesting. And it's only temporary. We're hoping to open a vintage boutique with some of her old couture dresses, and if that works out, I'll be able to be independent again in a matter of months. Or years." She nibbled her lower lip, heedless of her makeup. "Someday."

He placed the glasses on the counter and gave her his full attention. "About that. I heard you guys need retail space."

She blinked. "You did? Already?"

"The grown-ups here gossip more than the high schoolers." He tilted his head. "Why didn't you ask me about leasing the space by the board-walk?"

She felt her face flush with shame. "Because I

can't afford the deposit, never mind the monthly rent."

"You didn't think I'd make an exception for you?"

"I didn't want to ask. Especially once you got that offer from the funnel cake place. I know how important it is for you to succeed. And then you've got the whole dynamic with your dad. I didn't want to get in the way of that."

He braced both hands on the counter behind him. "My dad and I went over the offer from the funnel cake people yesterday. We're going to pass."

"But why? I thought you said they were paying top dollar."

"They are, so in the short run, it seems like a great deal." He paused to pour the scotch. "But think about it: Why do people come to Black Dog Bay?"

Lila considered this. "To get over their breakups and be surrounded by strangers telling them to hydrate every two minutes?"

"To reinvent themselves. To try something they've never tried before. This town is one of a kind and a little bit quirky."

Lila had to laugh. "A *little* bit quirky?"

"Black Dog Bay is full of things you can't get anywhere else. We have an obligation to keep it that way and in the long run, it's good for business. A bunch of chain stores and restaurants would ruin the ambience."

"That's true. Although I told Jenna the other day that if she could turn the Whinery into a chain, she'd be a billionaire."

"I want you and your mom to have the store by the boardwalk for the summer." He named a monthly rent that was a stretch but probably (barely) doable. "No deposit necessary—I trust you not to trash the place."

"Ben." She had the odd sensation that her heart was breaking and healing at the same time. "I can't possibly let you do this."

He shrugged. "Can. Did. Already done."

"But you could get so much more from any other tenant." Lila surprised herself with the sincerity of her protests. As much as she'd wanted the space, she realized that she wanted her dignity more. It was time to stop squeaking by on the kindness of ex-boyfriends.

"It's not up for debate." He went all brusque and businesslike. "Pick a paint color for the walls, figure out what kind of flooring you'll need, and I'll get my guys on it on Monday."

She raised her fingertips to her throat. "How can I ever repay you?"

He touched her elbow. "Tell you what—forgive me for shattering your eighteen-year-old heart and we'll call it even."

Her eyes welled up. "You're forgiven."

"Good. Because my whole family wants to do this for you." He smiled at her, his eyes sweet and shining with pride. "Part of me is always going to love you."

He opened his arms to her.

She stepped closer, not sure if they were about to hug or kiss or what, and stumbled in her stilettos. In one fluid, practiced motion, she leaned down to adjust the ankle strap, which showcased all her best physical assets simultaneously. Until the sound of ripping fabric made her gasp.

"What was that?" Ben asked.

"I think . . ." Lila closed her eyes and stood up, terrified to inspect the damage. "I think I just tore my dress."

"Let me look." He took charge, placing his hands on her bare shoulders and turning her around.

"How bad is it?" She winced, her eyes squeezed shut. "It sounded bad. You know what? Don't tell me. I don't want to—"

"It's bad," he reported. "You ripped this thing apart at the seams."

"Oh my God."

He ran his finger along the thin slice of skin now exposed from her shoulder blade to her hip. She put her panic attack on hold for a moment and tried to focus on the feel of his hands on her skin. The delicate black lace of her panties was clearly visible. She glanced back at him, holding her breath, waiting for him to make his move.

Ben started laughing.

"Here." He walked over to the side door and pulled a baggy gray hoodie off a coat hook. "Put this on."

She gaped at him, heedless of the rush of cool air on her skin.

He kept his gaze averted as he pointed down the hall. "Bathroom's the second door on the left."

Lila stood there for a moment in her lipstick and her high heels and her Marilyn Monroe dress, and then she started laughing, too. "I knew I should have lined this sucker with duct tape."

"I'll pour you some more scotch while you're in there," he called as she retreated down the hall. "You want a double?"

"A triple."

She took her time in the bathroom, gingerly peeling off the dress, putting on the long, baggy sweatshirt that fell to midthigh, and trying to scrounge up some scrap of dignity. After a few minutes, she resigned herself to the fact that she was fresh out of dignity for the night, so she strolled barefoot to the kitchen, where she found Ben staring down at his cell phone with burning intensity. He didn't even acknowledge her.

She helped herself to the glass of scotch resting on the countertop. "Are you okay? You look—"

"Allison just texted me." His voice was tight, his words clipped.

"Allison? Allison who you wanted to marry? That Allison?" Lila went up on tiptoe and peered over his shoulder at the glowing screen. "What did she say?"

He showed her a text consisting of three little words: *I miss you.*

Lila gasped. "The plot thickens."

Ben slammed down the phone and turned to her with wild, panicked eyes. "What do I do?"

"I don't know." She rubbed his shoulder reassuringly. "What do you want to do?"

"I don't know." His whole body tensed. "Should I text her back? What should I say?"

Lila inhaled and exhaled, and encouraged him to do the same. "Let's take a step back for a second. You want to think about the long run, right? What would you like the outcome to be? Best-case scenario."

He didn't answer right away, but he didn't have to. She could see the answer in his eyes.

"Okay, so you want to get back together." She shoved her hands into the sweatshirt's pouch. "What you have to ask yourself, though, is whether it's a *good idea* to get back together. What will be different this time? What's to stop you two from breaking up again? Ben. Hello?" She tilted her head. "Are you hearing me?"

"She misses me." He looked elated and tortured and terrified all at the same time. "I'm texting her back. What should I say?"

"You love this woman?" she demanded. "You're determined to make this work?"

He looked at her with all the passion that had been missing from their attempts at romance. "I have to, Lila."

"Okay, then." She adopted a tone of supreme authority. "Put down the phone."

His forehead creased. "But I—"

"If you're really in love and you really want to reconnect, don't *text*. Be decisive, Ben. Be bold. Take action."

Chapter 17

"So then he strode out of the house, all charged up and alpha male, got into his truck, and peeled out of the driveway. And I haven't heard from him since." Lila walked down the front steps of the Jansens' house with Summer, who was hanging on to every word. "But he left dinner behind and it was really good."

Summer whistled. "So I guess you two won't be spontaneously combusting any time soon?"

"Nope, but we will be doing business. He's going to be my landlord for the summer."

"You got the lease!"

"I did." Lila stopped for a little victory dance.

"Oh, and you'll appreciate this—my dress practically fell off while I was standing in his kitchen. And not because he ripped it off me."

"I do appreciate that." Summer pulled a bag of M&M's out of her purse and offered it to Lila.

"You should have seen his face when he got that text. I don't know if he and Allison are meant to be, but I know that he and I are not."

"So you can be friends." Summer wriggled out of her heavy wool sweater and basked in the afternoon sun.

"I'd say that's our only option at this point." The gravel crunched as Lila walked over to the hulking white FUV. "My dress was literally in tatters, with naked skin and lacy lingerie everywhere, and he just handed me a sweatshirt and told me to cover up."

Summer went around to the passenger side door. "Like brother and sister."

"Pretty much." Lila hit the unlock button on the key fob.

"And you're fine with all this?"

Lila was thankful that she could hide her face behind the tinted glass. "Sure, I'm a grown-up. I'm mature. I understand that people and relationships change."

"But . . . ?" Summer prompted.

Lila's shoulders sagged. "But why do I always come in second? I'm like the placeholder girl."

Summer waited for her to elaborate.

"My ex-husband pursued me relentlessly," Lila said. "He asked me to marry him after our third date—yes, I now see that's a red flag, and no, I didn't say yes until we'd been together for a year. He bought me my dream house, he remembered my birthday, he gave me roses and jewelry on our anniversary."

Summer held up her index finger. "Wait. We hate this guy, right?"

"Right. Because one day, apparently, all his feelings for me turned off like a faucet. He met someone else, she was prettier and perkier and smarter, and that was it. He was done with me forever."

"We definitely hate this guy."

"He never had a moment's doubt or asked for a second chance." Lila gazed at the red and yellow rosebushes surrounding the gray-shingled house. "He never even apologized. He said it was beyond his control and there was nothing he could do." She paused to collect herself. "Her name's Jessica. They're still together."

She had to pause again. Finally, she regained her composure and continued. "Maybe they're meant to be. Maybe I was just some generic blond placeholder wife until the real thing came along."

Summer scoffed at that. "Fuck that guy. You're well rid of him."

"Why? So I can marry some guy like Ben?" Lila tossed her purse back into the bowels of the

FUV. "The problem with that is, Ben doesn't want me, either. He used to, back in the day. But now the real love of his life has come along."

"But you told him to take action and go to her!"

"Yeah, because I don't want to be the placeholder again. Maybe I am, though. Maybe that's my destiny: Lila Alders, permanent placeholder."

Summer thought this over for a moment. "Nah."

"No, I'm serious!" Lila really warmed up to the topic. "When I was on the shopping channel, I couldn't get out of the late-night slot. I did my best, I worked really hard, and I loved that job, but it just wasn't enough. They let me go, and now I can't even get a callback on an audition. Maybe I'm just not prime-time material, on TV or in real life."

"Or maybe that wasn't the right career for you," Summer countered. "And your ex-husband wasn't the right guy. And neither is Ben."

Lila was horrified. "What if there *is* no right guy for me?"

"So you'll be single. Calm down."

"Calm down? You listen to me, Summer Benson: My ex-husband cannot be the last person I have sex with. I cannot go to my grave knowing Carl McCune was the last man to touch me."

Summer made a face. "These are your options? Shackled to your soul mate or celibate forever?"

"Easy for you to say. You have a soul mate to be shackled to."

"Yeah, I do. But you know what? For years and years, I didn't. And you know what I did all those years? I lived." Summer's eyes lit up at the memories. "I got up early and stayed out late and had adventures and saw the world. I made friends with all kinds of women; I dated all kinds of men. And I learned something from every single one of them."

"So what are you saying? I should go be the female equivalent of Jake Sorensen?"

"God, no. Do you think Jake Sorensen is happy or well-adjusted?"

Lila nodded. "He's rich and good-looking."

"Oh, my child, you have so much to learn." Summer crumpled up her M&M's wrapper and stashed it in the side door cup holder. "Stop with the soul mates—figure out what *you* want. Live your life. Make mistakes. Don't worry about destiny." Summer folded her hands as she concluded her sermon. "Besides, it could be fun to have Ben as a friend."

"That's true." Lila clambered into the driver's seat, managing to avoid the treacherous running boards. "We can hang out, drink scotch, talk trash about the funnel cake corporations of the world. I can give him decorating advice, and he can remind me to get my car fixed every time I see him."

"What's wrong with your car?" Summer asked as she climbed in and buckled up.

"A better question would be, what *isn't* wrong with my car?"

Lila started the ignition and glowered. "Now, where are you taking me, again?"

Summer made herself comfortable in the cushy leather seat. "To a treasure trove of vintage clothing."

"And why is this so cloak-and-dagger?"

"Because everybody talks in this town, and we need to keep this quiet."

Before Lila could put the car in gear, the front door to the house opened and Ingrid dashed down the stairs, waving both arms.

Summer sighed and cracked the window. "Here we go."

"Where are you going?" Ingrid demanded.

"I already told you—none of your business."

Ingrid craned her neck, trying to peer into the backseat. "Think about what I said at breakfast. Only twenty-three days until graduation. That's barely a month. Tick tock."

"I heard you," Summer assured the mussy-haired teenager.

"Well, then . . ." Ingrid pulled a glossy bridal magazine out of her tote bag. "I thought you should start looking at dresses."

Summer turned to Lila. "Floor it."

"Just look at them!" Ingrid implored.

"No."

"Yes!"

"You're eighteen years old! You're not the boss of me!" Summer closed the window.

Ingrid strode around to the other side of the car and appealed to Lila. "She's impossible. What could it hurt to just take a peek?"

"I'll take a peek," Lila volunteered.

"Thank you." Ingrid gave Lila a world-weary, mom-to-mom look as she passed the magazine through the window.

Lila examined the wedding gown Ingrid had marked with a yellow sticky note. "Oh, that's lovely."

"*I know.*" Ingrid fumed. "No lace, no big skirt, no bows anywhere. It's got gold edging! She likes gold."

"You have great taste," Lila assured the high schooler.

"Do me a favor and work on her, okay? If we're going to have a summer wedding, it's time to get serious." Ingrid glanced at the field of roses in the backyard. "I guess we could clear out the yard and have the reception here, but Dutch is kind of attached to his garden."

"Bye, now!" Summer made shooing motions with both hands.

After a flurry of meaningful glances, Ingrid went.

"Here." Lila handed over the photo of the gown.

"Thanks." Summer tossed the magazine into the backseat without even glancing at it.

"What was that all about? Or should I even ask?"

"Ugh. She's trying to get Dutch and me married off before she goes to college." Summer rolled her eyes. "She's very old-fashioned."

Lila raised her eyebrow at the Jansen home's traditional architecture and the conservative sedan parked next to the red convertible by the garage. "Dutch isn't old-fashioned?"

Summer threw her a saucy little wink. "Don't let the cuff links and the blazers fool you."

Lila smiled. "You guys have quite the cute little family thing going here."

"That kid has been trying to get Dutch and me down the aisle since our first date, practically. And we might go ahead and do it one of these days; I won't deny it. But if we do, I'm not wearing a gown that can be found in any bridal magazine, ever."

"It had gold trim," Lila pointed out.

"Is that supposed to be some sort of selling point?"

"Ingrid seemed to think it was right up your alley."

Summer sighed, unbuckled her seat belt, and heaved herself over the console and into the backseat to retrieve the magazine. She flipped through the pages and examined the gown in question. "Dude. No. That shit has a train and costs three thousand dollars. If I'm spending three thousand dollars, I'm spending it on liquor for an open bar, not some twee little frock."

Lila nodded. "Got it."

"When *Ingrid* gets married, I'll be happy to truss her up in a bustle and petticoats and a veil." Summer shook her head. "But she needs to wait her turn."

"Well, let me know if you ever want help finding a fabulous, au courant, *non*traditional wedding gown."

"I'll be sure to do that." Summer slid on her sunglasses. "Are we going or what?"

"Yeah." Lila rested both hands on the steering wheel. "But there's not enough room here to do a three-point turn, so I'll have to back up all the way to the street."

"Which requires superhuman spatial skills," Summer finished for her.

Lila jabbed her thumb over her shoulder. "It's kind of a big car."

Summer peered back through the rows of seats and the windshield. "You're not kidding. I think I can see the Pacific Ocean back there. It's like the trunk is in another time zone. No backup camera?"

"It's broken."

"Well, there's only one solution to this problem." Summer stuck her head out the window and hollered toward the porch. "Dutch!"

"You don't have to call Dutch," Lila admonished. "We can do this together."

"No way. I have a bad track record with those trellises."

While the mayor of Black Dog Bay put himself to good use maneuvering the FUV back to the main road, Lila and Summer sat in the backseat, chatting away and obstructing his view of the driveway.

"Now that the boutique is really happening, I need to find a way to get the word out," Lila said. "I'd hire a PR firm or something, but we have a very limited publicity budget."

"What's the budget?" Dutch asked.

"Zero point zero dollars."

"That is tight," Summer agreed.

Dutch didn't even flinch as he missed the mailbox by millimeters. "It's obvious." He nodded at Summer. "You keep saying you want to organize a fund-raiser for the historical society." He nodded at Lila. "You need to spread the word about a store that's going to appeal to women with disposable income. You need to join forces."

Lila and Summer glanced at each other. "Yes. Yes, we do."

"Figure out your demographic and create a target-rich environment." Dutch turned the wheel and angled the car to the side of the road. "Something like a fashion show."

"That's genius," Lila said.

He put the SUV in park and got out. "I have to

193

run. City council meeting." He opened the back door and helped Summer out. "See you at dinner?"

Summer gave him a kiss and sent him on his way.

"Spatial skills, resourceful, *and* able to chair a city council meeting?" Lila shook her head in amazement as she climbed back into the driver's seat. "That's why he's the mayor."

"That's why I'm marrying him." Summer held up one hand. "Don't say anything to Ingrid. Don't say anything to anybody. And don't get excited—"

"Too late!"

"—because nothing's official. And nothing's really going to change—it's just a bureaucratic formality."

"Awww." Lila batted her eyelashes. "You're so cute when you pretend you're not desperately in love."

Summer rolled her eyes while trying—and failing—to suppress a smile. "Stop harassing me and let's brainstorm. If we're going to plan a fund-raiser in a few weeks, we'd better get cracking. And we should probably stop and pick up your mom. She's definitely going to want to see this."

Chapter 18

"Are you *sure* she's not coming home soon?" Daphne whispered.

"I'm sure." Pauline Huntington, a plump, rosy-cheeked woman who lived in the fanciest, ugliest house in Black Dog Bay and apparently thought of Summer as her daughter, led the way up the mansion's sweeping staircase.

"You better be sure," Summer said. "Because I know how that woman deals with surprises, and I'm all out of horse tranquilizers."

"And your sister and I don't have the best history," Daphne told Pauline. "There was a little, ahem, falling-out a few years ago at one of my holiday parties and I'm afraid Hattie's held a grudge against me."

"You and everyone else in town," Summer said.

"Don't worry. She's meeting the senator in Dover for dinner, and she'll be gone for hours. I swear." Pauline opened a door and led Summer, Lila, and Daphne into a palatial bedroom suite with a coffered white ceiling, heavy damask drapes, and a massive four-poster bed made up with sunny yellow linens. "Hattie will never know about any of this as long as we all keep our own counsel. Pinkie swear?"

"Pinkie swear." Lila, Daphne, Summer, and Pauline gathered under the ornate hanging lantern and hooked their little fingers together. "Hattie Huntington will never hear a word about this."

"Good. Now let's crack open the vault." Pauline rested one hand on a set of double doors that presumably led to a closet. "Tell me a bit more about what you girls need."

"We're putting on a fashion show," Lila explained. "At the country club. To raise money for the historical society and get press for the boutique."

"I called the event coordinator on the ride here, and she booked us for Memorial Day weekend," Summer reported.

"But that's only a few weeks away!" Daphne's eyebrows shot up. "A few weeks to put together a fashion show is—"

"Ambitious but totally doable," Summer said. "The Huntington sisters have many minions at their disposal."

"Oh, don't call them 'minions,' darling." Pauline crinkled her nose. "They're our trusted and beloved household staff. We consider them family."

"Excuse me? I know for a fact that Hattie treats the hired help a million times better than she treats her family."

196

Pauline smiled angelically. "Why do you think I'm donating all her old clothes?"

"Anyway, I was thinking." Lila turned to her mother. "Could you get in touch with Cedric What's-His-Name?"

"Jameson," Daphne supplied.

"Right. And ask him if he'd be willing to lend us some clothes or even make an appearance?"

Pauline went all fluttery and fangirl. "You know Cedric Jameson?"

"I was the love of his life." Daphne fluffed her sleek black hair. "His muse."

Pauline clasped Daphne's hands in hers and gave a little hop of joy. "I just adore his designs. I have several of his pieces from the late sixties. Of course, he didn't do his best work until the eighties."

Daphne glowed. "That's when I was his muse."

"Focus, ladies." Summer grinned at Lila. "We need to figure out what kind of styles we need for the show. I'm thinking fun, fresh, and flirty."

"Well, the clothes are going to depend on the models," Daphne said. "Where on earth are we going to book models on such late notice?"

"We're not." Lila braced herself for her mother's reaction. "We're going to get normal women to walk in the show."

"Normal women?" Daphne was appalled. "Why in heaven's name would you do that?"

"Because we want to involve summer residents

like Mimi Sinclair and her fancy friends," Summer said. "Memorial Day is the start of high season, and your clientele will be women like Mimi. Women who have sophisticated tastes. Women who will spend a lot of money at your store after they feel glamorous and special in your clothes."

Daphne paused. "I'm listening."

"So we need to find outfits in a variety of sizes," Lila said. "Not just twos and zeros."

"Look no further." Pauline flung open the doors to reveal a huge, climate-controlled closet. The word "closet" didn't really do it justice—it was more of a vault.

Daphne put both hands over her heart, too overcome with emotion to speak.

"Hattie and I both have a weakness for beautiful dresses." Pauline flipped on more lights, and the cold, cavernous space instantly filled with golden light. "I picked up some great pieces during my travels, but some of these are from my own wardrobe." She cleared her throat. "And Hattie's."

Daphne held up a beaded pink and white cocktail dress. "Look at the detail work."

"All hand sewn in Shanghai," Pauline informed them. "Would you like to take this?"

But Daphne had already abandoned the pink dress for a simple black sheath on the next rack. "Oh, my heavens. Is this what I think it is?"

Pauline nodded with evident pride. "You have an eye for quality."

Daphne beheld the black dress with reverence, all but genuflecting as she motioned Lila over. "Come here and look at this. You may never see another one in your lifetime."

Lila studied the delicate lace overlay on the bodice. "Nice."

"Nice? Watch your mouth, young lady! This is an *Adrian*." Daphne announced this as if she'd discovered a unicorn or a leprechaun.

"He designed for old Hollywood back in the thirties and forties," Pauline explained. "He started the whole wasp-waist and shoulder pads look. Think Joan Crawford and Greta Garbo."

"This is the holy grail of fashion," Daphne breathed.

Lila snatched her hand back. "Then I probably shouldn't be touching it."

"Go ahead." Pauline took the dress off the hanger. "It's meant to be touched. It's much stronger than it looks."

"Yeah, I'm still not touching it," Lila said.

"Yes, you are, because I'm donating it to Unfinished Business," Pauline said. "It's been tucked away in a closet for too long."

"Thank you." Daphne looked longingly at the black lace. "But we can't take this. It must be worth thousands."

"You're taking it. Adrian deserves better than

decades all alone in the dark. This dress is meant to be out in the world, stopping people in their tracks." Pauline's eyes lit up, and Lila could tell the older woman must have been a great beauty when she was young. Just like Daphne.

"So that's the appeal of vintage clothing." Summer sounded delighted. "It's not just Grandma's dowdy old dresses. It's what Grandma used to wear when she was a hot little vixen."

Lila held up a gorgeous crimson chiffon dress with intricate rhinestone beading accenting the Grecian-inspired neckline. "Ooh."

"Take it," Pauline said.

Daphne checked the label and shook her head. "I can't in good conscience take a mint-condition Malcolm Starr and not give you anything in return."

"Oh, don't worry—you're not taking that." Summer seized the dress. "I am. This dress and I were meant to be." She held it up to her shoulders. "Baby, where have you been all my life?"

"You can't have that," Pauline said.

"What? Lila can have it, but I can't?" Summer bared her teeth. "I'll fight you for it, if necessary. I will bite, scratch, shank, and maim for this dress."

"But that was Hattie's!" Pauline exclaimed. "What if she sees you wearing it?"

Summer's jaw dropped. "Get out. You're telling

me that *Hattie Huntington* used to wear this?" She reexamined the diaphanous material and dazzling beadwork. "Well, Hattie does a lot of things I can't wrap my mind around. But whatever, it's mine now. And don't worry; if she says anything about anything, I'll handle her. I didn't get where I am today by letting that old bat boss me around." She clutched the red dress to her chest.

Lila laughed. "Okay, so I guess we know what you're wearing at the fashion show."

Daphne flipped through the other dresses, which included a gorgeous silk "handkerchief dress" and a strapless black taffeta gown with a full skirt and tulle lining. "This is a Suzy Perette with the tags still on. Was this Hattie's?"

"Yes. She never even wore it." Pauline placed one hand on her hip. "She didn't really want it, but she didn't want anyone else to have it. Typical."

While Daphne and Pauline continued to inventory the cache of clothing, Lila and Summer started talking logistics.

"So who else can we get to walk in the show?" Lila sat down on the edge of Pauline's bed and started making notes on her phone. "You and Jenna, of course. And you think we can get Mimi Sinclair?"

"I'll get her," Summer vowed, still holding tight to the Malcolm Starr with both hands.

201

"I'm good at strong-arming bad-tempered rich women."

"If we get Mimi, we can get all her mean-girl friends, too." Lila tried to envision the event with glamorous guests milling around in the country club ballroom. "Do we want to try to pull in some of the younger crowd?"

"Good idea," Summer said. "We can ask the mean girls' daughters."

"Ooh." Daphne unearthed a long, drapey pink nylon nightgown. "Is this a Lucie Ann?"

"That's a hot dress," Summer said. "Can I try it on?"

"But of course." Pauline handed it over. "You know who used to wear Lucie Ann? Zsa Zsa Gabor on *Green Acres*, that old TV show."

"Actually, *Eva* Gabor was on *Green Acres*," Daphne corrected.

The four of them were laughing and bonding and trying on various dresses when a sleek dark blue Mercedes pulled up to the portico.

Summer glanced out the window and yanked the pastel nightgown off in one swift movement. "You guys, it's Hattie!"

"Oh, dear." Pauline started scooping up dresses and shoving them back in the closet.

"She's going to kill us all." Daphne paled. "Try not to bleed on the clothes."

"Hello?" a thin, reedy voice called from downstairs. "Pauline, do you have company?"

"You girls go out the back." Pauline hustled them into the hallway. "I'll stall her."

Lila heard the authoritative *click-clack* of Hattie's shoe heels on the marble floor. "Summer Benson, is that you up there? What on earth are you up to? Pauline? I demand an explanation right now!"

Summer barely stifled her laughter and pointed out a large pink and green room with French doors that opened up to a second-story balcony. "Climb down the drainpipe," she whispered. "Try not to fall and break your neck. Good luck."

Lila went first, scraping her palms and snagging her jeans as she shimmied down to the porch. Daphne tossed down a pair of priceless old gowns, giggling like a teenager, and began her descent.

"She's coming!" Summer screamed out the window, all dramatic. "Hurry!"

Lila held her arms out and caught the fluttering tiers of silk and lace.

Then they heard Hattie's voice, outraged and vehement: "Daphne Alders, is that you? And is that . . . Lila Alders? Come back here, both of you!"

"Save yourselves!" Summer yelled.

"This isn't over!" Hattie shouted. "You can run, but you can't hide!"

Daphne reached out and took Lila's hand and together they fled the scene, crashing through the underbrush and making sure that the beautiful old dresses didn't get torn or soiled. For the first time since she'd come back to Black Dog Bay, Lila saw a flicker of her mother's old spark—the willingness to run, to take a chance and push ahead . . . even if they weren't completely sure where they were going.

Late Sunday night, under cover of darkness and her dad's old Baltimore Orioles cap, Lila drove to the other side of town to pick up the leopard-print car coat. She cut the headlights as she turned into Malcolm's driveway, then kept her head down while she skulked around his porch, feeling like a junkie going to her dealer's house to score a hit.

A hit of haute couture.

When Malcolm opened the door, she pulled the ball cap's brim even lower on her forehead and murmured, "The password is 'Pucci.' "

He started to close the door. "That's not the password."

"Okay, the password is 'Prada.' "

"Wrong again." He sounded gruff, but she could tell he was trying not to smile. "The hat's a nice touch."

"I'm just doing my part to maintain confidentiality."

"Very thoughtful."

She waited for him to open the door wider than

six inches, then gave up and moved closer, trying to peer through the narrow gap. "I try. I was thinking we could cross-stitch a nondisclosure agreement, too. With red thread, so it looks like we wrote it in blood."

The door eased open another two inches. "I'll be sure to whip that up next time I have a spare minute."

"Speaking of red thread . . ." She revealed the ripped Ceil Chapman dress she'd been hiding behind her back.

As soon as he saw the ruched red fabric in the clear dry-cleaning bag, he tried to slam the door, but Lila had anticipated this and wedged her foot in front of the jamb.

"Wait!" she cried. "Let me explain."

"I already did emergency surgery on that thing in a gas station parking lot in the middle of my workday," Malcolm said. "I've fulfilled my obligations."

"You have, and I am deeply grateful. But—"

Malcolm used his deepest, most commanding SRT leader voice. "No means no, Lila."

She responded in her softest, sweetest prom queen voice. "Oh, come on! Don't you want to finish what you started?"

His jaw dropped. "What *I* started?"

"Okay, what *we* started."

There was a long pause. Lila took advantage of the silence to add, "There was a wee wardrobe malfunction. My mom doesn't know, and I'm hoping she never finds out because it will probably kill her if she does. Don't do it for me; do it for her. A bereaved, lonely old widow."

The door swung open. "I'll look, but I make no guarantees. And for future reference, the password is 'proliferation.'"

Lila grinned as she breezed by him. "The password is 'Pucci.'"

Malcolm took the dress from her and assessed the damage. "Damn, Alders. What'd you do?"

She flushed. "I didn't do anything!"

His eyebrows shot up. "What'd your *date* do?"

"He offered me a lease and then his ex-girlfriend texted him." Even though she was telling the truth, she knew she sounded like she was lying. She was all flustered and fidgety again. *Damn psy-ops.* "I told you before, it was just a friendly dinner. Ben and I had our moment, and it was back in high school. We're friends now. Or something."

Malcolm crossed his arms and gave her a stony stare. "Friends don't tear each other's clothes off."

"The dress tore itself." She held up her right hand. "Sartorial suicide. I'll take a polygraph if you want me to."

"I don't."

"Well, that's what happened. I have no idea why."

"Remember what I said about old thread?" He motioned her inside so he could inspect the dress's stitching in better light. "Silk deteriorates over time. You'll need to go back over the seams with new thread."

"Sounds like a pretty basic repair." Lila tried to sound all blithe and innocent. "If you won't do it, I guess I could just take some upholstery thread and—"

"Upholstery thread?" Malcolm's head jerked up.

"Well, yeah. That's what you used to reattach the button, right?"

"Buttons are completely different from side seams." He exhaled in evident disgust. "Upholstery thread? Come on."

"Well, I don't know!"

"No shit." He peeled off the clear dry cleaner bag. "And while we're on the subject, you can't store these in plastic. It's bad for the fabric. So is light."

"Sunlight?"

"Any kind of light."

Lila stared up at him. "You're kind of strict."

"This isn't some department store dress you want to wear for one season. These things are forty, fifty, sixty years old. If you want them to last another sixty years, you've got to treat them right."

"This is why I need you." Lila put the back of

her hand to her forehead. "Save me from myself, Malcolm. More importantly, save Ceil Chapman from me."

He exhaled again, loud and irritated. "I know what you're doing."

"Asking you to work from home?" She craned her neck, trying to see over his shoulder. "Where's your workstation, anyway?"

He shifted his body, blocking her view. "My what?"

"Sewing basket. Whatever."

His jaw dropped. "I don't have a *sewing basket*."

"Sorry." She backed off. "Didn't mean to offend. Where do you keep your testosterone-infused needle and your thread of manly might?"

He jerked his thumb over his shoulder. "By the TV."

She glimpsed a huge sewing machine, complete with a flatiron foot pedal, in the corner of the living room. "Wow. That looks like serious business."

"It's old-school," he informed her. "Older than me. Nineteen seventy-two Columbia. It's a workhorse. Sews leather, silk, everything in between. All you have to do is change the needle and you're ready to go."

"Does she have a name?"

"No."

"You've spent all these years with her. . . ."

He looked like he was inwardly praying for patience. "It's not a 'her.' It's an 'it.' "

"How about 'Rosa'?" Lila suggested. "Since she's Colombian and all."

Malcolm didn't deign to reply to that, so Lila picked up the plastic-handled scissors on the sewing machine's tabletop. "And these are your official sewing shears?"

"Four bucks at the drugstore."

"Oh." She glanced down at them. "Listen, I'll be the first to admit that I learned everything I know about sewing from *Project Runway*, but isn't cutting important?"

"Yeah." He nodded. "The *cutting* is what counts, not the scissors. Think of sewing like sports. The player is more important than the equipment."

Lila laughed. "So now sewing is like football?"

"Most of the game is mental." For the first time, his eyes softened. "My grandmother was Romanian, and growing up with her was excellent training for the Marines." He nodded at the sewing machine. "This was hers, originally."

"She was a master?" Lila asked.

"Oh, yeah. You know how she did it? She never said no. Women from the neighborhood would bring in dresses and ask for impossible things, like making a waistline five sizes larger. She said yes every time, and she always got it done." He tossed the Ceil Chapman dress onto the sewing table. "She was the one who taught me that I could do anything."

Lila looked at the sewing machine again, then looked back up at Malcolm and saw him—really *saw* him. She saw past the beer and the baseball and the muscles and the marine, to the heart and spirit that had always been there. The boy who had to become a man too soon, who had the soul of an artist but refused to admit that, even to himself.

When he looked back, she knew that he saw her, too—past her hair and her makeup and her carefully maintained physique. He saw all the flaws and the false starts. Both of them let down their guards in that moment, and they recognized each other as two people terrified of their own power, but slowly, slowly edging toward their potential.

Then they broke eye contact, trying to pretend it had never happened.

"Everyone needs that," Malcolm continued. "Someone who believes that they can do anything." He grinned. "Besides, it kept me out of trouble. Between that and running track and cross-country, I didn't have time to get tattoos and smoke a bunch of meth."

Everyone needs someone who believes they can do anything.

He'd said the words so casually, but Lila realized she'd never had that. She'd been so fortunate in so many ways; she'd always had someone to shelter her and protect her and bail her out of trouble. She'd spent her whole life buffered from reality, first by her parents and then her husband.

But she'd never had anyone who believed that she could bail *herself* out.

She noticed a thin black metal cylinder resting on the corner of the tabletop, draped with a looped fabric tape measure. "Is that a weapon?"

Malcolm followed her gaze, then nodded. "PR-24. Standard-issue."

"In civilian, please?"

"It's basically a sidearm baton." He went back to examining the dress seam.

"So you can beat back a riot while you hem your pants?"

"Hey, you never know."

"You are so . . ." Lila didn't know how to finish that sentence, so she started a new one. "So how *do* you make a waistline five sizes larger?"

Malcolm turned the red dress's bodice inside out and showed Lila the excess fabric edging the seams. "They used to make clothes with much bigger seam allowances. If we wanted to make this bigger, first we'd let out the side seams as much as possible, and then we'd have to add gussets on the sides."

"Gussets?" Lila searched the mental glossary of

sewing terms she'd accrued from six seasons of *Project Runway.*

"Extra fabric that you add to expand the waist or the skirt or whatever. Like . . ." He cast his eyes up, searching for an example. "Remember in *Silence of the Lambs*, when Jodie Foster goes into Buffalo Bill's house and sees those diamond-shaped sewing patterns hanging on the wall?"

"Stop." Lila made a face. "We're working with Ceil Chapman and Valentino. Can we please not talk about skin suits?"

"I'm trying to drop some knowledge on you."

She shook her head. "You're such a *boy.*"

"I'm a *man,*" he corrected.

She smiled sweetly. "And you do *beautiful* sewing work."

He pointed at the door. "Get out."

She scooped up the repaired coat and obliged, laughing as she went. "So you'll fix the dress?"

Malcolm picked up the TV remote and clicked onto a basketball game. "I'll think about it."

"Don't think about it—do it."

He managed to withstand a few more seconds of her shameless begging before relenting. "Okay, I'll do it."

She raised one fist in victory. "Yes!"

"On one condition."

"What?"

For a moment, the only sound was the low drone of the televised sportscaster.

Then Malcolm said, "I want a do-over."

Lila stared blankly back at him.

"Of our date," he clarified. "The one you don't remember. I demand a do-over."

Lila parted her lips to protest that this was crazy, this was doomed, this was an unwise pairing of personal and professional interests.

And then she looked at him with the red silk dress in his hands and the riot gear on his sewing table and the abs that she knew were hidden under his shirt. She remembered Summer's advice: *Live your life. Make mistakes. Don't worry so much about destiny.*

"Okay." She took off her cap and shook out her hair. "I'm game."

He looked a little surprised by her acquiescence.

"It'll be fun, right?"

"Right." The cagey smile was back. "We'll do the same thing we did on our date in high school."

"Refresh my memory," Lila said. "Where are we going? What're we doing?"

"That's for me to know and you to find out."

"You're impossible." She gave him a look. "At least give me a hint about what to wear."

He glanced down at the slinky crimson cocktail dress. "Your dress will be ready and waiting for you."

Chapter 19

"Sweet Bluette or Labrador Blue?" Lila stepped back to examine the patches of paint drying on the north wall of the empty storefront. "What'll it be?"

Daphne barely glanced at the pale blue splotches. "Oh, sweet pea, I don't care."

"Well, the contractor wants to start painting this afternoon. Pick a color."

"Yes. About that . . ." Daphne sat down on a sawhorse, suddenly looking very frail despite her formidable height and fashionable outfit. "I'm not sure you've really thought this through."

Lila gestured to the carpeted floor and bare walls. The store's front window afforded a partial view of the Atlantic. "We have the perfect retail location for the summer. We have great product to sell. What's to think through?"

"Well." Daphne cleared her throat. "Don't take this the wrong way, baby—"

"Oh, boy."

"—but the reality is, you're not qualified to run a business. Neither am I. We don't know the first thing about finance or marketing."

"That's not true," Lila countered. "When I

worked for the shopping channel, I learned a lot about how to move merchandise. I can talk about a hideous velvet scarf for forty-five minutes straight. I can *sell out* that hideous velvet scarf in forty-four minutes. That hideous velvet scarf has a waiting list by the time I'm through."

"But what about the business side?" Daphne pressed. "The budgeting, the bookkeeping, the payroll . . ."

"We won't have a payroll." Lila was making this up as she went along, but it sounded plausible. "You and I are the only employees. We'll use any profits to pay down your debt and keep the house afloat."

"Listen to what you're proposing." Daphne scoffed. "You're proposing that you and I work all day, every day, for free—"

"For profit," Lila reminded her.

"And sell off the things that are most precious to me in this world? And hope that by some miracle, we'll make enough money in a few months to undo years of financial catastrophe?"

"Well, it doesn't sound very realistic when you put it like that." Lila sighed and rubbed the small of her back. "But I don't see what other choice we have. Plus, we'll get an online component up and running. But if we have a storefront, we can get foot traffic and word of mouth." She thought about the recently divorced Bostonian who'd coveted the antique hair comb.

Daphne looked even more defeated. "Lila, I'm proud of what you're trying to do here. It's very independent of you. But if I learned anything from what happened with your father, it's that it's easy to get overextended with a business. And I don't mean to be harsh, but when you were on the shopping channel, you had producers to run everything behind the scenes. You had hair and makeup people to help you look good. You had an agent to negotiate your contracts. All you really had to do was show up and talk about linens and holiday china sets."

Lila flinched. "That's not meant to be harsh?"

"We're in way over our heads here and I don't want you to feel bad if we fail."

Lila put the paintbrush down. "Do you have any better ideas?"

"No."

"Then let's choose a paint color and move on. Daylight's burning."

"How can you expect me to choose a paint color when I'm about to lose everything?" Daphne's lips trembled as she folded her hands, the picture of martyred motherhood. "My clothing collection is my life's work. I've curated it like a museum exhibit and you want me to gamble it away on some reckless whim."

And Lila finally snapped. "Mom, we've been over this. Do you want to keep the house?"

"You know I do."

Lila moved in to confront her mother. "Then you have a choice. Which would you rather hang on to: your house or a bunch of old clothes you haven't even looked at in decades?"

"How can I possibly make that choice?" Daphne's trickle of tears turned into full-blown sobbing. "That's like asking me which hand I'd rather cut off."

"Labrador Blue it is." Lila pressed the round lid back onto the sample paint can, then headed to the tiny bathroom to wash her hands.

When she yanked on the ancient metal faucet lever, the entire spout tumbled into the sink, cracking the white porcelain. Before she could register what had happened, water sprayed every-where—up to the ceilings, all over the walls.

She threw up her hands in a futile attempt to shield herself from the cold water. Out of years of habit, her first instinct was to call for her mother.

Daphne took one look at the geyser and started to panic. "What should we do? Who should we call?"

"Find a wrench!" Lila exclaimed. "The crew left some tools in the main room. Look in the corner by the ladder."

Daphne didn't move. "I'm calling Ben."

"You can't call Ben—he's in Boston wooing his ex-girlfriend."

"He's what?"

"Mom!" Lila clapped her hands. "Wrench! Now!"

"Well, call his father, then. Call the contractor. We have to call *someone!*"

"I'm calling you. Go grab a wrench and jump in here."

To her amazement, her mother did just that.

After a minute of frenzied searching, Daphne approached the faucet, holding a pipe wrench as though it were a weapon. Water continued to splash the walls.

"Your father always used to say, 'righty tighty, lefty loosey.' "

"Sounds legit. You try that and I'll be over here, looking up plumbing tutorials on YouTube." Lila gagged as a spout of water went up her nostril.

Daphne commenced hand-to-hand combat with the sink. "Don't get my phone wet!"

"Don't backseat Google."

"I can't do this!" Daphne shrieked.

Lila frowned down at an instructional plumbing clip with nausea-inducing camerawork. "Okay, tighten that scrolly thing on the nubby thing and twist it toward the other thing."

"Got it." Daphne twisted the wrench. "Nothing's happening!"

"Twist again."

"Nothing's . . . Wait." Daphne gasped. "Something's happening." As she maneuvered the wrench, the geyser receded to a gush, which receded to a trickle, which receded to a tiny *drip, drip, drip.*

Lila put the phone aside and started jumping for joy. "You did it."

"I did it!" Daphne started jumping, too. "Careful, the floor's slippery."

"We did it." Lila hugged her mother, then gazed around at the sodden drywall and dismembered sink handle. "I don't think they'll be painting this afternoon."

"Probably not." Daphne sounded positively giddy. "But lo and behold! I can plumb!"

"Watch out, water heaters of the world." Lila's grin faded as she continued to survey the damage. "We should probably call Ben's office and tell them they'll need to send over a Shop-Vac and an ark."

"I'll call." Daphne reclaimed her phone with an air of calm capability. "In case they need someone to talk them through exactly what happened."

Lila gave her mother another hug. "Go for it."

They were drenched, they were desperate, but they were in this together.

". . . So that's why I look like crap and I'm drinking heavily on a weeknight," Lila concluded later that night as she pulled up a chair at the Whinery. She knew she shouldn't be out in public with her sweaty face, messy hair, and smudged shirt, but she was too exhausted to care.

Summer placed a glass of Tempranillo on the bar top. "You've earned this. Where's your mom? She's earned one, too."

"She went home and passed out early. Her nerves are shot, but she's really proud of herself. I'm proud of her, too. Wait, does that sound condescending?"

"Nah, you're just stating the facts," Summer said.

Lila waved to Jenna, who was on the other side of the bar chatting with Tyler about various wine distribution issues.

As soon as he noticed Lila, Tyler ducked his head and scurried away.

Lila returned her attention to Summer. "It's kind of funny that after years of obsessing about shoes and makeup and hair, we're bonding over pipe wrenches and broken faucets."

"Shoes, makeup, and hair can only get you so far."

"Actual and factual. My mom even said something about helping to paint the store. I've never seen her paint anything but her toenails. She's finally getting on board with Unfinished Business."

Summer held up her hands as though framing a camera shot. "A mother, a daughter, a pipe wrench, and a pipe dream."

"We should put that on our business cards. It was so awesome of Pauline to give us all those clothes, and so awesome of you to arrange it. I don't remember this town being so . . ."

"Awesome?"

Lila laughed. "Yeah. Being an adult here is different from being a teenager. When you're in high school, all you can think about is there's nothing to do and nowhere to go, and the nearest movie theater is like a forty-five-minute drive."

"That's why I'm encouraging Ingrid to go to college out of state." Summer nodded crisply. "She needs culture and adventure."

"And you want her to stop harping on the fact that you're living in sin with her brother."

"That, too. The girl is relentless. And crafty! She'll stop at nothing to get her way."

"So unlike yourself."

Summer tossed her choppy platinum hair. "I have no idea what you're talking about."

After two glasses of wine, Lila knew she was too tipsy to drive home, so she decided to go for a stroll on the boardwalk. On the way out the door, she noticed a patch of bright red in the Ex Box.

"Ooh." She reached in and pulled out a bold, almost garishly patterned dress that was so long, flat, and square, it looked like a paper doll cutout. "Do you know what this is?"

"Fugly?" Jenna ventured.

"It's a vintage Tori Richard in mint condition."

Lila pointed out the label, which specified that the dress had been made in Honolulu. "My mom loves Tori Richard. This thing has to be twenty or thirty years old. Do you mind if I snag it?"

Jenna lined up a row of glasses on the bar. "By all means, get that thing out of here before it blinds us all."

"It is a little . . . bright," Lila conceded. "I'll give you that. But I think it has potential. What if I sewed up the back, opened up the front, lopped off the hem, added some shape, and turned it into a cute little jacket?"

Jenna looked impressed as she poured pink champagne cocktails into the glasses. "You know how to do all that?"

"Well, no, not personally." Lila ran her fingers over the patterned patches of red and black and white. "I have people for that."

"You have people," Jenna repeated, looking amused.

"Yes, I do. I have people, and I have wine, and I have a plan." She excused herself, traipsed out to the sidewalk, and dialed her phone.

"What now?" was how Malcolm answered her call.

"I need you," she informed him loftily.

He waited a beat. "Are you drunk?"

"Kind of. Listen, I'm at the Whinery and I need a consult. Any chance your nightly marathon will bring you this way?"

"No."

"Okay, well, any chance your car will bring you this way? I'd come to you, but, you know. The whole drunk thing."

His side of the line went dead silent.

"Hello?" she said. "Is this thing on?"

"What's the magic word?" he said.

She screwed up her face and racked her brain. " 'Proliferation'?"

"Impressive. I'll be there in fifteen minutes."

Ten minutes later, Malcolm strode into the bar, all rugged and hard-bitten in a gray-on-gray ensemble of cargo pants and a T-shirt.

Lila held up the Tori Richard dress and waved it like a flag. "Just the man I was looking for."

Malcolm glanced at Jenna, completely poker-faced. "Is she sauced?"

Lila practically skipped across the room and pressed the dress into his hands. "Can you make this into a jacket?"

Jenna laughed and told Malcolm, "She's sauced." To Lila, she said, "Honey, when you start asking Malcolm Toth to do your tailoring, it's time to call it a night."

Summer, Jenna, and Malcolm all shared an indulgent chuckle.

Lila gasped and spun around on her heel. "Don't you dare laugh at me! I will have you know—"

"Time to go, chief." Malcolm slung an arm

around her shoulders and hauled her out to the sidewalk.

"Oof." She shook him off, nearly tripping over the curb in the process. "Is it necessary to be so rough?"

"Yes." He shook his head in disgust. "Because *someone* can't keep her mouth shut after a few sips of wine."

"Be fair—I had two glasses, and they were generous pours."

"Wow. You must have won all the drinking contests in college." He ushered her down around the side of the building to the parking lot and opened the door to his Jeep. "Get in the car. You're going home."

She complied, blowing out a loud, huffy breath. "Fine. But don't ever call me 'chief' again."

"Buckle your seat belt, please." He got into the driver's seat with an air of resignation.

She folded her arms and crossed her legs. "I will consider complying with that request when you ask politely."

He reached across the passenger side and buckled her in himself. Then he pried the Tori Richard dress out of her hands, tossed it behind his seat, and started the car.

Lila wrenched her neck as she tried to follow the garment's trajectory. "Ow. Hey, can you do something with that dress? Can you turn it into a jacket or something?"

He looked offended she'd even ask. "You know I can."

She rolled her eyes. "Okay, then, *will* you?"

"You know I will." He turned onto Main Street and headed for her neighborhood. "But we don't talk about it, remember?"

"Right." She tried to look very serious. "Our dirty little secret."

"Right."

She let her sensibilities segue back into tipsy. "Speaking of dirty . . ."

He waited.

"I fixed a faucet today. Well, that's not entirely true—my mother fixed a faucet while I watched YouTube videos and yelled instructions. I've never done that before." She lowered her voice and confided, "I've never called a boy, either."

"Ever?"

She shook her head. "It's desperate. Unseemly."

He nodded.

"But I called you tonight." She watched his reaction closely. "And the day we met out by the Dumpster."

"Glad I could be part of your milestone." He pulled up in front of her house and turned off the ignition.

She hopped out of the car, humming a happy tune. "I have a good feeling about all this. Things are really starting to turn around."

He climbed out of the driver's side and walked

her to the front door. "Don't forget to drink some water before you pass out tonight."

She gestured grandly toward the ocean. "So I guess our date thing or whatever is off."

He stopped walking. "What? Why?"

"Because I'm all . . ." She indicated her sloppy ponytail and paint-spattered clothes and bare face. "And also, I called you. Twice."

He started walking again. "Are you trying to get out of it?"

She shook her head so vehemently, she nearly lost her balance. "No."

"Good." He steadied her with a hand on her shoulder. "Because as soon as I fix your dress, we're going."

"But I don't even have lipstick on," she reminded him.

He looked at her lips.

"And I'm needy and desperate."

He kept looking at her lips.

"And I look like *this*." She threw out her arms.

They had reached the front door. He made his stand on the welcome mat and held her face in both his hands. "Lila. It's not about what you look like."

She wrapped her fingers around his wrists. "Then what is it about?"

The door opened, and they both dropped their arms.

"Lila Jane, there you are. I've been—" Daphne

broke off as she noticed the tall, broad-shouldered man on her porch. "Well, hello."

"Hi, Mrs. Alders. I'm Malcolm Toth." He offered a handshake and a disarming smile.

"Malcolm, of course. How are you?" She beamed. "It's been a while, but I never forget a face."

"I'm fine, thank you." He was working a whole officer-and-a-gentleman routine that left Lila stunned and a little tingly.

Daphne glanced from Lila to Malcolm. "You brought Lila home from a date once, didn't you?"

"Mother!" Lila groaned.

"Didn't you?"

"Yes, ma'am." He inclined his head. "Lila's sophomore year."

"I thought so. I have an excellent memory."

"Stop talking," Lila hissed.

"Don't be rude to your mother," Malcolm said.

Lila shot him a death glare.

Daphne glowed. "Thank you."

"I'll be finished with that project we talked about in a few days." Malcolm turned and headed back to his truck. "Don't forget to hydrate."

"Well, well, well. Your ex-boyfriends just get better and better with age," Daphne said to Lila.

"Good night." Lila ducked inside and retreated into the foyer.

Daphne stayed right on her heels. "I'll bring

you a bottle of water. What a nice young man."

Lila snorted. "He's not that nice."

"He drove you home, he told you to drink water. . . ."

"He used to be a military SWAT team leader, Mom. His own sister said he could kill someone with a paper clip."

Daphne fanned her face. "That just makes him even more attractive."

Lila dashed up the steps, swaying a bit on her feet. "See you in the morning."

"We'll talk more about Malcolm then."

Lila looked over her shoulder at her man-eating, ex-model mother. "You don't want to hear what I have to say about him."

"Why not?"

"Because in addition to hanging out with him looking like this, I call him. He never calls me; I always call him."

Daphne looked queasy. "Oh, dear."

"And that's not all. I show up at his house unannounced. Late at night."

Daphne clutched the balustrade for support.

Lila delivered the coup de grâce. "And I badgered him into meeting me at a gas station Dumpster in the middle of the afternoon."

"Why?" Daphne's voice was barely audible. "Why would you do such a thing?"

"I'm not at liberty to say." Lila faced forward and continued up to the second floor.

"Well, if you've been acting like that and he still wants to see you," her mother yelled after her, "that means he only wants one thing."

Lila did a little shimmy as she rounded the corner into her room. *"Good."*

"Excuse me?!"

"I said, 'Good night'!"

Chapter 20

True to their word, Ben's work crew pulled off a miracle and finished renovating the storefront in a matter of days. They painted the walls, replaced the worn carpeting with hardwood, and made sure all the faucet handles were secure. Then Daphne took charge of the decorating, arranging the display cases and commissioning a local artist to paint "Unfinished Business" on the building's exterior.

While the construction team saw to the final details, Lila spent fifteen-hour days selecting and prepping the inventory from Daphne's and Pauline Huntington's collections, making count-less trips to the dry cleaner, and learning how to use the computer software and cash register.

Daphne, who deferred to her daughter about most of the financial and merchandising deci-sions, showed unexpected moxie when it came to designing the window displays and outfitting the in-store mannequins.

"You'd never even heard of Ceil Chapman or Odicini or Samuel Winston until mere weeks ago." Daphne shooed Lila away from the piles of dresses in her bedroom. "Go sit in the corner and look pretty."

"Actually, I hadn't heard about Samuel Winston until right this very moment."

"Don't flaunt your ignorance." Daphne deliberated about her options for a moment, then draped a blue silk gazar strapless gown onto a dress form.

"I have to admit, your taste is impeccable," Lila said. "Who made that one?"

"Givenchy Haute Couture. It's numbered."

"Like an art print?"

"That's right. Because it's art."

"Okay, that gown is art; that I will grant you. But this?" Lila held up a garish checkered pantsuit. "What hellish cocktail of hallucinogenic drugs were you on when you bought this?" She shook her head at the matching shirt and pants, both of which were patterned in a huge red and white gingham check. The pants were hemmed with a three-inch cuff, and the top was cut to reveal an inch or two of bare midriff.

Daphne's whole face lit up when she saw the garments. "The gingham pantsuit! I forgot all about that! Isn't it fun?"

"It's . . ." Lila trailed off as words failed her. "It's like Lady Gaga meets *Little House on the Prairie.*"

"Don't blaspheme, sweet pea; it's French. High-concept." Daphne pointed out the label sewn into the waistline of the pants.

"What was the concept?" Lila's eyes hurt from looking at the print. She spread the shirt out on the bed. "We put a bowl of potato salad and a few watermelon slices on this thing and it's a Memorial Day barbecue."

"You know what your problem is?" her mother asked.

"So many answers, so little time."

"You lack creative vision."

Lila laughed. "How can you say that? I can taste the potato salad and smell the charcoal!"

"Such a literalist." Daphne rolled her eyes. "You only see what's right in front of you."

"That's true—I can't see what's behind me or on the other side of solid walls," Lila allowed. "Guilty as charged."

Her mother shook her head in despair. "I mean, you only see what's on the hanger. If you want to be successful in the fashion business, you need to be able to imagine what an outfit will look like on an actual woman."

Lila eyed the gingham monstrosity, doing her best to envision it on her body. "I'm imagining what this will look like on me. And it makes me ashamed and afraid."

"Well, obviously." Daphne sniffed. "You're not the right person to wear this. You're too petite. This ensemble was designed for a tall, willowy figure. A woman with striking bone structure and a certain sense of panache."

"Whatever." Lila sat back in her chair. "We're not putting this out on the sales floor because no one's going to buy it."

Daphne ignored this. "A woman like . . ." She pursed her lips, considering.

"Mary Ann from *Gilligan's Island*?" Lila suggested.

"Ingrid," her mother concluded.

"Ingrid *Jansen?*"

"Yes, your friend Summer's stepdaughter."

"Well, technically, Summer's not—"

Daphne waved this away and handed Lila her phone. "Call her up and ask her to come over. We'll have her put on this so-called Memorial Day barbecue and you'll see. You'll see!"

"Well, damn." Lila stood next to her mother's vanity table, watching Ingrid model the red and white pantsuit. The slouchy, scowling teenager had wriggled into the cropped top and skintight pants and somehow pulled the whole thing off. "I have to admit, Mom, you were right."

"Of course I'm right."

Ingrid crossed her arms over her chest. "Can I take this off now?"

"I suppose," Daphne said. "But since you're here, I have a few more things I'd like you to try on. Just to get an idea of how they fit."

Ingrid appealed to Lila with her earnest gray eyes. "Do I have to?"

"No." Lila shot her mother a look.

"Yes." Daphne gave Ingrid a thorough once-over, her expression shrewd. "How tall are you, dear?"

"Um, five eight." Ingrid scrunched her shoulders up. "Okay, five ten."

"Excellent." The older woman circled the teenager, nodding and muttering to herself. "Nice shoulders, tiny waist, not too busy . . ."

"I know, I know, I'm flat as a board. Can I please change now?"

"You're model material," Daphne concluded.

Ingrid burst out laughing. "Yeah, right."

"You are. Listen to me—I know what I'm talking about."

"I don't even have a date for prom," Ingrid said.

"And someday, all the boys in your class will look you up on Facebook and weep with regret," Lila promised.

"I can't be a model," Ingrid protested. "I can't even put on eye shadow right. And also, I love doughnuts and Simone de Beauvoir."

"We'll pay you," Daphne offered. "You can come in once a week and try on new pieces so we can get an idea of how to style them. Now, I'm thinking we'll put this pink Chanel suit on display right by the register." She picked up a pink and black bouclé skirt. "Here, Ingrid, be a good girl and go put this on."

Ingrid looked to Lila for help, but before Lila could intervene, the doorbell rang.

Daphne rummaged through the closet in search of coordinating shoes. "Who could that be?"

Lila froze with the sudden, unfounded fear that creditors had come for her mother and would begin a round-the-clock campaign to harass them for money. That whatever she did to help her mother and herself, it would never be enough. Her recent attempts to take control of her own life were too little, too late.

While Daphne ignored the disturbance and Lila succumbed to an anxiety attack, Ingrid wandered out to the stair landing and peered out the window above the front door.

"Oh, no." The teenager scurried back into the bedroom and closed the door. "It's *her*."

"Her?" Lila whispered. "Her who?"

Ingrid made a face. "Mimi Sinclair."

Lila tried to recall what Summer had said about the seasonal resident. "The mean girl with the mean-girl daughter?"

Ingrid scrunched up her nose. "The whole family is awful."

"Why in heaven's name is Mimi Sinclair here?" Daphne waved a red patent belt threateningly. "I don't like that woman, never have."

"You know her?" Lila asked.

"It's impossible not to. She fancies herself some sort of high-society matron. Your father built her summer home fifteen years ago and she was insufferable even then." Daphne brandished the belt with both hands. "She thinks that just because she hired him to build her house, she has more money than we do."

"She probably does have more money than we do," Lila pointed out. "Everybody has more money than we do."

Daphne gasped and turned to Ingrid. "Don't repeat that."

Ingrid held up both palms. "I won't."

The doorbell rang again and everybody looked at Lila.

"You'd better get that, sweet pea."

"Don't tell her I'm here," Ingrid pleaded.

"Why not?" Lila asked as she headed for the hallway.

"Because. She's always trying to weasel information out of me because I'm the mayor's little sister." Ingrid shuddered. "And she's always *inviting* me places."

"What a bitch." Lila laughed as she hurried

down the stairs to the foyer. She opened the front door to find a tiny, tight-faced, perfectly coiffed woman decked out in pearls and a tweed blazer. A black Town Car idled in the driveway behind her.

"Hi." Lila extended her right hand. "I'm—"

"Lila Alders, of course I remember you, darling," Mimi said in a tone that suggested she did not find Lila darling at all. "Your mother and I have been friends for years. I was sorry to hear about your father; I trust you got the flower arrangement we sent?"

Lila summoned a vague memory of a vase full of lilies. "Oh, yes, they were lovely."

"Good. I'm so relieved to hear you received them." Mimi cleared her throat. "Since I never got a thank-you note, I wasn't sure."

Lila took a tiny, inadvertent step back. "Well, we—"

"Anyway, I can't stay long, but my dear friend Summer Benson mentioned that you and your mother were opening a consignment store down by the boardwalk?"

"Actually, it's more of a—"

"I'm always happy to help out Summer and Dutch—my husband and I are *very* close with them, you know—so I've brought some of my old handbags for you." She indicated two paper shopping bags on the step behind her.

"Thank you, Mrs. Sinclair, that's very—"

"They're in excellent condition." Mimi touched her fingers to her pearl necklace and laughed. "Except for the fact that they're last season, of course."

"Thank you so much." Lila finally managed to complete a sentence. "We aren't really operating on a consignment model, but I'll have my mother give you a quote if you like—she's the expert."

"Whatever you think is fair," Mimi trilled. "I'll swing by the store when it opens and you can give me a check. Oh, and be sure and tell Summer I dropped by. We'll all have to get together for lunch at the club." And with that, the mean-girl matron of Black Dog Bay pivoted and disappeared into the depths of the Town Car while her driver held the door for her.

Lila lugged the shopping bags up to the bedroom. "That woman *really* loves Summer."

"Told you." Ingrid had changed into a chartreuse sequined cocktail dress.

Daphne peeked inside the shopping bags and examined the contents. "What on earth are these?"

"Her fancy designer handbags. She wants to unload them because they're from—gasp!—*last season.*" A note of judgment crept into Lila's voice before she realized that, just a few months ago, she, too, would have refused to tote a year-old handbag.

Daphne looked up, confused. "But she's okay with carrying knockoffs?"

Lila's jaw dropped. *"What?"*

"These are fakes, sweet pea. All of them."

"No *way*," Ingrid breathed.

"No way." Lila's mind flashed back to Mimi's smug, superior smile and huge, lustrous pearls. "She has a summer house and a chauffeur and a diamond ring that could gouge your eye out."

Daphne held up what appeared to Lila to be a mint-condition Balenciaga. "Look at the hardware—cheap and light. Feel the canvas and the leather. See what I mean?"

Lila ran her fingers along the side of the bag. "No."

"It's obvious." Daphne pulled out a logo-printed satchel and examined the straps. "These handles are the wrong color. The cowhide should develop a lovely, golden, honey-colored patina, but this . . ." She made a face as she indicated the dull shade of brown. "That's a slap in the face to God, man, and handbags everywhere."

"Mimi Sinclair carries fakes," Ingrid murmured. "Up is down and black is white."

"Maybe it's just a fluke," Lila argued. "Maybe the salt in the air out here affects leather in some weird way."

"Don't be naive." Daphne examined a black quilted leather flap bag. "Here, look. This one seems fine at first glance, but see how the stitching lines up—or, rather, doesn't line up—

above the pockets and middle seam?" She opened the flap and inspected the lining. "And the material in here is cheap—listen."

Lila and Ingrid fell silent while her mother rubbed folds of material together.

"Hear that? Sounds like paper rustling. That's the mark of poor quality. And . . ." Daphne brought the bag closer to a window so she could get a better look at the interior. "Aha! Look at the tag here. It says 'Made in Paris.' " She crammed the purse back into the paper bag. "If it had actually been made in Paris, the tag would say, 'Made in France.' Authentic labels list the country, never the city. Everyone knows that."

"I didn't." Lila turned to Ingrid. "Did you know that?"

Ingrid shook her head. "No, but I carry a reusable cloth grocery bag as my purse."

"You do?" Daphne looked horrified. "We're going to pay you in purses, then. Every girl needs at least one good-quality bag by the time she starts college." To Lila, she said, "You're going to have to learn how to spot counterfeit bags, because there's a ton of them out there."

Ingrid twisted her arms behind her back and tried to unzip the sequined dress. "This town is nothing but scandals and secrets. If people only knew."

"Someone's going to have to tell the queen of the mean girls that she's been carrying fake bags to the country club all this time." Daphne looked a bit giddy at the prospect.

"Not it," Ingrid said quickly.

"Well, it's not my jurisdiction," Daphne declared. "I handle the fashion and beauty; you handle the business. That's how this partnership works."

"What? When did we vote on that? I demand a recount!" Lila took her mother's hand. "Be reasonable. I cannot tell Mimi Sinclair—"

"Summer calls her the Terrorist in Tweed," Ingrid threw in.

"I cannot tell the Terrorist in Tweed that she's been swanning around town with a bunch of knockoffs. You should see her eyes, Mom! And her hair. She's scary."

"Which is why you're going to be the one to tell her," Daphne said. "You know I don't do well with confrontation."

"But I . . ."

"You mowed the lawn," Daphne pointed out. "You found the space for the store. You got someone to do alterations. You can do this." She gave Lila a sunny smile and then bragged to Ingrid, "My daughter can do *anything*."

"*You* fixed the faucet," Lila lobbed back.

Ingrid shook her head. "It's a suicide mission. Nice knowing you, Lila."

"Thanks." Lila helped the teenager with the dress zipper. "Will you take a check?"

"No." Ingrid pulled her hair up and out of the way. "I'll try on whatever you want, but I don't want you to pay me. Not with money, anyway."

"Then what is it that you want?" Lila asked.

"I want you to find Summer a wedding dress."

Chapter 21

Unfinished Business officially opened its doors on a cool, gray Thursday morning. Lila didn't sleep at all the night before; she lay awake in the darkness, tossing and turning and wondering what she had gotten herself into. She hadn't been able to make a success of her career or her marriage—did she really expect this venture to be any different?

Who do you think you are?

In a vain attempt to silence the voices of self-doubt, she'd turned on her laptop and started skimming some of the online vintage fashion forums. After five solid hours of poring over posts about designers and stitching and the importance of original tags and labels, she started to understand how much she truly didn't know. It would take years to attain her mother's level of expertise. She didn't have years, so she tried to pick up the main concepts and catchphrases. Sometimes in life, as in late-night shopping channel broadcasts, concepts and catchphrases could carry you through.

She headed downstairs at dawn, brewed a strong pot of coffee, and went to rouse her mother.

"Wake up, Mom." She curled up in the shadows at the foot of Daphne's bed and waited for her mother to share her jitters and anticipation.

Daphne responded by piling two pillows over her face.

"Good morning? Up and at 'em?"

Daphne peeked out from beneath the pillows. "It's the middle of the night."

"*Au contraire*—it's the beginning of a new day. Go time, Mom. Look alive!"

"I can't." Her complexion looked ashen. "I thought I could do this, but I can't."

"Of course you can. You fixed the faucet, remember? You can do anything!" Lila held out the coffee mug. "Have some caffeine. You'll feel better."

"It's just too much. Your father's death, the money worries, selling off my clothes from my old life . . . I know you're trying to help me, and I appreciate it, but I can't do this. Not today. I'm sorry, sweet pea."

Lila rested her hand on her mother's shoulder and listened.

"I can't stand the thought of doing this over and

over for the rest of my life." Daphne's voice was muffled. "Getting up while it's still dark, trying to figure out all the computer stuff, struggling to scrape together property tax payments and car insurance payments and grocery and gas and water bills . . ."

"I know it feels overwhelming right now, but we can't look at it like that." Lila realized she was making another sales pitch—to get her mother to invest in the future. "Twenty-four hours at a time. One hour at a time. Hell, I'll be taking today five minutes at a time. Don't think about working and paying bills for years to come. Just ask yourself, can I make it through the next five minutes?"

Daphne paused. "Maybe I don't want to. I wish . . . sometimes I wish I had died, instead of your father."

Lila squeezed her shoulder.

"I know that's terrible to say, but it's true. I'm too tired to keep going like this. There are too many memories, and it's just too painful."

Lila wasn't sure how to respond. She didn't think that her mother would do anything to actually harm herself, but then again, she had started to realize that there was a lot she didn't know about her mother.

As if reading her thoughts, Daphne sighed and patted her hand. "You go ahead. Don't worry about me—I'll stop feeling sorry for myself in a bit, and then I'll meet you at the store."

Before Lila could argue, her mother pulled the covers up over her head and dismissed her with a regal wave of her hand. "That's an order."

So Lila did her hair and makeup to perfection, put on a simple navy sheath dress with a long coral beaded necklace, and drove down to the store by herself. One advantage to getting up at this hour was that there was plenty of room to park the obnoxiously oversize SUV.

She entered through the shop's back door and took a moment to savor the faint, lingering smell of fresh paint, the hum of the ventilation system, the soft, subtle blue of the walls that offset the colorful clothes arranged on the racks. This space, this moment, represented the culmination of a lot of hard work and optimism in the face of adversity. This was supposed to be her mother's dream come true.

But her mother couldn't bear to face it.

So Lila turned on the lights, unlocked the front door, hung the little wooden OPEN sign in the window, and waited for her first customer.

And waited.

And waited.

She told herself that she had very modest expectations—after all, tourist season wouldn't start for a month and most of her friends couldn't stop by on a Thursday morning. Jenna had to take inventory at the Whinery and Summer was working on grant proposals for the historical society. Ingrid was at school, Malcolm was doing whatever nebulous consulting work he did, and Ben was still MIA.

The first day is just a trial run, she told herself. *The beginning is the hardest part.*

She consoled herself with similar platitudes all morning, straightening dresses on hangers and wiping down display cases and rearranging the bouquet of fresh flowers by the dressing rooms. But when the clock struck noon, her resolve crumbled. The time had come to admit how misguided this whole idea had been, how much hubris she had exhibited in entertaining the delusion that she could make a living trying to sell ancient articles of clothing from her mother's attic to random strangers in a sleepy little town in Delaware.

The bell on the front door jingled as the first customer strolled in.

"Hey." A tall, tan brunette with frosted lipstick and an unmistakable air of ennui strolled in.

"Hi." Lila tried to hide her dismay as the teenager smacked her gum while flipping through a rack of delicate lacy evening gowns. "Welcome to Unfinished Business. What may I help you find?"

"Um . . ." The teenager wandered around, popping gum. "Nothing, really. I'm just kinda looking."

The bell rang again, and Lila was delighted to see that her mother had finally arrived.

Daphne took one look at the aimless adolescent and swooped in. "Young lady, you are stunning."

The gum snapping stopped and a faint smile appeared on those frosted pink lips. "Yeah?"

"You remind me of myself when I was your age," Daphne declared. She crossed the showroom and confided, "I was a model, you know."

And just like that, the teenager was Daphne's biddable groupie. "I go to school over in Wilmington. My sorority's having an eighties party next month and I need something hot and retro."

Lila opened her mouth to suggest a yellow cocktail dress, but Daphne silenced her with a mere look.

"I know just the thing." Daphne plucked a shiny, cherry red minidress from the rack by the fitting room. "This will be perfect on you."

Lila recognized the vinyl dress with the gold metal rings on the shoulder straps and the low scoop neckline. "Wait, we can't sell that."

Her mother ignored her and focused on the customer. A little spark lit up her dark eyes. "You know, I was wearing this dress when I met the love of my life."

The girl's eyes started to shine, too. "You were?"

"I was. And we were happy together for thirty years."

"So you think it's good luck?"

"I know it is. I have a good feeling about this party, especially if you tie everything together with the right footwear. May I suggest knee-high white boots?" Daphne ushered the girl to the dressing room and closed the curtain, wiping away a tear as she did so. "I can't wait to see it on you."

"Mom!" Lila whispered. "How can you sell that dress?"

Daphne looked at Lila, and her eyes were still shining—with tears, but most of all, love. "How can I not? It's special to me, but I can't ever wear it again."

"Ohmigod!" The college student was practically hyperventilating in the dressing room. "I look *so* good! Everyone else is going to be so jealous!"

Daphne laughed softly. "See? Why would I leave it boxed up in a storage unit when it could be back in circulation? That dress was made for first dates and whirlwind romances. I love it, but I have to let it go." She dried her eyes carefully to avoid smudging her mascara. "Even if I spend the rest of my life in Black Dog Bay, I'll know that my favorite Paco Rabanne is still traveling the world, having adventures."

The sorority girl bought the Paco Rabanne—plus a gold and black Lanvin evening dress from the seventies and a short, strapless green Gucci dress featuring a skirt covered in feathers.

"My friends are going to D-I-E *die* when they see this stuff." The coed didn't even flinch when Lila announced her total—more than three thousand dollars.

"As they should," Daphne said. "Your legs look fantastic in that Gucci."

"Please spread the word about us if you're happy with your purchases." Lila tucked a few business cards in with the tissue paper as she folded and bagged the purchases.

The teenager whipped out her phone. "I'm tweeting about you guys right now." She sashayed out with a newfound spring in her step, swinging her pink paper bag in one hand.

"Look at her go." Daphne smiled wistfully. "Working Main Street like it's a Milan catwalk."

Lila wished she'd had the foresight to buy champagne for this moment. All they had to drink was a few cans of diet soda in the back room refrigerator, but they made do, clinking the cans together with a dull, sloshy thud.

The door chime sounded again, and Daphne put down her can. "Here we go! On to sale number two!"

They hurried back out to the sales floor to find Ben Collier standing in the doorway. He looked a little more rugged than the last time Lila had seen him, owing to a two-day stubble and clothes that had clearly been slept in. The harsh noon sunlight accentuated the fatigue evident in his face.

"You're back!" She dashed around the counter and gave him a hug.

"I'm back." He squeezed her tightly. "Thank God you're here. I need your help."

She was afraid to ask the question, given his dishevelment, but she had to know. "How'd it go with Allison?"

"Yes, tell us everything." Daphne crowded into the hug.

"Well." He tried to disentangle himself, but Daphne held fast. "I think we're getting back together."

"Ugh." Daphne released her grip on his arms. "That's too bad."

"Mother!" Lila looked pointedly toward the back room. "Would you give us a moment, please?"

Daphne glowered, motioned from Ben to Lila and back again, then mouthed, "Meant to be."

"Play the landlord card," Lila advised Ben. "Tell her you're raising our rent if she doesn't make herself scarce."

But Ben, ever the gentleman, took off his hat and gave Daphne a placating smile. "How are you, Mrs. Alders? I hope your water heater's not giving you any more trouble."

Daphne beamed. "Not a bit, thanks to you." All sunshine and light, she turned and headed for the back room. "I'll leave you kids to chat."

Lila rolled her eyes. "You two are perfect for each other. Bringing up the water heater? Shameless."

Ben chuckled. "It worked, didn't it?" He straightened up and got serious. "I took your advice. I was bold. I took action. I drove straight to Boston and showed up at Allison's door in the middle of the night."

Lila sucked in her breath. "I said be bold, not be the cause of a panic attack and a 911 call."

"No, she was okay with it." His eyes darkened with intensity at the memory. "We talked and talked . . . and then we did some other things . . . and then we talked some more."

Lila made loops with her hand, prompting him to continue. "And?"

"And she says she wants to finish grad school before she makes any huge life decisions."

"Ben!" Lila smacked his shoulder. "You didn't tell me she was in grad school!"

"Yeah, she's finishing up her master's degree. She graduates at the end of May. You were right."

"I was?"

"Yeah." Ben turned his cap over and over in his hands. "About my deadlines being arbitrary and selfish. I was focused on my goals and what I wanted, and I didn't stop to think that her goals were just as important."

Lila was impressed with herself. "I said all that?"

"You would have if I'd told you about her

going to grad school. Anyway, we both agreed that we need to work together. What we have is worth it."

Lila felt a pang of love, but it wasn't the kind of love she used to have for him. "Aww. You look so happy."

"Happy" might have been an overstatement—he actually looked completely and totally focused. Almost frighteningly focused.

"She's coming to visit this weekend." His voice turned grim. "And I want everything to be perfect. My house, my family, the whole town."

"Sounds like a realistic goal."

He didn't crack a smile. "Allison's special. I don't know how to explain it, but . . ." He gazed down at Lila. "When you and I were hanging out, it was great. It was like old times. But also it made me realize how much I missed Allison."

Lila tried not to flinch. "Oh."

"What I have with her is so different from what I had with you. It's so much better!"

She flinched. "I think I liked it better when you didn't know how to explain it."

He looked horrified as he reached out to her. "I'm sorry. I didn't mean—"

She waved away his apology. "It's fine. I know what you're trying to say. Besides, I could never stay mad at you."

"You're not just saying that because I'm the landlord now?"

She threw him a little wink. "Ben Collier, you will always be more to me than just my landlord."

He finally took a minute to look around the rest of the boutique. "The place looks great."

"Your team did a great job." She summarized all the work they'd done while he'd been gone. "And my mom fixed the bathroom faucet."

His eyes widened. "Your mom fixed a faucet?"

"Mm-hmmm. Used a wrench and everything. She has many hidden talents, apparently. So you'll have to bring Allison by this weekend. I'm dying to meet her."

Ben hesitated. "It won't be weird?"

"Don't be ridiculous! I think it's fantastic. As long as you're happy, I'm happy." Lila tilted her head. "So what do you need help with?"

He looked determined and daunted all at once. "I want to get her something."

"Like a present?"

He nodded. "Something really cool. One of a kind."

"That pretty much describes everything in this store." Lila scanned the racks and shelves. "Help me narrow it down. What's her style like?"

"Uh . . . she wears jeans a lot."

"Fancy jeans or regular jeans?"

"Uh . . ." He was starting to panic.

Lila switched tactics. "What's her favorite color?"

He stared back at her like a job candidate who

had just been asked to identify his greatest weakness. "When she's working, she mostly wears black and white. I think?"

"Okay, so classic." Lila patted his forearm. "Simple. Understated. We can work with that."

"We can?"

"Absolutely. Do you know her dress size?"

"No." His expression segued from panic to guilt.

"All right, then we're probably better off staying away from clothes. Let's consider accessories. Does she like shoes? Handbags?"

"I don't know. She's not into all that stuff." A sheen of sweat appeared on his forehead. "She's had the same purse the whole time I've known her. And she wears the same silver hoop earrings every day."

Lila's ears pricked up. "She likes earrings?"

He nodded.

Before Lila could ask her next question, her cell phone rang. She glanced at the caller ID name and held up her index finger. "Hang on one second. I'm so sorry, but this is important." She turned her back on Ben and answered with a husky murmur. "Proliferation."

"Actually, this time, the password is Pucci," Malcolm drawled on the other end of the line.

She frowned. "What?"

"Stand by. I'm sending you a picture."

Lila held out her phone and clicked over to her

texts, where she saw the photo: a rumpled cocktail dress beaded with abstract shapes of gold, magenta, and dark blue.

She raised the phone back to her ear. "What am I looking at?"

"I just left the thrift store in Lewes," Malcolm said. "Some woman tossed that in the donation bin as I was walking out the door. Thought you might be interested."

"When did this happen?"

"About fifteen minutes ago." He paused. "Tag says Pucci."

"And you just left it there?" She could feel adrenaline surging through her body. "You left *Pucci* to fend for itself?"

"I had to go. I'm on a tight work deadline."

"Then why were you at the thrift store?" she demanded.

"None of your business." His calmness only served to fuel her agitation. "If you want it, I'd get a move on. I saw a couple of old ladies eyeing it."

She held out the phone again, scrutinizing the picture. "You're sure it's authentic?"

"Looked authentic to me. It's gonna go fast at fifteen dollars."

"I'm leaving for Lewes right now." She dropped her voice even lower. "And if someone else buys it before I get there, I'm going to come to your house and kick your ass."

"Looking forward to it."

"Oh, and Malcolm?"

"Yes?"

"Thank you."

"You're welcome." She could hear the smile in his voice.

Lila clicked off the line and beckoned to Ben. "Walk with me." She ducked under the counter and grabbed her keys. "I have to go on an emergency fashion rescue mission. Let's talk in the car."

"Where are we going?" he asked.

"Lewes." She hollered toward the back room. "Mom? I have to go. I'll be back in half an hour."

Daphne emerged, wringing her hands. "But what am I supposed to do if a customer comes in?"

"Be your usual charming self. Talk about the clothes. Reminisce about your modeling days." Lila started toward the front exit.

"You can't leave me here alone!"

"Thirty minutes." Lila put one hand on the door. "Just don't let the place burn down."

"But what if someone wants to buy something?" Her mother's voice shook. "I don't know how to work the cash register, or the credit card swiper thing."

"I'll stay," Ben volunteered.

"You're sure?"

"Go. Hurry back."

Daphne visibly relaxed.

Lila waved as she stepped into the sunlight. "You're the best ex-boyfriend ever."

Ben waved back. "I know."

"Call me if you need anything, guys. And Mom, Ben needs a grand-gesture gift for his girlfriend. She likes classic jewelry. Help him out, and remember, he passed up corporate funnel cake money for us." As the door closed behind her, Lila glanced down at the picture Malcolm had sent. "Hold on, beautiful. I'm on my way."

Chapter 22

Thirty-five minutes later, with the fifteen-dollar designer dress purchased and locked in her car, Lila pounded on the door of Malcolm's house.

"Who is it?" he called from inside.

"It's your partner in Pucci." *Pound, pound, pound.* Lila winced and shook out her hand. "Open up!"

"It's unlocked."

Lila charged in, prepared to upbraid him for abandoning vintage couture in mint condition, and found him hunched over his sewing table while the Golf Channel droned in the background. For a moment, she hung back, admiring the view of his shoulders and his back and his forearms. . . . Then she spied the wedding dress.

She approached the sewing machine with mounting dismay, staring at the piles of shiny white satin. "What is that?"

His voice was nearly drowned out by the clatter of the treadle. "A dress."

She clutched her car keys in trembling hands. "That's why you were too busy to go back for the Pucci this morning?"

"Yeah. I have to have this done by five."

Lila couldn't hold back a little squeak of indignation. "How could you?"

He stopped sewing and glanced up at her. "Uh . . . how could I what?"

"How could you do this to me?" She planted her hands on her hips. "To Rosa?"

"For the last time, she doesn't have a name. I mean, *it* doesn't have a name."

"Don't try to change the subject! I demand answers! Who is she?" Lila grabbed a handful of fabric.

A glint of amusement appeared in his blue eyes. "My sister's best friend. She needs an emergency alteration. My sister begged. Then she got my niece to beg. The kid can barely talk; it was pathetic. How could I say no?"

Lila scoffed. "A likely story."

"It's true. I'm taking the hem up and lowering the neckline."

"Oh really? And what's the rush?"

"She's eloping this weekend."

"Dressed like Britney Spears at the VMA awards?"

"I don't ask questions; I just make the repairs." Malcolm moved the scissors out of her reach. "What's wrong with you?"

Lila let go of the fabric with a dramatic flourish. "I'm in a jealous rage, okay?"

"I can see that."

"Are you *laughing* at me? Well, I'm glad one of us finds this entertaining." She clicked her tongue at the deconstructed dress. "Look at this! Cheap, tacky polyester. Stiff, scratchy lace. This is going to crease. This is going to stain. We both know it. How could you sully yourself with this when I've given you the very best? Silk thread and hand embroidery and generous seam allowances." She had to stop to catch her breath. "You can't try to tell me that *this* is in the same league as what I bring every time I see you."

He started stitching again. "Not to be rude, but I have to keep working while we talk. Time is of the essence."

"We had an understanding!" she cried. "And a nondisclosure agreement."

"Yeah, but we don't have a noncompete clause."

"So all that stuff you said about keeping your secret and taking it to the grave and death before dishonor? Those were just empty words?" She gritted her teeth. *"Stop laughing."*

He couldn't keep a straight face for more than half a second. "I've never seen anyone get so worked up about a little polyester."

"Because I'm offering you timeless craftsmanship by Ceil Chapman and you throw me aside for some no-name, mass-produced, one-season wonder!"

"This from the woman who doesn't even remember our date." He launched into that sardonic drawl again. "You completely forgot about me for over a decade."

She threw out both arms. "Well, I remember you now! You want a do-over? You've got one. You fix that Ceil Chapman dress and I will put it on and we will finish our unfinished business!"

He lifted his chin to indicate a white garment bag hanging on the closet door. "It's finished."

"Oh." She unzipped the bag and looked over the side seam she'd ripped. The repair was masterful. Undetectable.

Flawless.

"Oh." All her bluster disappeared as she realized how much time and care he must have devoted to the dress she would wear on their date. "Thank you. It looks great."

He muttered something under his breath and resumed sewing.

She hooked her index finger under the top of

the hanger, swung the garment bag over her shoulder like a cape, and got up into Malcolm's personal space. "All right, then. Tomorrow night. Pick me up at seven."

He gave her a curt nod. "See you tomorrow at seven."

"Yes, you will." She leaned down and whispered right into his ear, soft and sultry. "And by the end of the night, you won't be thinking about anybody's dress but mine."

Chapter 23

Just before lunchtime on Friday, a frazzled-looking pregnant woman walked into Unfinished Business with a zippered garment bag folded over one arm and a wriggly, redheaded little boy in each hand.

"Hi." She flashed Lila a dazzling smile, then turned to her little boys with a dour, well-practiced "mom face." "You two. I need you to be on your best behavior. We'll only be here for a few minutes, and I need to you to be *good*. Got it?"

The boys nodded.

"Let me be clear: no running, no fighting, no touching anything. I mean it. Now go sit in that chair over there." She pulled a tattered picture book out of her bag. "You can look at this while you're waiting."

The boys raced over to the upholstered chair and immediately started wrestling for prime position on the seat.

"Blake! Beckett!" The woman clapped her hands. "What did I just say? You are both—" She looked at Lila with a sigh. "Never mind. Let's just move this along as quickly as we can."

"They're adorable," Lila said, managing not to react as the smaller boy started licking the Azzedine Alaïa sequined camouflage satchel hanging on the wall next to the chair.

"I know you have to say that." The woman laughed. "But thank you, anyway." She unzipped the garment bag. "I'd like to consign this evening gown, please, if you think you can find a buyer."

"We don't typically do consignment sales, but let's have a look," Lila said. "I take it you don't have much call for evening gowns at this stage of your life?"

"I'm having twins." The woman rubbed her belly. "Twin boys."

"Oh, congratulations!"

The woman nodded. "Blake and Beckett here are two and three. And before you ask, yes, I do have my hands full; no, I don't remember what it's like to get a full night's sleep."

Lila could hear the frustration in the woman's voice. She smiled gently and urged, "Tell me about your gown."

The woman immediately brightened. "It's custom-made. I wore it for the evening gown portion of the Miss America pageant." She paused to let that sink in, the same way Daphne paused after she announced she'd been a model. "I was Miss Delaware. Fourth runner-up overall. I lost to Miss Texas."

"That is so cool." Lila peeled back the flaps of the garment bag to reveal a one-shoulder column gown crafted of royal blue silk crepe over two whisper-thin layers of chiffon. The dress featured tiny clusters of silver rhinestones and a tasteful cutout shaped like abstract floral petals on one side of the waistline. It didn't really fit in, style-wise, with the other dresses in the boutique, but it had an allure all its own. This gown clearly had a story, and Lila had started to figure out that the story was really what sold customers on vintage pieces.

"Delaware almost never gets into the top five finalists." When the gown's owner smiled, Lila could see a vestige of the glamorous beauty queen. "I'm Shannon, by the way."

Lila introduced herself, then asked, "So, what was your talent?"

"I danced. Jazz *en pointe*."

Lila ran her hand over the fabric's sequin

detailing. "I used to watch Miss America every year with my mom."

"Me, too. In fact, my mom grew up doing pageants. She taught me everything I know. She was Miss Maryland back in the day, but she didn't make it to the finals." Shannon sighed, her eyes wistful. "We got closer to the crown with every generation, and the plan was, my daughter was going to win the whole shebang." She patted her protruding belly. "Except it turns out I'm never going to have a daughter."

"So you're not going to try again?" Lila asked.

Shannon stared back as if Lila had started speaking in tongues. "After four boys in four years? No. And I've informed my husband that he will be making a surgical appointment to that end."

"Got it." Lila held up the gown to admire the draping. "It's beautiful. Are you sure you don't want to hang on to it? I'm sure it means a lot to you, and who knows? Maybe someday you'll have a niece or a granddaughter who wants to wear it."

"It's not about the actual dress," Shannon explained. "It's more about the *idea,* you know? The idea that I could have a little girl who would care about all this stuff. Who would want to carry on our family tradition." The former beauty queen smiled wistfully. "I know I probably sound ridiculous to you, and maybe I am. My husband says that even if we did have a daughter, she might be a tomboy who just wants to play baseball and go hunting."

Lila nodded.

"It's not that I don't love my boys. I adore them." She got a haunted look in her eyes. "There're just . . . *so many* Legos. And the Matchbox cars—they're everywhere."

Lila tried to hand back the blue gown. "Are you sure you don't want to have this preserved and stored?"

Shannon shook her head, her lips thinning. "I don't want to stash it away somewhere. I want to share it. I want it to mean something to someone, the way it meant something to me."

Lila reexamined the dress, exclaiming over the cutting and the stitching and the beadwork. "It's gorgeous." She hesitated before continuing. "But it's going to take a very special woman to carry this off."

"I know." Shannon lifted her chin with an air of regal grace. "Being a pageant winner requires a lot of poise and confidence."

"Right." Lila was starting to understand how the salesclerk at the estate jewelers' must have felt when offering to buy her engagement ring for a pittance. "So we might have to hang on to it for a while, and we might not be able to get you what you think it's worth. I mean, pageant gowns cost beaucoup bucks, right?"

Shannon nodded. "This one was made in Philadelphia to my exact specifications. It cost . . . actually, I'm embarrassed to tell you how much it cost. But it was worth it."

"You're *sure* you want to sell it?"

"I'm sure." The former Miss Delaware leaned in and confided, "Now, the tiaras, I'm keeping forever. They can pry those out of my cold, dead hands."

"Obviously." Lila felt the same way about her homecoming crown. "Well, I'd be thrilled to put this out on the floor, but I can only give you fifty dollars for it." She braced herself for outrage and protest, but the woman didn't miss a beat.

"Fifty is fine, as long as you find the right owner. Someone who will love it."

Lila raised her hand and gave her word. "Now, while you're here, can I interest you in some fabulous handbags or maybe a necklace?"

"No, thank you. My last necklace ended up doubling as a teething aid." The woman eyed the camouflage Alaïa bag with interest. "Well, okay, maybe I'll take this. It's big enough to double as a diaper bag, right?"

"Heck, yeah." Lila rang up the bag and found a padded hanger for the pageant gown.

Shannon gave the silk chiffon gown one last fond pat as she prepared to wrangle her boys back outside. "It just doesn't look quite as good when it's not in the spotlight."

• • •

"Two days down, and we're still standing," Lila said to her mother as they locked the front door and tallied the receipts.

Daphne collapsed into a plush purple velvet chair. "I'm exhausted, but it feels kind of nice. It feels like we're getting something done."

"We are." Lila opened the cash register and started counting the money. "We're rallying. Dad would be impressed."

Daphne got back on her feet and started straightening the dresses on the rack. "I couldn't have done any of this without you. I never thought I'd say this, but I'm glad you forced me to sell all these clothes. I feel . . . lighter."

"And think of the money we're saving on storage unit fees," Lila pointed out.

"Wait. What happened to this jacket?" Daphne held up the black and pink Chanel suit. "All the buttons are missing."

Lila glanced up from the cash register. "Are you sure? I double-checked everything before we put it out on the floor."

"What do you mean, am I sure? I'm not blind, sweet pea. The buttons are gone."

Lila inspected the jaunty wool blazer and skirt. Sure enough, the buttons had vanished, leaving loose threads on the black edging along the tops of the pockets and the front of the jacket.

Daphne checked the blazer cuffs, which had also been denuded of buttons.

"Why on earth would anyone cut off the buttons?" Lila asked.

"To sell." Daphne rubbed her forehead. "Chanel pieces are worth a lot more if they have the original stamped buttons. There's huge demand for hardware and fasteners. Someone must have come in here with a pocketknife and cut them off."

"Shut up; there's a black market for *buttons* now?"

"If it says Chanel, there's a black market for it." Daphne fumed. "We're going to have to start keeping the really good stuff in a separate area. A VIP back room."

Lila stared mournfully at the blazer. "So you're saying this suit is . . ."

"Worth about half of what it was worth when you opened the doors this morning." Daphne raised her index fingers to her temples. "I need a drink. Let's stop at the Whinery on our way home."

"You want to go to the Whinery?" Lila asked. "I thought you said that place was tacky and touristy."

"Well, maybe it's time I stopped being such a snob. Every time I drive by, it looks like everyone inside is having fun."

"They are." Lila stopped fretting about button

larceny for a moment. "There's free-flowing chocolate and a lovely chandelier and every breakup song you could think of. I'm sure they'd let you make a request."

"Sounds delightful. Let's go!"

"Can't." Lila studied the varnished hardwood floor. "I've got plans."

Daphne pounced. "What plans? With whom?"

Lila couldn't suppress a little smile. "Remember Malcolm Toth?"

"The delectable ex-marine who dropped you off the other night?"

Lila shot her mother a look of reproach. "Don't call him the delectable ex-marine."

"Why not? It's not demeaning; I'm merely stating the facts."

"Once a marine, always a marine, Mom. He's a delectable marine, period. Now, I'm going home to get ready. Want me to drop you off at the Whinery?"

"No, no," Daphne singsonged. "I can have a glass of wine in the comfort of my living room."

"You just want to meddle in my personal life and scope out the delectable marine."

Daphne pressed her hand to her chest. "You wound me. I'm going to help you get ready."

"Thanks, but I don't need help."

"I'll be the judge of that." Daphne rubbed her palms together at the prospect of playing stylist. "Where are you kids going on your big date?"

"No idea."

"Well, how can you get ready if you don't know where you'll be going?"

It was all Lila could do to restrain herself from flinging out her arms and twirling around the showroom, *Sound of Music*-style. "Doesn't matter where we're going. I already know what I'm wearing."

"Don't be ridiculous; of course it matters." Daphne frowned in consternation. "Your hair and makeup and outfit have to be just perfect."

"It doesn't have to be perfect, Mom. It has to be *right*."

Chapter 24

"For the last time, Lila, stop peeking out the window and go back upstairs." Daphne jabbed her index finger at the staircase. "You're not supposed to be raring to go at the front door when your date arrives. You're supposed to be upstairs, finishing up your *toilette*."

"But I'm already ready." Lila double-checked her reflection in the gilt-framed mirror next to the front door. She'd donned the sexy red Ceil Chapman dress, swept her hair up into a simple twist, and opted for smoky eyes and nude, shiny lips. She looked about ten times too fancy for any venue in Black Dog Bay, let alone anywhere she might have gone on a high school date.

But she wasn't going for subtlety tonight. She was going for shock and awe. Malcolm had challenged her to wear this dress, and she intended to wear the hell out of it.

Ever since she'd zipped up the back, she couldn't stop thinking about the fact that he'd worked on this dress. He'd had his hands all over the silk, inside and outside and . . .

"Letting men cool their heels is a time-honored tradition for a reason. Go upstairs!" Daphne implored. "Don't be too eager."

"The jig is up, Mother." Lila blew her reflection a little kiss and straightened up. "I already called him and showed up at his house uninvited, remember?"

"So you just have to keep making things worse?"

Lila spied headlights turning into the driveway. "Ooh, he's here." She grabbed her handbag and dashed out the door. As she navigated the steps
in precariously high heels, she heard her mother wailing behind her: *"Where have I gone wrong?"*

Despite her initial bravado, Lila was surprised to find herself hesitant once Malcolm got out of the car. Darkness had fallen, but the Jeep headlights were bright and harsh, illuminating her every imperfection.

They stood a few feet apart, taking stock, getting their bearings as the dynamics between them shifted yet again.

He cleared his throat. "Hi. You look—"

She took a step toward him. "Overeager and shameless?"

He relaxed. "I was going to say 'great.' "

"You, too." He wore dark pants and a crisp white shirt. Not a trace of sweat or visible abs anywhere. *But the night is still young.* "So where are we going?" She suddenly wished she had stashed her aviator sunglasses and possibly a pair of walkie-talkies in her bag. "Is it covert? Top secret?"

He closed the gap between them and opened the passenger side door for her. "Not especially."

Lila had learned at an early age how to enter and exit a car while preserving her modesty in a short skirt. She utilized roughly fifty percent of her skill set and asked, "Are you going to blindfold me on the way? So I can't retrace our steps and betray you to the opposition?"

Malcolm walked around the car, settled into his seat, put both hands on the wheel, then gave her his full attention. "Do you want me to blindfold you?"

She crossed her legs and stacked her hands on her bare knee.

He waited.

The way he was looking at her was actually making her feel a bit breathless. "I do now."

"I'll keep that in mind." He put the car into gear and headed back to the main road.

She tried to recover her composure and remember what it was you were supposed to talk about in the first five minutes of a first date. *Hint: not blindfolds.*

"Let's try that again: Where are we going?" she asked, then held up her hand. "On second thought, don't tell me. I'm enjoying the mystery."

"Fair enough." He headed north on the highway bordering the beach. "How was the first day of business?"

She told him about the Paco Rabanne minidress and the Miss America gown and the pilfered Chanel buttons, then asked, "How did the polyester elopement go?"

He shrugged one shoulder. "I'm assuming it went fine."

"You didn't get any details?"

"You saw the dress. I didn't want any details."

Lila sat back for a moment, then started bouncing in her seat. "Okay, I take back everything I said about wanting to be surprised. The suspense is killing me. Where are we going?"

"You'll find out soon enough."

"Don't toy with me," she warned. "I'm wearing this dress and these shoes and I have ways of making you talk."

He tortured her for a few more minutes before relenting. "We're going to Gull's Point."

"Gull's Point?" She glanced at him, confused. Gull's Point had been the popular Friday night hangout back in their high school days. Teenagers would build bonfires, drink beer, and then dare one another to leap off the windswept cliff into the ocean. It had been the backdrop of budding romances, bitter breakups, enduring friendships, and eternal feuds. Until, eighteen months ago, a real estate corporation had bought the land and started construction on an exclusive gated community for wealthy summer residents.

"We can't go there anymore," Lila pointed out as they reached the ornate metal gate that now sealed off the area. The houses were still under construction, so the neighborhood looked like a ghost town in the moonlight.

"Yeah, we can." Malcolm drove up to the gates and punched a code into the keypad. The tall metal panel slid open.

"How do you know the code?" Lila asked.

"One of the guys I work for invested in the development."

"And that would be . . . ?"

"Jake Sorensen."

Her eyebrows shot up. "You work with Jake? He never mentioned that."

"I do some contract work for him. You know him?" Malcolm seemed both stunned and disturbed by this prospect.

"A little bit, yeah. He showed me one of his

retail spaces as a favor to Summer. And he helped us list one of my mom's old dresses on eBay."

Malcolm stopped the car. "Was it white?"

"Yes."

He nodded. "*I* helped you list one of your mom's old dresses on eBay."

Lila twisted around in her seat to face him. "That was you? But I thought you said you did cybersecurity?"

"Which means I'm qualified to throw together an eBay listing if my very generous employer asks for it."

"So our couture collaboration goes back further than we thought," Lila mused. She lapsed into silence as she surveyed the tall, sprawling skeletons of homes in progress. The trees and boulders and bonfire pits had been leveled to accommodate a string of mega-mansions that took up every available inch of each lot. "This is kind of sad. I mean, I know this place was a fire hazard and it's a miracle no one ever broke their neck jumping off that cliff, but we had so much fun here."

His voice deepened. "I remember."

She gazed at him through the shadows, trying to put the pieces together in her memory. "We came here on a date in high school?"

"Sort of," he admitted. "You came with your friends, but then they drank a six-pack of spritzers and started pushing each other off the cliff, and you didn't want to get wet, so I hung out with you and drove you home."

"That's right." She stared past the half-built houses at the endless black ocean. "I didn't want to mess up my hair or my makeup or my clothes." Lila felt a familiar sinking sense of disappointment in herself. Even as a teenager, when she was supposedly young and reckless, she'd been too concerned about appearances to take chances. She'd been too caught up in what everyone might think to go after what she really wanted.

And now it was too late—Gull's Point was gone and she was old enough to know better.

Malcolm glanced toward the backseat. "I brought food and wine and a blanket. I was thinking we could go out by the edge of the cliff and—" He broke off when he saw the expression on her face. "You know what? Screw that. Let's jump."

Lila hesitated for a moment, then leaped into action. She opened the door and swung her legs out onto the uneven packed dirt. "Hurry up, before I come to my senses."

"Now or never." He yanked the keys out of the ignition.

She leaned down to take off her shoes. This time, her dress didn't rip. Because Malcolm had secured the seam with strong, sure stitches that would probably hold up for another sixty years.

He stepped out of the other side of the car, stripped off his shirt, then unbuckled his belt and yanked that off, too.

She froze in place, nearly blinded by the headlights in her face but very much enjoying the view.

"What?" Apparently, he'd taken off as much as he was going to, despite the fact that he still had his pants on. *Damn.* "You're losing your nerve?"

"No, no." The night wind swept in, making her shiver.

They made their way across the concrete slab framing what would soon be the grandest, fanciest house on the cliff. Malcolm guided her through the beams silhouetted against the starry sky, until they stood at the very edge of the precipice.

It was too dark to see the water below, but she could hear waves crashing against the rocks that bordered the beach.

"Ready?" He took her hand in his. She reveled in the feel of his warm skin against her chilled arm and shoulder.

She nodded and edged closer. Then she closed her eyes and pictured the dark, churning depths below. What it would feel like to fall. What it would feel like to break the surface. What might be underneath the surface in the frigid depths.

He stepped forward.

She hung back.

"Wait, wait." She opened her eyes and stared into the void. "Maybe we should stop and think this through."

"Too late, we already skipped that step."

"What if there are sharks down there?"

He laughed. "Stop stalling. Let's go."

She edged two inches closer to the drop-off. "The water is going to be freezing."

"The adrenaline will kick in and you won't feel a thing."

"What if I get a concussion? What if I'm paralyzed for life?"

"You'll be fine."

"What if—"

"Imagine you're fifteen right now," he urged. "You have no fear."

But fifteen had been an anxiety-ridden age for Lila. Despite her pretty face and popularity, she'd always held herself back, trying to be who her friends, her parents, her boyfriend, needed her to be. And she'd tried so hard to live up to all those expectations that she'd never figured out who she really was.

Malcolm stopped trying to convince her. Instead, he kept holding her hand at the edge of the cliff and said, "Tell me when you're ready."

All Lila could feel was the wind on her cheeks and the damp ocean spray and the solid, steady presence of him next to her. She lifted her face up to the sky. "I'm not fifteen. I'm twenty-nine." She looked back down at her dress. "And I still don't want to mess up my clothes. This is sixty-year-old silk that you worked on for hours."

"Easy solution. Take it off."

"That's your answer to everything, isn't it?"

"Yep." He grasped her shoulders, spun her around, and yanked the recently reinforced zipper down. The shoulder straps slipped off and the fabric pooled around her ankles.

"Done," he announced. "Ready?"

She reached for his hand again. "Ready."

They stepped off the sandy ledge together and after a nanosecond of weightlessness, they plunged into the sea.

It was freezing and dark beyond anything Lila had ever known. She could feel the burn of salt water in her eyes and throat, the power of the waves tossing her body around. Malcolm held fast to her hand.

With a gasp, she broke the surface, then let go of him to start swimming toward shore.

Her hair was plastered over her eyes as she started for shore. It wasn't far, but she had to fight for every inch of progress against the drag of the undertow. Malcolm stayed right there with her, ready to help if she needed it.

But she didn't need help. And when she finally staggered onto the sand, her teeth chattering and her whole body shaking, she realized that the day had finally come: After decades of empty threats and false alarms, her mother's advice about always wearing matching bras and panties had paid off.

Champagne-colored silk-satin finished with Leavers lace for the win.

"Come on." Malcolm strode up behind her and wrapped one arm around her shoulders. "Let's get you dried off."

"Y-you were right." She was shivering so much she could hardly get the words out. "The adrenaline kicked in."

"Move it along." He hustled her across the rocky beach and up the narrow dirt path to the cliff top, where he opened the car door, turned the heater on full blast, and grabbed the picnic blanket out of the back.

"Here." He wrapped the thin cotton blanket around her shoulders and ushered her into the passenger seat. "Get in there and warm up."

"But if I'm under a blanket, you can't see my fancy underwear," she protested.

"Don't worry—I saw it." He gave her a smoldering once-over before he closed her door. Then he jogged to the cliff's edge, retrieved the red dress, got into the driver's seat, and handed her his dry shirt.

"Put this on," he commanded.

She obliged, sliding her arms into the long sleeves and snuggling into the soft fabric, taking a little bit longer to cover herself than was strictly necessary. "I'm never giving this back," she informed him.

"Good. Get over here."

She rested her head on his bare shoulder, basking in the heat blasting out of the air vents, jacked up on adrenaline, and dripping all over the leather seats. The nerves in her toes and fingertips tingled at the sudden change in temperature.

"That was worth a fifteen-year wait." She hesitated, afraid to say what she was feeling. Then she went ahead and said it anyway: "*You* were worth a fifteen-year wait."

He ran his fingertip along her lower lip, then turned her face up to kiss her. She met him halfway, and the moment his lips touched hers, she was keenly aware that she wasn't wearing pants.

And he wasn't wearing a shirt.

Life was good.

They shifted positions, starting to get comfortable, starting to explore each other.

He deepened the kiss and she parted her lips and both of them tasted like salt from the ocean, and then . . .

The real fifteen-year-olds arrived.

Flashlight beams bounced through the car's interior, followed by a pack of kids who were laughing and yelling and swearing at one another at the top of their lungs. Judging by the number of voices Lila heard, there must have been at least four boys and three girls . . . plus at least three six-packs.

In addition to beer, these kids were also apparently drunk on Friday-night freedom and they were not pleased to find adult interlopers in their midst. They made a dramatic show of stopping and speculating as to why two "grown-ass adults" would be fogging up the car windows in the middle of a half-constructed luxury home community.

"They're probably pretending they live here," the alpha female opined loudly. "Like, giant, empty houses turn them on. Sick and twisted."

"Damn kids." Lila pulled away from Malcolm and straightened the front of the shirt. "How did they even get in here?"

He laughed. "Since when can six-foot-high walls and a fancy gate stop a bunch of high schoolers?"

"Do they not understand that we're trying to make up for lost time here?" She rolled down her window and yelled, "Don't be selfish! You guys still have time. *We're old!*"

All she got in response were some catcalls and a series of loud popping sounds.

She stuck her head out into the darkness. "Fireworks are illegal, you . . . you hooligans!"

Malcolm tugged her back into the car and rolled

her window back up. "Stop harassing the teen-agers."

"Why should I?" she demanded. "We were here first."

He started the car and drove back toward the gate. "They're bored, they're hormonal, and their cliff is being turned into a bunch of McMansions. Let them have fun while they can."

"Whatever." She finished buttoning the shirt and buckled her seat belt. "I want to have fun, too."

He stopped the car and gave her his full attention. "Lila, I don't make a lot of promises, but I promise you this: We are going to have fun."

Her whole body thrilled at the undertone of dark sensuality in his voice. "Yeah?"

Slowly and deliberately, he leaned over and pressed a soft kiss onto the hollow of her throat. "Baby, I am going to show you such a good time."

For a moment, all she heard was the rustling of fabric, but then she thought she heard a muffled bark.

Both of them startled.

As they straightened up in their seats, a giant, shaggy black dog trotted in front of the head-lights.

Lila told herself that she couldn't possibly have seen what she just saw. The famous phantom of

Black Dog Bay. The town legend she'd always dismissed as a bunch of hooey. According to lore, the black dog appeared when your life was changing forever. When your past mistakes were behind you and a new life was unfolding, whether you liked it or not.

The black dog appeared when things were meant to be.

Malcolm stared straight ahead at the now-empty path. "What was that?"

Something in his voice made her think he knew exactly what that was.

Lila tried to sound causal. "Um, I think it was a bear?"

He shook his head. "Too small to be a bear."

Her voice dropped to a whisper. "Was it . . . was it a dog?"

"Maybe it was a badger," he suggested.

"Maybe it was a skunk," she said. "Or a runaway pony."

"Maybe it was a wolverine."

"Yeah, probably a wolverine."

They lapsed into silence on the drive back into town, one pantless, one shirtless, both of them struggling to make sense of what they'd just witnessed.

By the time they pulled into the Alderses' driveway, they had agreed upon the only possible conclusion:

"Never happened," Malcolm declared.

"Never happened," Lila agreed. On impulse, she leaned over and gave him two more kisses on the lips.

"One for tonight, and one for sophomore year." She wrapped her arms around his neck and delivered one more. "And a little something to hold you over till next time."

He caught her arm as she pulled away, then kissed her again, slowly and thoroughly, as though he had all the time in the world and knew exactly what he was going to do with it. "*That's* to hold me over."

Lila scooped up her shoes and dashed up the porch steps, perfectly aware that the hemline of his shirt was creeping up as she went.

Daphne, who was waiting for a full report in the front hall, regarded her daughter's bedraggled state with dismay. "What on earth happened to you?"

Lila tucked her damp hair behind her ear. "Love, lust, delayed adolescence. 'Night!"

"Wait! Where's my Ceil Chapman dress?"

"Backseat of Malcolm's Jeep. I'll get it back next time I show up unannounced at his house."

"Come back here, young lady! What are you *wearing?*"

"The delectable marine's shirt." Lila couldn't stop smiling. "He managed to keep his pants on— for tonight. We're sharing an outfit."

"You . . . He . . . I . . ." Daphne sputtered

through a whole cycle of emotions. "I've never seen you like this."

"Neither have I." Lila pulled a strand of sea-weed out of her hair. "What can I say? I'm a late bloomer."

Chapter 25

Lila awakened at sunrise to the sound of pans and glassware clattering in the kitchen and the smell of something cinnamony. She ran a brush through her hair, threw on jeans and a sweater (and lip-stick and mascara, because God forbid she should greet unexpected houseguests at seven a.m. looking less than perfectly put together), then went downstairs to find Summer chowing down at the breakfast bar while her mother made pancakes at the huge stainless steel, gourmet-restaurant-quality stove.

"Good morning. You guys are up early." Lila dropped the bright-eyed-and-bushy-tailed routine and yawned when she realized there was no one who needed to be dazzled and impressed.

"Hi." Summer, sporting a bedhead Mohawk, handed her a mug of coffee. "We're having a power breakfast. Planning for the fashion show."

"It's going to be great." Daphne looked as though she'd been up for hours in her diamond earrings and patent red loafers.

Lila accepted the coffee gratefully. "That sounds —hey, why does she get to have pancakes but I couldn't have waffles the other day?"

Daphne brandished the spatula. "Because *she's* not trying to seduce an ex-boyfriend in a Marilyn Monroe dress."

"She's getting married," Lila said. This had the intended effect of taking all the heat off her.

Daphne spun over to Summer, still armed with the spatula. "Ooh, you are? Why haven't I heard about this? When's the big day?"

"You'd have to ask Ingrid." Summer tried to look disgusted, but couldn't quite conceal her excitement. "It's really her wedding. I'll just show up and say the vows."

"Let me see the ring."

Summer held out her bare hands. "Haven't gotten around to that yet."

Daphne gave a little *hmph* of disapproval. "Where are you and Dutch registered?"

Summer's expression changed from excited to horrified. "We're not. We're keeping this low-key. Two slackers in love."

"But you have to register for gifts, darling."

"I don't want gifts." Summer took a huge swig of coffee. "I just want to be done with the wedding." She shot an accusatory look at Lila, who responded with an angelic smile. "Anyway, back to the fashion show."

"I can help you with your gift registry," Daphne offered. "Not to toot my own horn, but I have exquisite taste. Just point me to a Web site and I'll choose the best linens, the most classic china patterns, the finest crystal."

At the mention of china patterns, Summer looked physically nauseated. "Can't I just register at the liquor store and be done with it?"

"Yes." Lila gave her mother a look. "Don't terrorize the bride-to-be."

Summer flashed her a thumbs-up and slipped her a contraband pancake wrapped in a paper towel. "As I was saying, we need to get an initial head count for the fashion show by the end of the month because—"

"That's what I don't get," Lila interjected. "You're fine with working the runway in a bright pink nightgown in front of hundreds of people, but you're allergic to weddings?"

Summer heaved an exaggerated, put-upon sigh. "Strutting around in sex-kitten pajamas that Zsa Zsa Gabor would wear is one thing—"

"*Eva* Gabor," Daphne corrected.

"—but walking down the aisle in a big mess of tulle is quite another." Summer gagged. "And then the whole deal with the garter and the bouquet toss and the veil . . . it's all so antiquated and patriarchal." She paused. "Oh my God, Ingrid's rubbing off on me."

"Don't spook her," Daphne admonished Lila.

"She and Ingrid are going to be the stars of the fashion show."

"Ingrid's in the show now?" Lila laughed. "Have you broken the news to her yet?"

"No, because I know she'll try to use it as leverage against me. She'll probably make me agree to a harpist at the wedding." Summer clutched the countertop. "Or a string quartet. That girl is a ruthless negotiator."

"Well, give her whatever she wants, because that beaded Pucci minidress Lila found at the thrift store will be divine on her." Daphne patted her daughter's hand. "That was a great score, sweet pea. I don't think it's ever been worn."

"You found a mint-condition Pucci at a thrift store?" Summer looked impressed. "How did that happen?"

Lila brushed her hair back over her shoulder. "Just lucky, I guess."

"Oh, that reminds me." Summer turned to Daphne. "I saw some signs for an estate sale that starts at nine. We should go check it out and see if there's any jewelry or luggage."

Lila made a slicing motion across her throat. "She's not allowed to shop."

"It's not shopping; it's business," Daphne said.

"We should leave as soon as possible." Summer got a competitive gleam in her eyes. "You have to get there early if you want the good stuff."

"Sounds like a plan." Daphne jumped as her cell phone chirped. "What was that?"

"You have a text," Summer informed her.

"Mom, you finally learned to text?" Lila put down her pancake and gave a little golf clap.

"Not really." Daphne handed her phone to Summer. "Summer's been corresponding with Cedric all morning."

"Ooh, is he coming for the fashion show?" Lila asked.

Summer glanced down at the phone. "No."

Daphne's perfect posture gave way to a pouty slouch.

Summer skimmed the text. "But he says he wants you to come see him in Belgium—"

"Right." Daphne sniffed. "With all my disposable income."

"—and he says he's spreading the word about Unfinished Business to 'buyers who matter.' " Summer set the phone aside. "What does that mean?"

Daphne perked up again. "Vintage couture is big business overseas, you know. Dealers in New York and Paris and London send buyers around the world to find important pieces."

Lila sipped her coffee. "We do have some important pieces."

"But no one's ever going to look for them in Black Dog Bay, Delaware." Daphne sighed.

"What we need is a satellite store in New York. Chelsea or the West Village."

"I'll get right on that," Lila said. "Right after I find out if we're going to make rent next month."

"I suppose you're right." Yet another weary sigh. "We're not a model and a TV star anymore; we're just a widow and a divorcée."

"Well, when you put it that way . . ."

"Be careful how you talk about yourself." Summer pointed her fork at Daphne. "What you think, you become. I believe the Buddha said that. Or a bumper sticker."

"Facts are facts. And the fact is, I just don't have the moxie to make it in New York anymore," Daphne said. "Besides, I've been in this house for thirty-five years now. It's who I am. It's where I belong."

Lila devoured the rest of her pancake, then excused herself to go shower and change. "I have to go vacuum the shop and clean the windows before we open for the day." She gave her mother a hug after she rinsed her plate. "Keep it up with the texting lessons and stay out of trouble, you two."

"You're the one who needs to stay out of trouble." Daphne stage-whispered to Summer, "She came home from a date last night with no pants on."

"I approve," Summer said, then stage-whispered

back to Daphne. "Who's the guy? Not the high school boyfriend again?"

"No, no, she's moved on to a delectable marine."

"Ooh, then I *definitely* approve."

Lila watched them with her eyes narrowed. "I don't think I like you guys hanging out together."

"We'll be sure to bear that in mind next time we're taking a vote," Summer said.

Daphne crossed the kitchen and gave her daughter a kiss on the cheek. "Thank you for taking care of the opening today, sweet pea. I'll be over right after we hit the estate sale."

"Don't spend any money," Lila warned.

"I'll only make wise investments," Daphne promised.

"That makes me feel so much better."

"Toodle-oo! Anyone here?" a clear, high voice called out from the front of Unfinished Business.

Lila emerged from the back room with a Jacques Fath pantsuit in one hand and a Romeo Gigli beaded halter top in the other. She had to fight the impulse to turn tail and flee when she saw Mimi Sinclair waving at her.

"Mrs. Sinclair!" She mustered a half smile. "Lovely to see you again. How are you?"

"Very well, thank you for asking. Summer mentioned that you and your mother officially opened your little shop—I was so very sorry to hear that Daphne has to go back to work; you have my deepest sympathies—and I thought I'd drop in and show my support."

"Gee. Thanks."

Mimi, oblivious to the sarcasm, flitted around the boutique, examining one-of-a-kind garments with an air of blasé sophistication.

Then she studied the hat-and-handbag display lining one wall and uttered the question that Lila had been dreading: "You don't have my handbags displayed yet?"

Lila swallowed hard. "Well, we—"

"Or have you sold them all already?"

"Hey, has Summer talked to you yet about the fashion show? She and my mother are putting a fun little fete together at the country club and they would so love for you to model."

"Me? Really? Well, I hate to call attention to myself, but I *have* been told I have a certain star quality."

"You'd be a fantastic addition to the show. Why don't you look around and see if there's something you'd like to wear?"

"This is nice." Mimi held up a Nettie Rosenstein evening gown made of oyster-colored silk.

"It's gorgeous." Lila walked Mimi toward the dressing room. "Not many women could fit into that waistline, but you're so trim and petite. Why don't you try it on?"

But Mimi could not be deterred from her mission. "And you know what would look fabulous with it? The enameled clutch I dropped off the other day. Do you still have it, or did some fashion-forward customer snap it up the second you put it out?"

"We still have it," Lila said. "Why? Have you changed your mind? I can return the bags to you, if you'd like. I understand why you'd hate to let them go."

"Heavens, no. I told you—they're from last season. I only carry the latest and best." Mimi patted her pink leather satchel, which, thanks to Daphne's tutelage, Lila now recognized as a knockoff.

"That's lovely," she told Mimi.

"Isn't it? My husband brought it back from a consulting trip in Europe. He goes to such lengths to spoil me!" Mimi handed the ball gown to Lila and continued to browse, touching everything just enough that Lila would have to straighten all the hangers after she left. "I'm only at the beach house for the weekend—I've got so many social engagements back in D.C., you know—so why don't you go get those purses and we'll look at them right now. Together."

Lila prayed for a sudden sinkhole to appear in the floor or an errant bolt of lightning to strike her dead on the spot.

She didn't get an official act of God, but she did get her mother.

"I'm finally here!" The shop's back door slammed as Daphne traipsed in. "And I struck gold at the estate sale! Wait until you see—"

"Mom!" Lila whirled around with wild eyes. "I'm so glad you're back! Mrs. Sinclair here has dropped by to wish us well on our grand opening—"

"I think you're *so* brave." Mimi took one of Daphne's hands.

"—and to ask about the resale value of those handbags she dropped off the other morning."

Daphne took a breath, then frowned in an almost comical display of confusion. "Handbags? Which handbags are those, sweet pea?"

Lila glared at her mother. "I'm sure you remember. The bags you said you were going to appraise?"

"Silly me, I must have forgotten in all the excitement!" Daphne turned to Mimi with her ditziest smile. "You can't imagine how distracted I've been lately with the construction and the inventory and the financial documents. I had no idea how much was involved in starting a business. My brain has absolutely turned to mush!"

"Well, when do you think you might be able to give me a number?" Mimi asked, not bothering to disguise her impatience. "I told my daughter she could use the proceeds from my old bags for a new phone." She rolled her eyes. "Natalie lost a few phones this year, and my husband refuses to buy her another one until she quote-unquote 'learns some responsibility.' But, obviously, she can't be the only one of her friends without her own phone—she's *very* popular—and my husband goes over all the credit card statements with a fine-tooth comb, so I told her I'd get cash and we'd just Enron the whole thing."

Daphne and Lila avoided making eye contact.

"We'll get to it in the next few days," Daphne vowed. "I promise. We'll give you a call."

"When?" Mimi pressed.

"Soon," Daphne swore.

"Are you sure you don't want the bags back?" Lila asked. "It might be more convenient to take them to a vintage store in D.C."

"Absolutely not. I told Summer Benson I would patronize your business, and that's exactly what I intend to do."

At this point, Daphne realized that Mimi's "patronage" had nothing to do with her and everything to do with social climbing. So she gave the terrorist in tweed exactly what she wanted: She begged her to try on the ball gown. She oohed and aahed and played the adoring supplicant to the lady of the manor. Finally, she threw in some truly shameless hyperbole about Mimi missing her calling as a supermodel, and Mimi was mollified. Temporarily.

"Please contact me about the bags at your earliest convenience." She gave Lila and Daphne one last look of reproach as she prepared to leave without buying anything. "I realize you're still new to this, but customer service is your most valuable asset."

Lila nodded, wide-eyed. "We'll keep that in mind, Mrs. Sinclair."

Daphne's smile sharpened. "We'll call you just as soon as we get a chance."

As Mimi flounced out of the shop, Lila turned to her mother. "How dare she tell us how to run our business? She's never worked a day in her life!"

"I know!" Daphne fumed. "And I've worked at least five now!"

"Why didn't you just tell her they're fakes? You can't put it off forever, you know."

"I'm not telling her," Daphne vowed. "Not today, not ever. You tell her!"

"You're the handbag expert," Lila argued.

"That's right. I deal with handbags, not wretched, self-important snobs." Daphne gazed fondly at her daughter. "Besides, you're so good at handling people."

"Insincere flattery won't work on me."

"It's sincere!"

"Still not working."

"Damn. That woman's got some nerve." Daphne tsked. "But you and I know the truth:

She's all designer logos on the outside and cheap, synthetic material on the inside."

"Agreed."

Mother and daughter stared each other down for a moment, then said, at exactly the same moment, "Not it."

Daphne surprised Lila by laughing. "We can stall her for a few more days."

"Yeah, and then what?" Lila demanded.

"You worry too much. Speaking of which, guess what I found at the estate sale?" Daphne opened her leather satchel and pulled out a ragged cardboard jewelry box. "Some old woman died and left a house full of stuff that nobody in her family wants!"

"Try not to sound so gleeful," Lila advised.

"I can't help it! Look what I found in a pile of plastic clip-on earrings and colored glass brooches." Daphne opened the box to reveal a bib necklace dripping with large golden links and massive clear crystals with sharp points.

Lila stared at the 1970s glitz. "That is *hideous*."

"Forgive her; she knows not of what she speaks," Daphne appealed to the heavens. "Lila, you're not seeing this for what it really is."

"And what is it, really?"

"It's a one-of-a-kind find."

Lila's eyes narrowed as suspicion sank in. "I hope you didn't pay a lot for this, Mom, because fine jewelry's not an investment. Diamond rings and gold necklaces lose half their value before the ink's dry on the receipt. Learned that the hard way."

Daphne dismissed this with a wave of her hand. "Oh, this isn't fine jewelry. The metal is some sort of alloy, and the crystals are just Lucite."

Lila couldn't stop staring at the sheer *volume* of the beads. "Then why'd you buy it?"

"Because even though the materials aren't high-end, the designer is." Daphne turned over the necklace and pointed out a tiny oval engraving on the back of one of the wide golden links. "This is a deLillo. I got it for seventy-five dollars because the fools running the estate sale had no idea what they had."

"Seventy-five dollars?" Lila made a face. "You were robbed."

"We can resell it for three thousand," Daphne decreed. "Maybe thirty-five hundred."

"You're delusional," Lila shot back. "No one's going to pay three thousand dollars for this thing. It's so . . . so . . . There aren't even adjectives to describe it."

"William deLillo used to work for Harry Winston and Tiffany's." Daphne reached for Lila's smartphone. "Look it up. Look up 'William deLillo necklaces' and prepare to eat your words, young lady."

Lila looked it up, and after scrolling through several vintage jewelry Web sites, she concluded,

"Okay, so . . . thirty-five hundred might actually be a little on the low side."

"You can apologize any time now."

Lila picked up the necklace and dangled it in the sunlight. It looked substantial but weighed less than she would have predicted, probably because the "crystals" weren't really crystal at all.

"I can't believe there are people out there willing to pay thousands of dollars for this," she murmured. "It looks like something I'd find on clearance at T.J.Maxx."

"Blasphemy. This is why I'm the curator and you run the cash register."

Lila laughed and reached for the battered jewelry box. "Do you want me to put this in the display case by the register?"

Daphne clutched the box to her chest. "Not yet."

"Why? Are you planning to wear it?"

"No."

Lila arched one eyebrow. "Then . . . ?"

"I want to hold on to it for a little while. And don't give me a guilt trip about credit card bills and mortgage payments. I'll sell it when I'm ready." Daphne tightened her grip on the box. "I'm just not ready."

"You want to hold on to it? You just finished telling me about some old woman who died and left—and I quote—'a house full of stuff that nobody in her family wants.' "

Daphne seemed mystified. "What's your point?"

"My point is, don't let that be you."

"What does any of that have to do with me? I still look thirty-five and I have no plans to die any time soon, thank you very much."

"Okay, then, what if you keep the necklace in exchange for learning to text?"

Daphne sighed. "Fine."

"*And* learning how to check voice mail," Lila added. "Knowing how to work your own cell phone is kind of the bare minimum for a business owner."

Daphne folded her arms in a display of adolescent defiance. "I never wanted to be a business owner."

"Then here's the part where I have to give you a guilt trip about all the credit card bills and the business loans and the personal loans and the cost of heating and cooling a gigantic house. . . ."

"Fine." Her mother sulked. "I'll learn to check voice mail. But I won't like it."

"You don't have to like it; you just have to do it." Lila maintained her cheerful, can-do facade, but she had reviewed the files from the estate attorney again yesterday. And no matter how much the new business made over the summer, her mother's mountain of debt would keep growing as the interest accrued. No matter how many extras they cut, the basic expenses of maintaining the house would eat up any profits. Lila had started to think about how to explain to her mother that all their hard work was too little, too late.

Their best efforts simply wouldn't be enough.

Chapter 26

Malcolm called just before lunch.

Lila motioned to her mother that she was going to the back room, then answered her cell phone with what her mother would deem an unladylike degree of enthusiasm. But it wasn't as if she'd been waiting for his call—she *just happened* to be keeping her phone on her person at all times today.

She greeted him with the most seductive "Hello" she could manage through a huge smile.

"Hey." Just the sound of his voice was inspiring more unladylike thoughts. "I don't know if you remember me, but we went out once."

She laughed and sat down on a gray metal folding chair next to an empty clothes rack. "Refresh my memory."

"We went to Gull's Point. I'm the guy who took you out trespassing on private property."

"Hmm, I seem to have some vague recollection."

His voice dropped even lower. "I ripped your dress off before kissing you good night. Ring any bells?"

"Oh, that's right, you're the boy with the shoulder muscles," she said. "And the back muscles. And the . . . sparkling personality."

"Yeah. I was wondering if you might want to come over to my place tonight and . . ."

Lila stood up and pressed the phone to her ear. "Yes?"

"Sign my yearbook."

She laughed so loudly, her mother opened the door and shushed her.

"Is that a yes?" Malcolm asked.

"It's a yes. I'll be there as soon as I lock up the store tonight."

Lila was still basking in a post-phone-call glow when a blonde with a *Jersey Shore* tan, scraggly hair extensions, and even more scraggly cutoffs strutted into the boutique. She was followed by two burly men toting garbage bags and a black-and-white spaniel with a red collar.

Lila exchanged a quick glance with her mother before launching into her greeting spiel: "Welcome to Unfinished Business. Are you looking for anything special?"

"Oh, I'm not looking to buy anything; I'm looking to unload a bunch of stuff. I brought in

302

some clothes you might want." The blonde patted the countertop, and the display case shuddered as the men heaved the trash bags onto the spotless glass surface.

Lila assessed the woman's outfit: threadbare white tank top, booty-baring denim shorts, oversize flannel shirt à la Kurt Cobain, and red Converse sneakers with a hole in the toe. "I'm so glad you came in today, but we don't usually take unsolicited stock. Typically, our inventory acquisition involves—"

The blonde sneezed onto a mannequin wearing a Thierry Mugler petal dress. "Sorry. I'm allergic to this dog."

"We don't allow dogs in the store." Daphne dabbed at the petal dress with a tissue. "The fur, the drool, the . . . other bodily fluids. We can't risk it with the clothes."

Before the girl and her henchmen could reply, the door opened again, and a fashionista with thick black hair and the body of a Teutonic goddess swept in.

"I've heard about you," the goddess announced without preamble. "You're the mother-daughter team, yes? The Dior doyennes of Delaware?"

"I'm Daphne Alders." Lila's mother disposed of the tissue and offered a ladylike handshake. "Dior doyenne at your service."

The fashionista clasped Daphne's hand for the briefest moment before letting go. "I'm Tara

Rassas. I'm a buyer for several vintage boutiques in London and New York, and I'm also an acquaintance of Cedric James—"

"Excuse me." The blonde draped herself over the counter. "I was here first."

Tara's gaze flitted over the overstuffed garbage bags. "So I see."

The burly henchmen turned and exited the shop without a word.

"Wait!" Lila called after them.

Tara ignored all of this and continued speaking to Daphne. The tattered blonde shot the older women a death glare.

Lila stifled a sigh and tugged at the frayed twist tie on the first trash bag. "Since you're here, might as well take a look."

"I don't really know what's in there." The girl geared up for another sneeze. Lila handed her the whole box of Kleenex. "Just that it's old and not my style."

Lila steeled herself as best she could and peeled back one edge of the bag. She said a silent prayer that she wasn't about to catch fleas or the bubonic plague, and pulled out the first garment her hand touched.

"Mom?" she murmured when she saw what she was holding.

Daphne and Tara were now talking shop about James Galanos and Treacy Lowe.

The blonde started playing on her cell phone

and the dog sniffed the hem of a Pauline Trigère tapestry dress.

"Mom!" Lila hissed. She beckoned her mother over to bear witness to the fashion miracle unfolding before their very eyes.

"Look." Lila pulled out a 1940s blue velvet dress in perfect condition with yellowed cardboard tags still dangling from the label and tried out one of her newly acquired catchphrases. "It's the holy grail of dead stock."

Daphne gasped and peered over Lila's shoulder. "Is that . . . ?"

"It is." Tara the fashion buyer peered over Lila's other shoulder. "That's a Gloria Swanson with the original label."

Daphne shoved Lila aside, reached into the bag, and pulled out a navy lace cocktail dress with an illusion bodice and a full skirt.

"Oh my God," breathed Tara. "A Peggy Hunt."

Daphne rescued a dozen more dresses from the depths of the trash bag, each more detailed and gorgeous than the last.

"Carolyn Schnurer," Tara guessed before checking the label of a boatneck sundress patterned in cream and grass green. "It has to be."

"There's so many of them," Lila said. "In so many sizes."

"Where did you get this?" Daphne demanded.

The blonde glanced up from her phone with evident annoyance. "My aunt owned a clothing store back in the day. When she closed up shop, my uncle threw everything in storage. And now they're dead, so it's my problem." She resumed texting. "You want this stuff or not?"

"*I* want it," Tara interjected, running her hands over a black-and-white strapless A-line frock. "I want it all."

Daphne looked around, presumably for a deadly weapon with which to defend her merchandise. "I'm sure you do, but you can't have it. My store, my score."

Tara pulled a fancy gray wallet out of her fancy gray handbag and addressed the blonde. "I'll pay cash."

Daphne gasped. "How dare you? You can't sashay in here and poach a bag full of Peggy Hunts and Carolyn Schnurers!"

"I'm not poaching; I'm paying."

Lila stepped in between them, hoping to avert bloodshed and wondering if she should call Malcolm for backup. This was rapidly devolving into a SWAT team situation.

Daphne pointed to the door. "Please leave immediately."

The client leaned against the counter and watched with growing interest. "Don't get all dramatic; there's plenty to go around."

"No. Wrong. There are *not* plenty of dead-stock Peggy Hunt dresses to go around." Daphne gathered them up in her arms and clutched them to

306

her bosom. "How long have these been in storage?"

"Dunno." *Achoo!* "A couple of years, I guess?"

"Use a tissue!" Lila cried. *"Please!"*

"And they've been in"—Daphne could barely force the words out—"garbage bags all this time?"

"No, my aunt had them in a bunch of boxes, but they wouldn't fit in my car so I had to unpack them."

"Thank God," Daphne murmured.

Tara waved a fistful of cash. "Two thousand dollars. Right here, right now."

"Get out!" Daphne screamed. "Before I call the police!"

Tara responded with, "Three thousand."

Lila held up her hand and called for a cease-fire. "Wait. What on earth is this?" She picked out a stretchy black piece of fabric that looked like high-waisted boy shorts attached to suspenders, which met in the middle in a V.

Tara put down her money and gaped.

Daphne curled up her hand and bit her knuckle. "That, sweet pea, is a monokini."

And just like that, the fashionistas stopped fighting and started conferring in hushed, reverent tones.

"I've seen photos, but I've never seen one in person outside a museum," Tara said.

Lila held the item at arm's length, puzzled. "Where's the rest of it?"

"That's it," Tara said. "Simple. Severe. Brilliant."

"No, I mean, where's the top?" Lila asked.

"There is no top," Daphne explained. "That's the point."

"So it's a topless bikini? Hot," the blonde said. She held out her hand. "Maybe I'll hold on to that one."

Daphne swatted her hand down. "This piece is iconic. Rudi Gernreich designed it in protest against American puritanism."

"Peggy Moffitt modeled it in *Women's Wear Daily*," Tara added.

Lila stared at her mother. "You use words like 'puritanism'?"

"I do when I'm talking about Rudi Gernreich."

Tara rounded on the blonde. "Do you have any more of those?"

"I don't think so."

"How do you propose we display this, Mom?" Lila draped the monokini across the counter. "Maybe on one of the mannequins? With a wide-brimmed hat or something?"

The blonde grabbed it back. "You know, I don't think I'm going to sell that one. I kind of want to keep it for myself."

Tara and Daphne were all but frothing at the mouth.

"What? No. You can't keep that."

"What on earth would you do with a Rudi Gernreich, anyway?"

The blonde smiled and adjusted her white tank

top. "Wear it to the beach this summer. Totally Euro-style. Aww yeah."

Daphne's whole face tightened. "You don't *wear* this out in the sand and sun. Shame on you! This is an important piece of fashion history. It's meant to be preserved and displayed, and . . ."

"It's a swimsuit," the blonde said. "Last I checked, swimsuits belong at the beach. And let's face it—I totally have the body for it."

"Let's not get irrational, ladies." Lila started inventorying the contents of the other garbage bag. "I'm sure we can come to an agreement."

The girl rocked back on her heels and hooked her thumbs through her belt loops, obviously enjoying the power struggle in progress. "Tell you what," she said to Daphne. "You can have the—what did you call this, again?"

"Monokini."

"Yeah, you can have the monokini if you take the dog. Package deal." She held out the red leash. "He was my aunt's, too. She left me a bunch of old clothes, a bunch of ratty old furniture, and this dog." One corner of her lip curled up in a sneer. "But no trust fund."

"Well, we will be delighted to take the clothes off your hands." Daphne piled the dresses on the counter. "But as for the dog—"

"I'll take the dog," Tara volunteered. She reached out for the leash and the monokini.

The blonde looked stunned. "You will?"

"Absolutely. I adore dogs," Tara said.

"You don't even live here!" Daphne cried. "She flies around from London to New York to Timbuktu."

"She's lying," Tara said. "There's no vintage fashion scene in Timbuktu."

"I'll take the dog!" Daphne said.

"I'm taking the dog and I said it first!"

The two elegant, perfectly groomed women were about thirty seconds away from taking off their earrings and brawling amid the Balenciaga. In the absence of a SWAT team, Lila did her best to play negotiator. "What's the customs situation with taking a dog to London?"

Tara blinked. "Pardon?"

"Do they have to stay in a kennel?" Lila asked. "Is there a waiting period? Do they need vaccination records?"

"I . . . don't know."

"Ha!" Daphne tossed her head in triumph. "She doesn't know." Then she paused and took a deep breath. "Fine, I'll take the dog. Anything for fashion."

"You'll never love that dog like I will," Tara shot back.

"Listen." Lila turned to the blonde. "You don't want to leave your dog with either one of them."

But the girl had segued from enjoyment back to boredom. "For the last time: It's not my dog; it's my aunt's."

Lila smiled down at the little black-and-white spaniel, who had curled up next to the girl's red sneakers. "Well, then." She held out her palm for the leash. "*I'll* take the dog."

"That's my girl!" Daphne cooed, then lowered her voice and whispered, "We'll figure out what to do with it later."

Lila ignored her mother. "Is it a he or a she?"

The girl appeared to be deeply immersed in a text debate. "Dunno."

"What's its name?" Lila tried.

"Whatever you want."

"Oookay." Lila knelt down and scratched the spaniel's soft, curly-furred ears. The dog responded by pressing its head against her hand, seeking more affection. "We'll take you to the vet and get this all sorted out. And in the meantime, you need a name. How about Rudi?"

"I like it." Daphne seized the monokini and shot Tara a look of triumph. "Rudi works for a boy or a girl."

"Great." The blonde surrendered the leash and wiped her nose on the back of her hand. "So how much will you give me for all this stuff?"

Daphne produced her calculator and eyeglasses (which she insisted on wearing during financial transactions because they made her "look and feel smarter"). She motioned the girl closer and they went back and forth for about three seconds.

"Done." The girl gasped at her newest text

message and responded with such vehemence, Lila was surprised she didn't sprain her thumbs.

Tara turned on her heel and strode toward the door. "You haven't seen the last of me."

"I look forward to our rematch." Daphne retreated into the back room with the Peggy Hunts and Carolyn Schnurers, openly gloating and congratulating herself.

Lila found herself alone in the showroom with Rudi. "So I guess I'll take the dog outside?" she called after her mother.

"Have fun!"

"And you're okay with being in here alone while I'm gone?"

"Don't be silly, sweet pea. I'm not helpless."

"Then I'll be back after lunch. Maybe you can help me figure out what to wear tonight."

Her mother reappeared in the doorframe. "Another date with the delectable marine?"

"Yeah, but this time I'm not sharing his outfit. I want to wear my own, and I want to look hot. Like, spontaneous-combustion hot."

"Consider it done," Daphne said. "Give me some context. What's the occasion?"

"Yearbook signing."

"What?"

"I need a little something that says, 'Have a great summer' with a wink and a smile. Don't let me down."

Chapter 27

"Rudi, you're adorable." Jenna had located a packet of oyster crackers somewhere in the Whinery's stockroom and offered a handful of snacks to the spaniel on the pink and black welcome mat outside the bar. "How could anyone ever give you up?"

"It was brutal. His owner didn't even kiss him good-bye," Lila said. The little dog rolled over for a belly rub, and Lila obliged.

Summer walked over from the historical society building to join them. "Who is this little cutie paws?"

"Rudi," Lila replied.

Summer knelt next to Lila and took over belly rub duty. Rudi wriggled with joy, his stubby little tail thumping against the concrete. "I didn't know you were getting a dog."

"I wasn't planning on it. But my mother agreed to take him in exchange for a topless swimsuit from the sixties. Just another day in the vintage clothing business."

"I wish I could take him home with me." Summer moved on to scratching the underside of Rudi's jaw, which elicited near paroxysms of canine glee. "Ingrid would love to have a dog, but Dutch is allergic. He had to mainline Claritin the last time we went to a Humane Society fundraiser."

"But *he* probably had the common decency to use Kleenex instead of Thierry Mugler," Lila muttered.

"What, now?"

"Nothing."

"Tell me more about this topless swimsuit," Jenna said.

"Yeah," Summer chimed in. "Isn't 'topless swimsuit' really just another term for 'bikini bottoms'?"

"No. It's . . ." Lila turned up her palms. "Words alone can't do it justice. You have to see it to believe it."

"I'm free until two." Summer got to her feet. "Let's go. My spring wardrobe could use a little pizzazz. Oh, and speaking of pizzazz, that reminds me—one of Ingrid's friends is signing up for some sort of pageant. She needs a fancy evening gown for the formal wear competition, but her budget is practically nonexistent. I don't suppose you guys have anything you could lend her?"

Lila's mind flashed to the former Miss Delaware. "Call Ingrid and ask her if she can drop by the store. I may have exactly what she's looking for. Sash and tiara sold separately."

"Wow, check it out." Half an hour later, Ingrid ran her hands along the crystal beading on the bodice of the royal blue gown. The tiny facets reflected the light and cast flecks of gold across the walls. "I think I'm blind in one eye now."

"That's a lot of dress," Summer marveled.

"This gown got a former Miss Delaware all the way to the top five in the Miss America pageant," Lila informed them.

Ingrid got right down to business. "How much? It's for my friend Mia."

"Mia Lintz?" Summer kind of choked. "The girl who helped you study for AP chemistry? The one with the eyebrows?"

"She's getting them waxed," Ingrid said defensively.

"Eyebrows wants to enter some teen miss thing?"

Ingrid nodded. "She wants the prize money. I guess they offer pretty good scholarships."

"Well, I'd be happy to give her the dress for free," Lila said, "since it's you guys—"

"Thanks," Summer said. "We'll make it up to you in post-fashion-show revenue."

"—but according to Miss Delaware, you need more than a sparkly gown to win these things."

"Oh, Mia has a great platform," Ingrid assured them. "Her whole thing is getting girls involved in science and engineering programs. Dutch is helping her with her public speaking skills."

Summer remained skeptical. "What's her talent?"

"Reciting the periodic table of elements."

Lila and Summer exchanged a look. "She really thinks she can win with an eight-year-old gown and the periodic table of elements?"

Ingrid shrugged. "It was either that or play the banjo. And, I mean, it's just walking around in heels and a pretty dress. How hard can it be?"

Lila, who had often heard her television job described as "just smiling and talking for a few hours," knew exactly how hard such undertakings could be. "I'll wrap up the dress and you can take it home with you. Mia can try it on and decide if it's what she's looking for. If it's not, just bring her in and we'll find her something else."

Summer shook her head. "I'm sure it'll be great. This whole plan is foolproof; what could go wrong?!"

"You're such a cynic," Ingrid said.

Summer wandered back toward the dressing room, where Daphne was changing a mannequin's outfit from the sneezed-upon petal dress to a freshly dry-cleaned black mermaid gown. "So I heard a rumor about a monokini?"

Daphne dropped everything and clutched Summer's forearms. "Have you ever seen one?"

"I've never even heard of one until today."

"Well, prepare to have your breath taken away. Follow me—it's in the back room."

While Daphne practically dragged Summer off to the storage area, Ingrid remained by the cash register.

"Well?" she asked Lila. "Did you find the perfect wedding gown yet?"

" 'Perfect' might be a tall order," Lila hedged. "How about this?" She pulled out a navy silk chiffon gown painted with metallic streaks. "You said she likes gold."

Ingrid dismissed it with toss of her head. "Eh."

"Eh? This is a Zandra Rhodes! There's nothing 'eh' about Zandra Rhodes."

"It's not right for Summer and Dutch's wedding. Nothing in here is right." Ingrid's big gray eyes managed to look both disdainful and disappointed at the same time. "We'll know it when we see it."

"I'll keep my eyes open," Lila promised. "In the meantime, I might be able to hook you up with a few pageant tips for your friend." She flipped through the store records and dialed up the former Miss Delaware. "Hi, Shannon, it's Lila at Unfinished Business. Yes, we found a buyer for your dress. . . . Well, it's a local teenager who's about to enter her first pageant and I was wondering if you—what's that? What's her talent?" Lila cleared her throat. "I believe it will involve"—she tried to slur her words—"reciting the periodic table of the elements. . . ."

Ingrid watched while Lila listened to Shannon go on a five-minute, epic rant.

"Yep." Lila held the phone a few centimeters

317

away from her ear. "Got it. Absolutely. I will pass that along."

When she finally hung up the phone, Ingrid asked, "Pass what along?"

"The bad news is, Miss Delaware says there's no way the periodic table of the elements is going to get your friend to the semifinals, let alone the crown. She says it's going to be a waste of her dress."

"Whatever. It's not even *her* dress anymore." Ingrid nodded toward the phone. "You call her back and you tell her—"

"Hang on, hang on. She also asked me to pass along her phone number and tell Mia to give her a call."

"For what?" Ingrid sneered. "Tips on blonde-on-blonde hazing and double-sided tape?"

"Hold your fire," Lila counseled. "Because the good news is, she's offering to be Mia's pageant coach."

Ingrid looked confused and somewhat suspicious. "That's a real thing?"

"Apparently. She's offering to do it on a volunteer basis."

Ingrid gave her a sideways glance. "Why?"

Lila shrugged. "She doesn't have a daughter and I think she wants to share all her pageant wisdom. Think of it like a secret sale: buy a gown, get a free consultation from a state champion."

"What's the catch?" Ingrid demanded.

"How did you know there's a catch?"

"There's always a catch."

"And you say Summer's a cynic." Lila smiled. "Well, remember how I said she doesn't have a daughter? She has two sons, with two more on the way. So the catch is, you guys will have to coordinate pageant training with nap time. Do you think Mia can do that?"

"I'm sure she can." Ingrid looked around the little shop with an air of wonder. "That's pretty amazing, that she just offered to help like that."

"Yeah, well, this town has some pretty amazing people in it. And they're very attached to their old dresses."

"Yeah, but that's incredible, right? It's like fate. It's like it was meant to be."

"Maybe it is," Lila replied as her mother and Summer reemerged from the back room. "Or maybe it's all just a question of luck and timing."

As if to prove her point, the little bell on the boutique's door chimed and Lila's ex-boyfriend/ water-heater repairman/landlord walked in, accompanied by an outdoorsy-looking young woman with wild dark curls, kind hazel eyes, and not a trace of makeup. She wore sturdy hiking boots, tattered olive shorts, and a baggy magenta tank top layered over a black sports bra. Lila would bet good money that this woman's panties didn't match her bra.

She could also tell from a single glance at Ben's face that this woman was the love of his life.

And when the love of his life smiled back at him, she didn't look at him as though he were a varsity football star or the golden boy who'd inherited his father's company. She treated him like a man who was determined to prove himself and build his own future. She saw him in a completely different light than Lila ever would.

These two didn't know each other's entire life histories, but they had their own shared story that no one else would ever be privy to.

"Ben!" Daphne rushed forward and threw her arms around him. "What a lovely surprise!"

"You must be Allison." Lila stepped forward to give Ben's companion a perfunctory, show-business-style hug.

"And you must be Lila," Allison said. She even *smelled* fresh and wholesome, like lavender shampoo or laundry soap.

Daphne glanced from Lila to Ben to Allison, first with confusion, then with a bit of dismay. "Welcome to our little corner of the world, Allison. You must be Ben's . . ."

"Girlfriend." She took his hand and they looked at each other with adolescent adoration. "Soon-to-be fiancée. Maybe."

"Definitely," Ben said. "I was telling her about the new properties we're working with, so I thought we'd drop by. Sorry to interrupt."

"You're not interrupting," Summer assured them. "We were just leaving. I've got to get back to grant proposal prison."

Ingrid waited until Summer was out the door, then regarded Lila with those big gray doe eyes. "Wedding dress."

"I'm on it," Lila vowed.

"Sooner rather than later."

"I hear you!"

Ingrid exited, carrying the pageant gown in a bulky paper shopping bag, and Daphne turned back to the man she had desperately hoped might be meant for her daughter.

"So, Allison!" She clapped her hands. "How are you enjoying your visit?"

Allison glanced over at Ben before answering. "It's great."

"Mm-hmm?" Daphne prompted.

"It's really . . . different." She adjusted the shoulder strap of her tank top. "I've met Ben's parents before, but I've never been to his hometown."

"And how long will you be staying?" Daphne pressed.

Lila nudged her mother's ankle with the side of her shoe. "Mom."

Daphne batted her eyelashes, all inquisitive innocence. "What?"

"I'm just here for the weekend," Allison said.

"Allison's finishing her master's program," Ben

bragged. "I'm trying to convince her to move here afterward."

"Goodness, isn't that a bit fast?" Daphne wondered aloud. "How long have you two been together?"

This time, it was less of a nudge and more of a kick. *"Mom."*

"Calm down, pumpkin," Daphne whispered. "I'm just making conversation."

"I have to be back in Boston on Monday afternoon," Allison said. "But I have finals in a few weeks, and after that . . ." Her eyes sparkled and her cheeks flushed. "We'll see. Ben's been very convincing."

Ben caught Lila's gaze and mouthed, "Thanks."

"If you're used to big-city life, Black Dog Bay might be a bit of a shock," Daphne cautioned. "I moved here from New York, and it was quite an adjustment. Thirty-five years later, I'm *still* waiting for a decent sushi place."

"But small-town life is great in other ways," Ben added heartily.

"Absolutely," Lila agreed. "The ocean is right there. . . ."

Allison's smile wavered. "I can go to the ocean in Boston."

Daphne kept going. "There are no gourmet restaurants, no museums, no independent theaters; all the stores close so early. . . ."

Lila barely restrained herself from physically

covering her mother's mouth. "We have a ghost dog. And a wine bar that serves free candy."

Allison turned to admire a printed floral dress in the window display. "Well, the fashion scene seems to be thriving. Look at these pieces."

"You appreciate fashion?" Daphne sounded surprised.

Allison glanced down at her baggy shorts and scuffed boots with an apologetic smile. "I can't keep up with all the trends, but I appreciate good craftsmanship. And there's a point where it really stops being about clothes and becomes an art form, right?"

"Yes." Daphne looked close to tears. "Exactly. It *is* an art form. A well-made gown has beauty and structure and a distinct point of view."

Lila gave Ben a look. "See? I told you—designers have a point of view. It's a real thing."

He hovered near Daphne and Allison, ready to quell any further talk about the lack of sushi and sophistication.

A little bark emanated from the back room, and Lila excused herself to go check on Rudi.

"Is there a dog back there?" Allison sounded delighted.

"Yes." Lila discovered Rudi systematically shredding the towels she'd put down for him on the tiled floor. "A very bored dog who is finding ways to entertain himself."

"Bring him out!" Allison urged. The moment

she set eyes on Rudi, she opened her arms to him. "Is he a springer spaniel?"

"I'm not sure." Lila gave them a quick summary of Rudi's history. "I don't know how old he is, or what breed. All I know at this point is that he enjoys belly rubs and towel tug-of-war."

"I always wanted a springer spaniel." Allison cuddled the black-and-white dog like a baby.

Lila turned to Ben and winked. "Okay, so you'll have the wife, the kids, the Subaru, and a springer spaniel instead of the golden retriever."

"Works for me."

Daphne seemed disgruntled that a dog was stealing the spotlight. She turned to Lila and announced with great authority, "It's all settled. Allison and Ben are coming over to our house for dinner."

"Tonight?" Lila asked.

Daphne nodded. "Seven o'clock. Which means I'd better leave now to start cooking."

Lila started to laugh, then realized her mother was serious. "You're cooking?"

"Oh, sweet pea, you're so droll. Of course I'm cooking." Daphne touched Allison's arm and confided, "I make the best scallops you'll ever taste this side of Paris."

"Um . . ." Lila ignored these outrageous culinary lies and focused on the important matters. "I have plans tonight."

"You do?"

"Yes." Lila cleared her throat and willed her mother to remember their earlier conversation. "The yearbook thing?"

"Oh, we don't want to impose," Allison said, still snuggling Rudi. "We'll find another time to get together."

"Absolutely not," Daphne trilled. "Lila can join us for appetizers and drinks before her big date."

Ben gave Lila a look she couldn't quite decipher. "Who's the guy?" he asked.

Her mother, her ex-boyfriend, and her ex-boyfriend's new girlfriend all stared at her.

"Go ahead," Daphne urged. "Tell them."

Lila demurred for a moment, not sure if she was ready to face all the opinions and questions. Afraid of what everyone might think.

And then she realized that she didn't care what anyone else thought. She lifted her head and spoke in a loud, clear voice. "Malcolm Toth."

"That guy from high school?" Ben looked incredulous. "The quiet guy who was on the track team?"

"I don't really know what he was like in high school," Lila said. "I just know what he's like now."

Ben nodded as if his darkest suspicions had been confirmed. "I always knew he had a thing for you."

Lila grinned. "And now I have a thing for him, too."

Allison shot a sidelong glance at Ben. "You know him?"

"See? That's another thing about small-town life," Daphne advised Allison. "Everyone knows everyone, and no one minds their own business."

Lila escorted her mother to the door. "You'd better get going on those scallops, Mom. We'll see you at dinner. Bye, now."

"I'm going to get the scallops from that seafood place in Bethany," Daphne confided in a whisper. "Don't tell."

Allison was still giving a full-body rubdown to Rudi, who leaned against her shin and gazed up at her with pure canine adoration. "Do you want us to take this little guy for the rest of the afternoon? We could walk him on the beach, buy him some treats and some food."

"She's a dog lover," Ben said.

"I can see that." Lila hesitated for reasons she couldn't quite articulate, then capitulated. "If you want to dog-sit, knock yourself out."

"I think he likes me," Allison announced to the room at large. "I think we have a bond."

"Black Dog Bay's a great place to have a dog," Lila said. "It's in the name and everything."

"Score one for small-town life." Ben shared a conspiratorial smile with Lila, but as he started for the door, she heard him muttering, "Malcolm Toth?"

"Hey." She stopped him with a hand on his shoulder. "What's going on with you?"

He avoided eye contact. "Nothing."

"You're being weird," she pointed out. "About Malcolm. Are you . . . I mean, I know how this sounds, but are you *jealous?*"

"No." When he met her gaze, he looked confused and a bit embarrassed. "But it's still weird. I can't explain it."

"I know exactly what you mean." She closed the distance between them and gave him a quick, sisterly hug. "See you later."

And just when Lila thought she'd wrapped up the busiest, strangest day in Unfinished Business's short history, a diminutive but formidable figure appeared in the doorway.

"Miss Alders." Hattie Huntington wore sensible black pumps, a fur-trimmed gray coat, and the air of an executioner. "We meet again."

Chapter 28

Lila stood motionless by the mermaid gown, too intimidated to speak or move.

"Hello? Miss Alders?" Hattie walked in with a very sure stride for such a frail-looking old lady. "You could at least pay me the courtesy of a verbal response."

Lila forced out a little squeak of assent. "Yes, Miss Huntington."

"The last time you were at my home, we didn't get a chance to speak properly." Hattie's glacial blue eyes glittered. "I told you our conversation wasn't over, and I meant it."

Lila swallowed. "Yes, well . . ."

"Don't interrupt me, young lady. I'll let you know when it's your turn to speak." Hattie let a long pause ensue. "You seem to enjoy the thrill of the search and the thrill of the chase."

Lila endured another moment of agonizing silence, then asked, "Am I allowed to talk now?"

"No. I've got something to hand off to you."

Is it a lawsuit? Lila didn't dare ask.

"My car is outside," Hattie announced. "Hold the door."

Lila did as she was told, propping open the glass door while Hattie's driver hauled a massive antique steamer trunk out of the navy sedan and carried it into the boutique.

The driver gave a curt nod to Hattie, then to Lila, and hastened back to the car.

Lila had learned enough from her mother and the online forums to know that she was looking at old-world French artistry. She reached out to touch the trunk's smooth, cognac-colored leather. "Ooh, is this—"

Hattie cut her off midsentence with a snap of her fingers. "I have a task that requires your assistance." Her lips thinned into a crimped white grimace. "It's the least you can do, considering the circumstances."

Lila bowed her head. "Yes, Miss Huntington."

"I'm aware that Pauline handed over half our couture collection to you and your mother." Hattie's heels clicked against the wooden floor as she stalked closer to Lila.

"If there's, um, anything you'd like to take back, I'd be happy to—"

"I don't want anything back. Quite the contrary. I have a particular gown I'd like you to pass along to Miss Benson."

Lila looked up, confused. "To Summer?"

"Yes. But she can never know it came from me. No one can ever know it came from me—not even Pauline. Is that understood?"

"Yes, ma'am." Lila's apprehension mounted as Hattie unlatched the trunk's brass fastenings. What sort of garment would a woman like Hattie keep secret from her own sister?

Hattie opened the trunk's lid. "Prepare yourself, Miss Alders."

Lila tried to steel herself. "I'm prepared."

"This is truly one of a kind." Hattie reached into the trunk and pulled out a pile of black sequins and lavender tulle. "*This* is how vintage style is done. It's a Bob Mackie original from the eighties. One of his more understated pieces."

Lila's heart rate sped up as she glimpsed the

exquisite beading and flawless stitching. The top of the dress was a snug, boned corset designed to hug the body, but the bottom flared out in a cascade of black and lavender tulle. "This is incredible." She examined the shimmering black sequins covering the seam between the bodice and the skirt. "Moulin Rouge meets Rodeo Drive." She glanced up at Hattie. "Summer will love it."

"Of course she will." Hattie sniffed. "I hand selected it for her."

"Where did you get this?"

"None of your business," the old lady snapped. "Your business is to get it to Miss Benson and to do so with discretion. Do I make myself clear?" For a moment, those hard blue eyes softened.

Lila stopped fawning over the dress and touched the older woman's hand. "But why don't you want her to know where we got it?"

Hattie snatched her hand away, regaining her customary hauteur. "As I'm sure you're aware, young lady, I have a reputation to uphold. This never happened."

"This never happened," Lila echoed, wondering exactly what it was about vintage clothes that elicited paranoia and vows of eternal silence.

She walked Hattie back out to the curb and tried to help the old woman get safely back into the car, which earned her a literal slap on the wrist for her efforts. "But wait. What about your trunk?"

"You may keep it. And for the record, it's Goyard." Hattie didn't say good-bye or even spare Lila another glance. She turned to her driver and commanded, "Go."

The driver obeyed, and the sleek sedan pulled away.

Lila, trying to process the reality of what had just happened, watched the car round the corner. Asking herself questions that she would never be able to ask anyone else, since she'd been sworn to silence. Yet again.

Then she raced back into the boutique, locked the front door, and grabbed her phone.

"Hello, Ingrid? Hey, this is Lila Alders. I've got some great news and I wanted you to be the first to hear: I think we just found Summer's wedding dress."

For once, Lila was grateful for the FUV's cavernous interior. Since she couldn't leave the Bob Mackie in the boutique—and no way would the Goyard trunk go unnoticed by her mother—she backed up her vehicle so that the liftgate was as close as possible to the store's back door, then wrestled the steamer trunk into the cargo space. It fit with plenty of room to spare. Lila was reasonably sure that the car's passenger area was eternally expanding, much like the universe itself.

Sweating and panting, she slammed the liftgate

down, climbed into the driver's seat, and plugged in her phone charger. She turned on the ignition, rolled down her window, scrolled through her music options to find an appropriate victory song, and was all ready to roll out of the parking lot like one of the teenagers she'd decried at Gull's Point . . . when the engine died.

The music went off. The dashboard lights dimmed. The window refused to roll back up.

"Are you kidding me?" She yanked the key out, then tried to start the car again. The music and the lights reactivated for half a second, then faded. Somewhere deep in the bowels of the engine, she heard an ominous grinding noise.

Still in rebellious high schooler mode, she rattled off a string of obscenities, then jumped down onto the pavement and kicked the nearest tire. The FUV just stood there, steely and sturdy and completely shut down.

She gave up, collected her handbag and cell phone from the console, locked the doors, and left the vehicle by Unfinished Business's back door.

"Tomorrow," she promised as she walked down the alley toward Main Street. "Rematch at eight a.m."

She could feel the first traces of summer in the late afternoon. The chill wind had given way to a gentle breeze, and the slowly setting sun cast all the shops and passersby in a warm golden glow. Lila knew that she could venture into any of the nearby businesses—the Whinery, the historical society, the bookstore, the bank—and find someone she knew who would be happy to give her a ride home, but she decided to walk. She strolled by the white gazebo and the bronze statue in the town square, down to the boardwalk. The last few weeks had been so jam-packed with struggles and worry and unexpected revelations that it felt luxurious to have some time alone to just enjoy the moment. To bask in the sunshine. To text the delectable marine.

She sat down on one of the weathered white benches overlooking the shoreline and wrote: *Command performance at dinner tonight, but I'm making a run for it before dessert. Meet you at the rendezvous point at 2000 hours.*

A few minutes later, he replied: *Let me know if you need a diversion.*

She laughed and put away her phone and gazed out at the horizon, wondering how she ever could have been so blind. Even at fifteen, caught up in a whirl of popularity and pretension, how could she have been immune to this immediate resonance, this rare connection?

How could she have *forgotten* this man existed?

She didn't know what would happen after tonight, but she understood with absolute certainty that she would never be able to forget him again. Not just because of who he was or what he'd done, but because of how they were together. Deeply flawed, yet somehow perfect.

When Lila got home, she found her mother subjecting Ben and Allison to a guided tour of the foyer.

"This house is amazing," Allison gushed. Her magenta tank top had amassed a sprinkling of black-and-white dog hair. "It feels so grand, but still warm and welcoming."

"Thank you." Daphne stopped to point out a vase she'd bought in Italy.

"Who was your decorator?" Allison reached over and took Ben's hand. "Just in case I ever happen to need one in town?"

"Oh, I did everything myself." Daphne didn't even attempt to sound modest. "Picked out every light fixture and curtain panel. All the rugs, all the furniture, all the artwork."

"You've really got an eye for style."

"That's what they tell me." Daphne swept into the living room. "Now, this sofa has a fascinating history. Bill and I were visiting historic homes in the Berkshires—"

"I'm home." Lila interrupted the monologue to kiss her mom's cheek and admire the freshly cut lilacs on the coffee table. "Ooh, those are beautiful."

"Ingrid stopped by with them earlier to say thank you for giving her some sort of pageant dress?" Daphne smiled quizzically at her daughter.

Lila recounted the tale of Shannon, Mia, and the upcoming pageant boot camp. "It was very serendipitous, and they all seem excited to be working together."

"I've got to go check on dinner," Daphne announced. "Sweet pea, you're the hostess while I'm gone."

"Yes, ma'am." She turned to Allison and Ben. "Vodka shots?"

"Lila! Behave yourself. Oh, and if the doorbell rings, it's probably Marla from the bed-and-breakfast. She called earlier and asked if she could borrow my crystal punch bowl. I put it on the side table in the dining room."

"Got it."

While Daphne disappeared into the kitchen to finish "cooking" the scallops, Lila sat down with Ben and Allison and re-extended her offer of hard liquor.

"I'd take it," she advised. "Once you get my mom started on decorating details, you're in for a long night."

"No, no, I asked because I'm genuinely interested." Allison adjusted one of her tiny silver hoop earrings. "I don't have an innate sense of style, but I really appreciate people who do."

Ben glanced toward the doorway to the kitchen, then cleared his throat and leaned toward Lila.

"Listen, now that it's just the three of us, there's something we need to ask you."

Lila struggled to keep her mind and expression totally blank.

Allison shifted in her seat. "I know you just met me and this is way overstepping my boundaries, but . . ."

She broke off and turned to Ben, who finished the sentence for her.

"It's Rudi."

Lila exhaled and sank back into the throw pillows. "What about him?"

"I love him." Allison proclaimed this with the conviction of a high schooler in the throes of her first crush. "And he loves me."

"It's true," Ben said. "You should have seen them on the beach together."

"And I was hoping, if you hadn't gotten too attached to him yet, that you might consider letting me keep him." Allison bit her lip and held her breath.

Ben hastened to sweeten the deal before Lila could give an answer. "If she moves here, you can still see him."

"That's right." Allison crossed her legs and jiggled her hiking boot. "*If* I move here."

Lila glanced around the room. "Where is Rudi, anyway?"

"At my place," Ben said. "In the crate we bought him this afternoon. Along with the dog bed and the little squeaky toy in the shape of a lobster."

"So you've basically kidnapped him already." Lila tried to look stern. "This whole 'asking permission' is merely a formality."

"You can come visit him any time you want," Allison offered. "We'll take such good care of him. Ben's already set up a checkup at the vet for Monday."

"You set up a checkup for my dog without even checking with me?" Lila shook her head at Ben. "You don't waste any time, do you?"

"We didn't mean for this to happen," Allison cried. "We just started playing fetch, and one thing led to another and now . . ."

Lila decided it was time to put them out of their misery. "You can keep him. I'm sure you and Ben and Rudi and the lobster squeaky toy will be very happy together."

"We already are!" Allison engulfed Lila in a surprisingly strong, lavender-scented hug. "Thank you, thank you, thank you."

"You're welcome." Lila smoothed her hair. "Now, if I can't sell you on vodka, who wants wine?"

"Dinner is served," Daphne called. Everyone trooped into the dining room and lavished compliments on the china, the crystal, and the perfectly plated meal Daphne had so lovingly prepared.

"A fashion model, a master decorator, an entrepreneur, *and* a gourmet chef," Allison marveled as Ben pulled out her chair. "You're quite a role model."

"I believe in living life to the fullest." Daphne simpered as Ben pulled out her chair, as well.

"Well, I have to tell you, this is not at all what I was expecting when Ben told me about this town." Allison unfolded a white linen napkin. "I had serious reservations about settling down way out here. I've always heard that small towns are cliquish and everybody's up in everybody's business and I'd never be able to find a job in my field."

"Um," Lila said.

Daphne shushed her daughter with a single look. "What do you do?"

"My degrees are in business, with an emphasis in nonprofit management." Allison looked out the huge bay window at the water. "It's beautiful here, but what are my long-term career prospects going to be like?"

Ben looked at Lila, silently entreating her to intercede. Allison looked at Lila, hoping for reassurance. Daphne concentrated on her wine.

So Lila did what she did best: She went into shopping channel host mode and sold Black Dog Bay.

She described everything she'd just passed on her walk home, all the independent businesses, the loyal, longtime residents, and the influx of seasonal tourists who contributed to the cultural dynamic. She recounted all the ways neighbors had helped her and her mother by fixing the water heater, by planning the fashion show, by donating priceless vintage dresses and agreeing to provide expert alteration services.

"Remind me who does our alterations, again?" Daphne said.

Lila kept going with her pitch. She told Allison about her new friends from the Whinery and her old friends at the country club and the evolving, complex relationships she had with her ex-boyfriends.

"When I came back here, I was worried that I'd have to go right back to being who I'd always been in high school. But I've changed, and so has everyone else."

"Like me," Ben said.

Lila nodded. "Some of my old friends have moved on, and that's okay. We're at different stages in our lives, but hopefully we'll reconnect someday. In the meantime, I've met some truly amazing people and done things I never would have gotten to do in Philadelphia."

"I haven't changed." Daphne sounded dejected.

"Yes, you have," Lila said firmly. "You're a business owner. You're working. You're learning to text."

"Against my will." Daphne turned to Allison and put down her silver-plated spoon. "As someone who's been through exactly what you're going through, let me tell you the truth."

Lila and Ben looked at each other with trepidation.

"Black Dog Bay is not the place to go if you want to be an internationally successful model. You're not going to get rich and famous here. You're not going to be able to see a midnight screening of an independent movie and then go out for a nightcap at a fabulous jazz club."

Allison's eyes got wider with every word out of Daphne's mouth. Lila started flailing her foot around under the table, hoping to make contact with her mother's shin.

"But this is the best place in the world to start a life and have a family," Daphne concluded. "If I had my life to live over again, I would still give up everything I had in Manhattan to move here. I'm not going to lie and say that everybody minds their own business, but that's the beauty of Black Dog Bay. Neighbors bring you fresh lilacs and lend each other punch bowls. People support local businesses. Ben gave up filthy lucre from the funnel cake company so Lila and I could start our boutique."

Allison regarded Ben with renewed admiration.

Daphne dabbed at one eye with the corner of

her napkin. "The years I had here in this house with my husband and my daughter were the happiest of my life."

Lila couldn't believe what she was hearing. "Really?"

"Yes. That's part of what makes it so hard to stay here without you and your dad."

Everyone took a moment to compose themselves, and then Daphne commanded, "Eat! My scallops are getting cold."

Lila obeyed, pausing between bites to inform Allison, "Oh, and FYI, I have a friend who heads up the local historical society, and she was just saying she needs someone to help her with grant proposals."

"I'm great at grant proposals."

"Perfect. Her name is Summer Benson. I'll put you two in touch." With that, Lila picked up her plate and pushed back her chair. "I'm sorry to run out like this, but if you'll excuse me . . ." She winked at her mother. "I've kept my date waiting long enough."

Daphne eyed her simple outfit of dark jeans and a white and navy striped top. "You're wearing that?"

Not for long. "Yep."

"Well, at least put on a fresh coat of lipstick. Are you going to the Whinery?"

Lila was already halfway across the room. "Not tonight."

"I keep hearing about the Whinery," Allison said. "What's so great about it?"

"I'm not sure," Daphne replied. "Can you believe I've lived here all this time and I've never once been inside?" She pushed her plate aside, too. "We should go."

"We should!" Allison looked delighted by this possibility. "Can we?"

"But of course!" Daphne said. "We can do whatever we want. I'm sure Ben here will be happy to take us. Won't you?"

Lila watched poor Ben's expression in her compact mirror while she applied her lipstick. He was the very picture of stoic resignation. "Hey, Mom, is it okay if I borrow your car?" she asked. "Mine's on strike."

"If you must." Daphne turned back to Allison. "I hope I'm not out of line, but you really should consider going a few shades brighter with your lipstick."

Lila cringed. "You're out of line."

"No, no, it's fine." Allison rested her chin on her hand, waiting for Daphne to finish.

"Wait until you see how a nice deep coral brightens up your whole face," Daphne told her hapless victim. "I'll give you some pointers."

"That's so sweet of you," Allison said. "I hardly ever wear makeup, so I need all the help I can get."

"Well, you came to the right place. We can

experiment with a few looks before we go to the Whinery."

Instead of making excuses and coming down with a sudden illness, Allison scooched her chair closer to Daphne's. "Hey, do you know anything about false eyelashes? I've always wanted to try them, but I don't have the first idea of where to start."

"Are you kidding? I'm the queen of false eyelashes. I have a *Ph.D.* in false eyelashes." Daphne glanced over at Ben. "This might take a few minutes. You might want to make yourself comfortable in the other room."

"Why don't you drive Lila to her date?" Allison suggested. "And I'll text you if we need you to stop at the drugstore for supplies."

"Good thinking." Daphne started collecting the plates. "You'd be surprised what you can do with drugstore makeup brands if you have the right tools."

"Let's go." Ben nearly toppled his chair in his enthusiasm to escape the conversation.

Lila grabbed her purse and followed him out to the car before any more decisions and directives could be handed down.

As Ben started the truck and headed for Main Street, Lila said, "Thanks for the ride."

"Least I can do after I dognapped Rudi. Thanks for convincing Allison this place is heaven on earth."

"Oh, I think you did that all by yourself." She smiled at him in the shadows, feeling a tiny bit wistful. "I just sealed the deal with the promise of grant proposals."

He rubbed his jawline. "You were always good at figuring out exactly what people want."

"It's pretty obvious most of the time." She wrapped her arms around herself, wishing she'd thought to grab a sweater. "Enjoy your new dog. And your night at the Whinery with your girlfriend and my mother."

"God." He tilted his head back as they braked for a stop sign. "What am I going to do?"

"You'll do what you always do. Be their rock."

"I don't want to be a rock," he protested. "I want to go home and watch *SportsCenter*."

"Too late." She directed him down the dark and winding road to Malcolm's house. "Tell Jenna I said hi and don't let my mom have more than a glass and a half of wine or you'll be very sorry. And no matter what she says, don't let her have tequila. Giving my mom tequila is like feeding a gremlin after midnight."

He groaned. "What have I gotten myself into?"

She couldn't stop laughing. "You're showing the love of your life what a fun and happening nightlife Black Dog Bay has!"

"Help me." He appealed to her in a display of manly misery.

She kept laughing. "I think Jenna mentioned something about karaoke this weekend."

"*SportsCenter*," he croaked.

"Don't forget to take pictures and video. I expect my in-box to be overflowing tomorrow morning." She pointed out Malcolm's mailbox. "Right here."

"Hot date in the middle of nowhere, huh?"

"Well, we can't *all* go to karaoke night at the Whinery."

He eased the truck down the tree-lined drive. "You're sure I can't beg or threaten or guilt-trip you into coming with us?"

"Nope." She opened the door and double-checked for ankle-snapping running boards out of habit. "Because I finally figured out exactly what *I* want."

She could hear the low rumble of the truck engine idling as she dashed up Malcolm's walkway. Ben was waiting to make sure she got inside safely. Because he wasn't in love with her anymore, but he would always care. And she would always care about him.

That was the way it was meant to be.

She climbed the porch steps, turned around, and blew her ex-boyfriend a kiss. Then she waved good-bye to her past, rang the doorbell, and prepared to face her future.

Chapter 29

Lila draped one arm along the doorframe and arranged herself in a vampy pinup pose while she waited for Malcolm to let her in.

She heard the lock click, and then the door opened—but only a few inches. "What's the password?"

She leaned even closer to the doorframe. "Aren't you the guy who keeps calling me and asking me to sign his yearbook?"

The door opened another inch. "I might be."

"Well, I'm here on official business. I'm running for student council, and I'd like your vote."

The door swung inward and Malcolm leaned forward to brush his lips over hers. "Come on in."

Ben's truck backed down the driveway to the main road.

"Who was that?" Malcolm asked.

"Ben dropped me off. He's procrastinating going to karaoke night at the Whinery with his soon-to-be fiancée and my mother, but he's not getting out of it. Poor thing."

Malcolm, delectable as ever in a faded Marines T-shirt, looked confused. "He has a soon-to-be fiancée?"

Lila tried to explain the situation with Allison. "I mean, she seems nice enough, but that girl moves pretty fast. She's been here less than twenty-four hours and she's commandeered my dog and my ex-boyfriend and now she's moving in on my mom." She planted her hands on her hips. "I'm trying to be a good neighbor and a good hostess, but I have my limits."

"You've been more than generous." Malcolm led her through the cottage and out to the back deck, which overlooked a small pond and the vast dark forest. At the very edge of the horizon, above the foliage and below the stars, she could see the golden dot of the lighthouse on the north edge of the bay.

He gestured to a roomy rattan chaise sofa set and asked, "What can I get you to drink?"

She ignored this and continued on her tirade. "Promise me this: If she ever asks you to do couture tailoring for her on the sly, you better say no."

He gave a single, curt nod. "I can commit to that."

"I'm serious."

"So am I."

"Good." She sidled into his personal space, so close she could feel his body heat against her bare arms. "Because if you sew so much as a single button of hers, let alone her zipper yoke, I will . . . I will . . ."

347

He leaned back against the railing and folded his arms. "I'm waiting."

She tried to come up with a fitting retaliation. "I will TP your house *and* write slanderous things about you on the walls of the girls' bathroom." She lifted her chin and he pulled her in for a kiss.

"I reserve my services only for your buttons and your zippers," he vowed.

"You better." She rubbed her cheek against the stubble on his jawline. "Speaking of these buttons of mine, will you be putting them on or taking them off?"

He threaded his fingers into her hair and inhaled deeply. She rested her open palm against his chest, feeling the steady beat of his heart, and for a moment, it was just the two of them together, without any pretense or expectation. It felt terrifying and thrilling and tender all at once, and Lila was suddenly suffused with self-doubt. She'd spent years trying to be the perfect girl-friend, then the perfect wife and the perfect lover. She'd become an expert at figuring out what a man wanted from her. She could be sweet and demure or sexy and bold, depending on what the situation called for.

But right now, with Malcolm, she wasn't gauging his responses and trying to anticipate his next move. It was all she could do to contain her own responses.

They kissed and kissed under the night sky, alternately tensing and relaxing as they moved to a cushioned rattan sofa. She had never felt more desired. She had never felt more desire.

"I don't know how to do this," she said softly into the darkness.

He stilled.

"I don't know how to do this with you," she amended. "I mean, if we . . . If things don't go well, and you don't like it . . ."

"I'll like it." He brushed her hair aside and kissed the nape of her neck.

But all she could think about was her ex-husband's expression, so detached and disappointed, as he explained to her that she hadn't met his expectations, that she would never be enough. All the pride and promise she'd once seen in his eyes had been replaced with a vague sense of pity. And then he'd walked away and found someone else.

Just like Lila had walked away from Malcolm all those years ago.

She loosened her hold on him, tracing the planes of his face with her fingers, and decided that even if tonight was all they ever had, even if the two of them weren't meant to last, she would survive. She would pick up and move on and find a way to be happy again.

She knew now that she could take care of herself. She wasn't afraid to be alone. But she hoped, oh how she hoped, that she could be with him.

Before she could communicate any of this to him, verbally or nonverbally, her cell phone rang.

"Leave it." Malcolm sounded so terse and unyielding that Lila had to laugh.

"It's probably my mom, drunk dialing me from the Whinery." She settled the contours of her body even closer against his and resumed kissing him in earnest.

Her phone rang again. And again. And again.

Without breaking the kiss, he picked up her whole purse and heaved it over the deck railing into the high grass.

She tugged off her shirt, then tugged his off, too. He skimmed his hands up her sides and fumbled with her bra clasp and then, just as the lacy straps gave way—

His phone started ringing.

He cursed under his breath, his palm still pressed against her back, and tossed his phone down next to hers.

And then, with the cool breeze blowing and the stars shining down, they finally finished their unfinished business.

"Talk about spontaneous combustion." Lila collapsed next to Malcolm on the scratchy all-weather cushions, her nerves tingling and her heart slamming in her chest.

He gathered her up in his arms, keeping her

warm as the night wind turned colder. "That was definitely worth waiting fifteen years for."

They sprawled out on the wide rattan lounge, still and silent, exactly where they were supposed to be.

She turned onto her side and snuggled even closer. Although she knew she should savor the moment, she couldn't help thinking about the future. "Can I ask you something?"

He lifted his head just long enough to kiss her temple. "Yeah, but you might have better luck after I've regained consciousness."

She smiled. "Does this mean . . . I don't know. Does this mean anything?"

He hauled her closer, until he could see her face. "Yes."

"So I've got your vote for student council?"

"I might need a little more convincing," he drawled.

Lila had never felt like this with a man after sex—playful and passionate and protected all at the same time.

He wrapped his arms more tightly around her. "Are you cold?"

"A little bit. But let's stay out here for a few more minutes. It's so beautiful."

"Be right back." Malcolm got up, located his discarded T-shirt on the deck, handed it to her, and then opened the sliding glass door to the house. While he was inside, Lila got up, too, and wandered down the porch steps to the grass. Her body shivered beneath the thin cotton shirt, but all her senses thrilled as she felt the tiny blades brush her feet. As she stared into the shadows, she heard a muffled chime from the handbag Malcolm had tossed off the deck. Her phone was ringing. Again.

She followed the sound and scooped up her purse. With a rueful sigh, she located her phone and scrolled through her missed calls.

All seventeen of them.

From Ben. From Summer. From several numbers she didn't recognize and one identified by caller ID as "Sussex County Emergency Services."

An icy wave of dread washed away her warm, happy afterglow as she dialed the code to her voice mail and pressed the phone to her ear. Before she even finished listening to the first message, she dropped the phone back into her bag and raced back up the stairs, yelling for Malcolm even though she knew it was already too late.

Chapter 30

"We believe the fire started in the vehicle, then spread to the building," the fire chief told Lila, Malcolm, and Ben as they gazed at the charred remains of Unfinished Business. "Our team is still working, so we're going to have to ask you to stay back."

Through the dim lighting afforded by the streetlamps and the nearby businesses, Lila could make out the hulking twist of metal that had once been her FUV.

"But how?" She coughed and pulled her sleeve over her mouth. The smell of ash and smoke was overwhelming. "How did this happen? My car wasn't even working." She turned and appealed to Ben, who seemed to be handling this news much better than she was. "Oh my God. I burned your building down."

Malcolm placed a steadying hand on her shoulder.

The firefighter's face was streaked with gray smudges. "We won't know for sure until we finish a full investigation, but we think there might have been an electrical short in the vehicle's wiring console." He stared at Lila. "Did you leave anything plugged into the dashboard?"

She tried to remember. Although she'd been here only a few hours ago, it felt like days. "My cell phone charger."

He nodded. "Was there anything flammable by the front seats? Maps, receipts, cardboard?"

"I might have left my coat on the passenger seat. It was so warm outside." Lila flinched, imagining the pink fabric igniting in a sudden burst of flame. Then she remembered the contents of the backseat. "The Bob Mackie!" She slipped on a puddle of filthy water and nearly fell down. "The Goyard trunk!"

"Ma'am, we're going to ask you to stay back."

"I need to check the cargo area!"

Malcolm put both hands on Lila's shoulders and pulled her back. "Stop. Whatever was in the backseat is burned to a crisp."

"But—"

"Lila." His voice was low but firm. "Look at your car."

There was hardly anything left to look at. The heated leather seats, backseat DVD player, endless array of cup holders—gone.

The side-impact air bags, wood-paneled dashboard, surround sound audio system—gone.

The broken backup camera, the engine glitches, the assist steps that had left all those bruises on her shins—gone.

And her mother's couture collection, fifty

years' worth of ball gowns and bustiers and boleros—*gone.*

Now she had nothing. No safety net. No way to keep the promises she'd made to her mother and herself. Their last chance to save themselves from financial ruin had literally gone up in smoke.

"I hope you had insurance for your merchandise," the firefighter said.

Lila didn't realize she was crying until she started laughing. At which point, Malcolm took her into his arms. He didn't try to comfort her or convince her it wasn't that bad. He just held on to her while her whole world rolled right off its axis.

She closed her eyes and leaned into him and felt the cool wind drying her damp cheeks.

"You okay?" he asked.

"I'll be fine." She was surprised to hear how steady her own voice sounded. "But what am I going to say to my mother?"

Daphne had already heard the news by the time Malcolm and Lila pulled up in front of her home. She was waiting, slender and slouched like a reed in a strong wind, on the front porch.

Lila put her hand over Malcolm's on the steering wheel. "Give us a minute," she said. "She won't want to break down in front of a man." The she slammed out of the Jeep and ran to her mother's side.

"I'm sorry, Mom. So, so, so sorry." Lila engulfed her in a hug and braced herself for tears and hysterics and laments that there was no way to save the house now.

Daphne didn't hug her back. Instead, she pulled out of Lila's embrace, got to her feet, and planted her hands on her hips.

"How did this *happen,* young lady?"

Lila could still smell traces of acrid smoke in her hair. "Well . . ."

"Deputy Sanderson said that ridiculous SUV of yours just burst into flames?"

"I don't understand it, either." Lila recounted what the firefighters had said about the FUV. "The electrical system was always wonky. Ben kept telling me to get it checked, and I meant to get around to it, but—"

"But you were too busy taking care of the house and the store." Daphne wrapped one hand around the porch railing. "And me."

Lila hung her head in shame. "I was also too busy to make sure we had inventory insurance." She didn't dare look up at her mother. "Everything's gone and it's my fault." She remembered the note of pride in her father's voice when he spoke of this house, the palace by the sea he'd built for his wife and daughter.

She could hear her mother sniffling, and sure enough, when she finally glanced up, tears were streaming down Daphne's face.

"Well, that's it, then," Daphne murmured, her body sagging against a support post. "It's over. It's done. This house is as good as gone." She gave herself a little shake, straightened up, and turned back toward the door.

"Wh-where are you going?" Lila trailed after her.

Daphne's stride barely slowed as she pushed open the front door. Then she stopped in the front hall to check her reflection in the antique Italian glass mirror. She smoothed back her hair, she pinched her cheeks, and then she announced, "I'm going to take a long, hot bath. I'm going to go to bed. And tomorrow morning, I'm going to call that Realtor and have her list the house for sale."

Her mother's sudden segue into brisk efficiency alarmed Lila more than tears and hysterics ever could. "Maybe there's still a way to save it," Lila said. "Give me a day or two to figure this out. There has to be some other option, something we haven't thought of yet."

"I spent thirty-three years decorating and redecorating these rooms." Daphne glanced around the darkened foyer, her expression unreadable. "Thirty-three *years*."

"I know." Lila's chest tightened as a whole new level of guilt and regret set in. "You poured your heart and soul into it."

"Wrong." Daphne cut her off with a swift chopping motion. "This is—was—my *house,*

Lila. Wood and metal and plaster. Not my heart. Not my soul."

"But you love it," Lila said.

Daphne's expression slackened as she stopped looking at the artwork and furniture and looked down at her hands. "I loved the people who lived here. But your father's gone and you've grown up, and I'm, well . . . I'm not exactly sure who I am these days. But I can't go back to who I was before I got married, and I can't stay here and pretend nothing's changed. This"—Daphne gestured to Lila's disheveled, soot-stained clothing—"is a sign."

"A sign?"

"A sign that it's time for me to move on."

"Move on to where?" Lila could hear the panic in her own voice.

"You know, I've been thinking about that." Daphne adopted the cool, calculating mannerisms she displayed when wearing her glasses. "And I think I'm going to call Cedric and ask if he knows of any vintage clothing dealers who need a buyer. Remember Tara, that woman I almost had to assault for the monokini? I could do her job."

"But she travels, Mom. Constantly. By herself. To, like, London and Shanghai and Dubai."

"I'm not afraid to go to Dubai by myself." Daphne hesitated. "All right, maybe I am, but I'll just have to deal with it. I traveled for work once upon a time and I'll learn to do it again. Because this house . . ." Her voice, her eyes, her whole body seemed lighter. "Is gone." She breathed in slowly and exhaled with evident relief. "We'll call Whitney tomorrow. She can fax me whatever I need to sign."

"Nobody faxes anything these days, Mom. We'll have to scan it."

"Whatever you think is best." Daphne turned to her daughter with a mix of fear and hope in her eyes. "Or do you think it's too late? Maybe I am too old to start over."

"You're not," Lila said firmly.

"You really think I can do it?"

"I know you can." Lila swallowed. *But what about me?*

As if she'd spoken aloud, her mother turned to her and cupped her cheeks. "I'll get to go back to the world I always loved. And you'll be free, sweet pea. You won't have to worry about me all the time."

Lila ruined the perfect mother-daughter moment by laughing. "Sorry, I know this is serious, but you smell like a tequila distillery."

Daphne burst out laughing, too. "We had such a good time at the Whinery. If I had known what it was like in there, I would have been going for margaritas every weekend!"

"Oh boy."

"I've been a well-behaved wife and mother for

a very long time." Daphne managed an off-balance little twirl. "I have a lot of time to make up for."

Lila rubbed her forehead with the heel of her hand. "I'm not sure how I feel about letting you loose in London and New York and Brussels."

"Feel however you want about it—I'm the mother, so it's my decision." Daphne's laugh turned into a diabolical little cackle. "Don't worry; I'll call you every day. Maybe I'll even text. Who knows what I'll do?" She was looking younger and more energized by the moment.

Lila, however, felt suddenly exhausted. "One thing at a time. Let's get cleaned up and go to bed. You can sleep on all this and reevaluate in the morning."

"There's nothing to reevaluate," Daphne declared. "My house, my boutique, my clothes— I know this was never your dream. It was mine. You put your life on hold to help me, but now it's your turn. You're free." Daphne patted Lila's cheek, then turned toward the staircase.

Lila glanced back toward the driveway, where Malcolm was waiting for her. "So . . . does this mean I can go spend the night at my boyfriend's house?"

Daphne looked over her shoulder and followed Lila's gaze. "Oh, it's official? The delectable marine has been promoted to boyfriend?"

"He's very persuasive." Lila hugged her mother

again and this time, Daphne hugged back. "I am really and truly sorry I burned up all your vintage couture."

"Well, look on the bright side: Neither one of us will ever have to tell Mimi Sinclair that her husband buys her fake handbags."

Chapter 31

The remains of the FUV looked even more stark and soulless in the cold light of day. The molten metal frame had collapsed in on itself and the fire department had ripped off the hood and the doors in their efforts to determine the cause of the blaze. Most of the boutique's wooden framework had been consumed by the fire, but part of the exterior south wall still stood, and a snarl of pipes and wires jutted from the ground.

Emergency crew workers were shoveling mounds of soot and debris, and Lila felt a pang as she considered that, just yesterday, this pile of rubble had been painstakingly preserved cocktail dresses and evening gowns and pantsuits.

One of the workers noticed her and waved her over. He tucked his helmet under his arm as he approached. "Are you the vehicle owner?"

Lila nodded.

"Tell me you have auto insurance."

"I have auto insurance," she confirmed. "The car dealership wouldn't let me drive off the lot without it."

"Call your insurance company and tell them it's a total loss," he said. "You'll have to check your coverage, but they'll probably replace your vehicle with one just like it."

Lila exhaled suddenly, almost choking on her laugh. "God forbid."

The man gave her a wary look, then stepped aside as two firefighters approached, lugging a rectangular container that was burned and blackened but still intact. "You're the vehicle owner? Here you go. Everything in the front seat was destroyed, but we did manage to salvage this from the back."

"Is that . . ." Lila tried to tamp down the excitement swirling up, warning herself not to hope. "Is that the Goyard?"

With the workers' help, she moved the trunk to a bare patch of asphalt on the far side of the alley. The hinges and latch had been welded shut by the heat, but someone produced a crowbar and pried off the lid. The exterior of the priceless antique trunk was scorched beyond repair, but inside . . .

"It survived." Lila pulled out the delicate black and lavender lace gown. "It's still perfect." She gazed at the airy, delicate tulle. Not so much as a single smudge. "I can't believe it."

"I can't believe it, either." One of the fire-fighters examined the construction of the trunk. "That thing must be lined in asbestos or something."

"That's how they made 'em back in the day," the other one replied.

"It's a miracle," Lila breathed. Her mother's words echoed in her mind: *You put your dreams on hold, but now it's your turn. You're free.*

Here was her chance to start fresh, without guilt or expectations. She could go anywhere, do anything.

But she found she didn't want to let go of her past and chase new dreams.

She wanted to stay here and finish what she'd started.

"Check it out—you made the front page of the *Black Dog Bay Bulletin*." Jenna waved from the other side of the wreckage, then made her way over to Lila. She had the local newspaper tucked under her arm and a stainless steel travel mug in her hand. "How're you holding up?"

Lila surveyed the destruction spread out before them. "I'm still in denial, which is working out pretty well for me."

"How's your mom?" Jenna asked.

"She's taking it in stride." Lila nibbled her lip, relieved to be able to share her concerns with someone. "Says she's going to sell the house, go hole up with her fashion icon ex-boyfriend in

Belgium for the summer, and try to get back into the vintage clothing business."

"Wow. Talk about bouncing back."

"Yeah. I thought she'd be devastated, but I think she's handling this better than I am, to be honest."

Jenna sighed, then sipped her coffee. "Maybe a fresh start is just what she needs."

"Maybe." Lila accepted the newspaper Jenna offered and skimmed the front-page article. "But she was *invested* in that house. Hours and hours and I don't want to even think how many thousands of dollars . . ."

Jenna took another slow sip of coffee. "Sometimes your biggest investments become burdens."

Lila glanced over at the bar owner. "Oh yeah?"

Jenna straightened her shoulders and put on a smile. "Don't listen to me—I'm just cranky and bitter because I haven't had enough caffeine yet. And I'm on my way to the Whinery to meet a plumber."

"That's never good."

Jenna rolled her eyes. "Everyone got a little carried away at karaoke last night, and a bunch of women stormed the ladies' room and held a mass burial at sea for some of the stuff their exes had given them."

"Oh, dear."

"Yeah. Watches and bracelets and an opera-length string of pearls and who knows what else.

Well, I guess the plumber will know if he can ever fish it all out of the pipes."

Lila wrinkled her nose. "Ew."

"Yeah. And plumbers are expensive." Jenna scowled. "You know what else is expensive? Gold and silver and diamonds. Those crazy broads basically flushed money down the toilet!"

"Not as much as you might think." Lila recounted her experience with the estate jeweler in Philadelphia.

"Well, with the number of freshly divorced women trying to unload their wedding rings around here, you'd think someone would have filled that market niche by now." Jenna folded the newspaper up and marched off to meet the plumber.

"Yes," Lila said slowly. "You'd think."

Chapter 32

Six weeks later

Summer Benson lifted up the layers of black and lavender tulle and let them fall back over her knees. "*Rowr*. I feel like I should be dancing the cancan in old-timey Paris."

"Isn't that the goal of every bride on her big

day?" Lila fluffed the sides of the skirt and sat down on the bed of the Jansens' guest room.

Summer and Dutch had set the date for a Saturday evening in late June. Well, to be precise, *Ingrid* set the date for a Saturday evening in June. Ingrid also chose the bouquets, the menu, and the invitations. Summer's only stipulation was that she would wear the black and lavender Bob Mackie gown—and Dutch would wear a lavender rose boutonniere.

Lila smiled at Ingrid, who was loitering in the doorway with a Virginia Woolf novel in one hand and *Bridal Guide* magazine in the other. "Please tell me you didn't skimp on the photographer, because you need this preserved for all eternity."

Summer swept back her platinum hair, experimenting with different styles. "Don't worry; your mom hooked us up with some fancy-pants fashion photographer who worked for *Vogue* back in the day, and he really seems to know what he's doing. And when I asked him how much it would cost, he just laughed and said he still owed your mother for sweet-talking the police out of pressing charges for some foolery that went down at CBGB back in the eighties."

Lila smiled like the proud daughter she was. "Some people read celebrity tabloids for juicy drama; other people watch reality TV. I have my mother."

"Do you miss her?" Summer asked.

"Every day. But she's much happier since she left for Europe, and she's got two vintage clothes dealers fighting over who will get to hire her."

"So basically, she's putting all of us twenty- and thirty-somethings to shame." Summer dropped her hands, bored of preening in the mirror. "Ingrid, do you want to pick out my hairstyle, too?"

"I'm on it." Ingrid scribbled a few notes onto the back cover of *Bridal Guide*. "I'll ask Shannon next time I see her. She gave Mia a brow-shaping lesson, and they're meeting for pageant boot camp every single day, and guess what they're prepping for the talent portion?" Too impatient to field any guesses, Ingrid kept right on talking. "Mia's going to play the banjo and sing a song about the periodic table by some guy from the sixties called Tom Lehrer."

"Never heard of him," Lila said.

"Me, neither, but the song's hilarious and Shannon says it's really offbeat and retro and the judges will love it."

"When's the big day?" Summer asked.

"Next Saturday." Ingrid dropped the magazine and held up crossed fingers. "As soon as we're done with the wedding, I have to switch into pageant mode."

"You need a hobby," Summer said.

"I have one," Ingrid shot back. "It's called running other people's lives. Which reminds me:

I heard a rumor that Jake Sorensen's back in town. I heard he was spotted by the boardwalk yesterday."

"All those women at the Whinery aren't going to rebound by themselves, you know." Summer glanced at her phone as her text alert beeped. "And of course he's coming to the wedding. I mean, it *is* the social event of the season."

"Ugh. That reminds me: Why'd you invite Mimi Sinclair?" Ingrid demanded.

Lila gaped at Summer. "You invited Mimi Sinclair? Why?"

Summer didn't even look up from her phone. "Because an invite to the social event of the season comes at a price, and the price for Mimi Sinclair is forgetting that her old handbags ever existed."

And suddenly, it all made sense. "Is that why she stopped calling me eight times a day like a bloodthirsty bill collector?" Lila asked. "Summer, you didn't have to do that."

"Yeah, now we'll all have to suffer at the wedding." Ingrid sulked.

"I figured that whatever money you have left could be better spent on, well, anything," Summer said to Lila. Then she addressed Ingrid. "And this wedding was your idea, so try to focus on the positive."

"Fine. If Jake Sorensen's coming, I'm going to make a few changes to the seating chart for the reception." Ingrid looked giddy at the prospect. "Forget the head table; I'm sitting next to him."

Summer put down her phone. "No."

"What?!"

"I'm sorry—I misspoke. What I meant to say is, *hell no*."

"So you're allowed to hang out with him, but I'm not?" Ingrid cried.

"Correct."

"That's such a double standard."

"My wedding, my rules. Deal with it."

"Oh my God, you're doing it." Ingrid gasped. "You're turning into a double-standard-having, curfew-setting, patriarchy-supporting evil step-mother."

Summer nodded. "And *you* planned the whole wedding and picked out the centerpieces. Oh, the irony."

"Don't worry," Lila told Ingrid. "We'll find you a cute high school senior at the reception you can flirt with."

"Don't patronize me." Ingrid set her jaw, glared at both women, then flounced out of the room in a huff.

Lila managed to hold in her laughter until Ingrid was out of earshot. "You guys are going to be quite the blended family."

"It'll be fine. I wouldn't even know what to do with a normal family and a white picket fence. Convention is for suckers." Summer batted her eyes at her own reflection. "Damn, I make this dress look good."

Lila had to agree. The gown fit Summer as if custom-made for her, and Lila couldn't be positive, but she thought Summer might have teared up a bit when she first tried it on last month. "It's just allergies," she had insisted. "I'm allergic to tulle."

But today, Summer was all smiles and moxie. "*Where* did you get this?"

Lila threw up her hands. "I already told you, I can't tell you."

"And *how* did it manage to not burn to the ground when everything else in the boutique did?"

"If you continue with this line of questioning, I'm going to call Ingrid back in here and tell her to start looking for a string quartet."

Summer side-eyed her. "You're bluffing. The wedding is less than thirty-six hours away."

"You don't think Ingrid Jansen can rustle up a string quartet in less than thirty-six hours? You'll look so beautiful walking down the aisle to Pachelbel's Canon in D."

A look of real panic crossed Summer's face. "No further questions, Your Honor." She waited patiently for Lila to unfasten the series of zippers and hook-and-eye closures at the back of the gown, but as the two of them worked together to lift the garment over her head, a small strand of black beads fell to the rug.

"No worries." Lila picked up the beads, made a note of where they belonged on the skirt, and tucked them into her pocket. "I'll have the tailor sew this back on tonight."

"Thank you." Summer succumbed to her "tulle allergy" again. "Thank you for finding this dress for me. I know you've been swamped with selling the house and starting the new business, and for you to make time to get a bunch of beads sewn back on . . ."

"It's no problem," Lila assured her, offering up the tissue box again as Summer changed back into her simple black sundress. "I'm just happy this dress has found an owner who really appreciates it."

Lila carried the dress down the stairs and draped it across the backseat of her new car. She'd used part of the insurance money from the FUV to buy a gently used sedan, which offered ample storage space, a mere half dozen cup holders, and braking speeds and turn radii that didn't require a working knowledge of upper-level physics. She'd put the rest of the insurance settlement into her new business.

The rows of red, pink, and white rosebushes in the Jansens' backyard were in full bloom. Around the curve of the bay, Lila could see a hulking moving truck in the driveway of what had once been her home. The house had sold within forty-eight hours of listing, and now it would set the scene for another couple trying to build their dreams and start a family in the idyllic little town by the bay: Ben and Allison. Allison had apparently been sincere in her admiration of Daphne's decor, and they had made a generous bid to purchase most of the downstairs furniture as part of the deal.

Daphne had been thrilled to turn over her home to someone who would love it as much as she had. Lila was thrilled, too—slightly icked out, but mostly thrilled.

"I'm serious, Alders." Summer followed her out to the car. Tear-spiked lashes belied the steely look in her blue eyes. "The last five minutes never happened."

Lila waved good-bye as she opened the driver's side door. "Never happened."

She backed the car out of the Jansens' driveway without incident, then dialed her cell phone and let the car's hands-free speaker system take over.

Malcolm answered with the two words that had become his standard greeting to Lila: "Status report?"

"Alive and well," she said. "But I've got a time-sensitive sewing situation on my hands."

"I thought you said you wouldn't be needing my services anymore."

"This is the last time. Promise."

"You say that every time."

"Yeah, but this time I mean it!"

"Uh-huh." His tone roughened. "Are you going to be wearing those black boots and the hot leather jacket?"

"Soon," she promised. "Right now I have business to attend to. Meet me at the Naked Finger in half an hour."

The Naked Finger was tucked away in the lower level of the Black Dog Bay Historical Society building, a tiny storefront that required passersby to take a flight of steps down from the sidewalk. The building's owner, Miss Hattie Huntington, had offered the use of the space for the summer after taking great pains to clarify that this gesture was made to ensure Lila's continued silence about the Bob Mackie gown and not out of any misguided sense of community or goodwill.

Thanks to extensive cleaning, minor renovations, and the addition of a few glass display cases, what had once been a basement storage space now served as a cozy resale jewelry boutique done up in soothing tones of blue and cream. Lila had commissioned the same artist who'd painted the Whinery's whimsical logo to create a hanging wooden sign that could be easily spotted from the street. The shop wasn't big or fancy, but it was hers, and she was going to make it work.

She worried, of course, that she should be trying to generate more publicity, more press, more word of mouth to bring in customers, but she had also come to accept that some things couldn't be bought. Some things were just meant to be.

And despite the fact that the store wouldn't officially open for business until July 1, the people who needed her were already finding her. The owner of the Better Off Bed-and-Breakfast had called just this morning to arrange a consultation.

She heard rapping on the shop's glass front door. Her two o'clock appointment had arrived: a bedraggled-looking woman waiting with slumped shoulders and reddened eyes.

"Are you Lila?" the woman asked when Lila unlocked the door.

"I am." She ushered the woman in and handed over the box of Kleenex she'd stationed next to the cash register.

The woman grabbed a fistful of tissues and swiped at her face. "You buy used engagement rings, right?"

"Well, I will, but the store doesn't technically open for business until—"

"Because I need to sell this." The woman slapped a diamond solitaire down so hard, she chipped the glass counter. "It's either sell it or throw it in the ocean, and right now, I'd rather throw it in the ocean, but the innkeeper said I should at least try to get some cash for it."

Lila looked down at the ring, bright and sparkly even in the shadows, and weighed her words. "How long ago was your breakup?"

The woman blew her nose. "Wednesday night."

Lila nodded, tucked the ring into a small padded envelope, and handed a pen to the woman. "Write your name and phone number on this."

"Why?"

"Because you're in no position to negotiate right now." She smiled sympathetically. "I have a mandatory cooling-off period for breakups less than a week old. When you're a little more rested and a little less devastated, we'll make a deal, but for now, I'll stash this in the safe and give you a receipt so you can claim it when you're ready." Lila grabbed a pen and started the documentation process. "Tell Marla I said hi, and if she offers you cookies, take them. Her oatmeal chocolate chip recipe is to die for."

The woman pushed the envelope across the counter to Lila. "I just want to be rid of this damn thing. Seriously, make me an offer."

"In a few days." Lila handed her a business card.

"I'll take five dollars. Hell, I'll take two fifty."

"Which is why I'm not making you an offer right now."

"I *hate* him." The woman paused, her lower lip trembling. "But I love him, too. And I'm afraid I'll never be able to stop."

"Totally normal. You came to the right town."

Another pause. "I can't believe this is my life. This shit is supposed to happen to other people."

"I know." Lila pulled a plastic bottle of water from the carton under the counter. She'd had the labels custom printed with the store's name. "Here, don't forget to hydrate. And please believe me when I tell you that it gets better."

The woman unscrewed the cap of the bottle, her eyes dark and haunted and hopeless. "Promise?"

Lila put one hand up in the air and the other on her chest. "Cross my heart."

By the time Malcolm arrived, Lila was waiting for him at the curb, basking in the warm ocean breeze under the clear blue sky. He parked the Jeep, gave her a kiss, and stowed the garment bag containing the Bob Mackie in the backseat.

"Ingrid Jansen was right: This town is rife with secrets," she informed him as he opened the passenger door for her. "It looks all wholesome and serene on the surface, but underneath, it's nothing but intrigue and scandal and covert ops."

"Covert ops?" he repeated.

"Yes. Hello?" She flipped back her hair. "That's official military talk."

"Right. I feel like I'm back in Okinawa."

"Don't mock me. Listen—that's Summer's wedding gown in the bag, and it needs a quick repair. Just a tiny little bead or two. Shouldn't take more than a few minutes."

He draped one arm across her shoulder and pulled her in for another quick kiss. "Says the woman who won't be doing the repair."

"Maybe I'm not at couture standards yet, but I'm learning," she admonished him. "I sewed that black silk blindfold just last week, remember?"

He moved his hand from her shoulder to her leg. "You did excellent work."

They drove through downtown Black Dog Bay and then out toward the nature preserve, chatting about Malcolm's latest project with Jake and Lila's attempts to find a part-time jewelry designer. When they passed the Alderses' old house, the move was in full swing. Boxes and bundled-up pieces of furniture were piled on the porch. Rudi the spaniel was racing around with a lobster squeaky toy in his mouth.

Lila waved as they cruised by. "Should we stop and say hi? Offer to help them unpack?"

Malcolm's hand inched up her thigh. "Nope."

"My ex-boyfriend is living happily ever after in my mom's dream house." Lila paused for a moment to absorb the reality. "That sounds so weird when I say it out loud."

"Is it hard to see someone else living there?"

"No. I thought it might be, but I'm genuinely happy for them." She put her hand over his and intertwined their fingers. "You know what I finally figured out after selling all that stuff to all those people for all those years? I'm a minimalist. I don't need a giant mansion or a massive SUV or two storage units' worth of designer clothes to be happy."

He shot her one of his trademark spontaneous-combustion looks. "Just you, me, and a blind-fold?"

She laughed. "Pretty much. I have everything I need right here: the amazing guy who hung out with me at the cliffs fifteen years ago, a new business dealing in old jewelry, and the town I thought I'd never come back to." She rolled down the window so she could enjoy the sun and the sea and the call of the gulls. "Who knew the secret to happiness could be so simple? Reduce, reuse, recycle."

Questions for Discussion

1. To what extent do you believe that certain relationships or events in your life were "meant to be"?

2. Lila and Ben's romantic relationship ended after high school, but they reconnect on a different level. Do you think the two of them could have made it work as husband and wife? How important is physical chemistry versus emotional/intellectual compatibility in a marriage?

3. Do you think Ben and Allison will have a happy marriage? Which factors are most likely to determine this?

4. If Lila and Daphne had been forced to break the news to Mimi Sinclair about her knockoff handbags, who do you think should have told her? What would Mimi's reaction likely have been?

5. Daphne considers her vintage couture as archived pieces of her own history. Are

there certain items of clothing that capture significant moments in your life? Are there certain pieces you've purposefully gotten rid of?

6. Lila buys the FUV in a spate of panic and revenge after her life falls apart. Several characters in the book talk about buying material goods as a way of seeking comfort. Can this work as a coping strategy, and should we place a value judgment on "retail therapy"?

7. Malcolm doesn't talk much about his memories of high school. What do you think he was like as a teenager?

8. Daphne and Lila name their boutique Unfinished Business because it acts as a bridge between their pasts and their futures. If you opened a shop to resell some of the most meaningful material possessions from your life, what would you call it?

9. Lila and Malcolm share a moment during which they are terrified not of their limitations but of their potential. Can you think of examples of this in your own life, when the idea of striving for fulfillment is more daunting than the idea of "settling"?

10. Daphne mentions several times that she gave up important parts of her identity when she married and moved to Black Dog Bay. Does one member of a couple typically have to sacrifice more in order for the relationship to work?

11. Lila and Malcolm see the "ghost dog" of Black Dog Bay right after their cliff-diving adventures by the point. Why do you think the dog appeared at that particular moment? What specifically had just changed or developed between the two of them?

About the Author

Beth Kendrick is the author of *Cure for the Common Breakup*, *The Week Before the Wedding*, *The Lucky Dog Matchmaking Service*, and *Nearlyweds*, which was turned into a Hallmark Channel original movie. Although she lives in Arizona, she loves to vacation at the Delaware shore, where she brakes for turtles, eats boardwalk fries, and wishes that the Whinery really existed.

Connect online.
bethkendrick.com
facebook.com/bethkendrickbooks
twitter.com/bkendrickbooks

Center Point Large Print
600 Brooks Road / PO Box 1
Thorndike, ME 04986-0001 USA

(207) 568-3717

US & Canada:
1 800 929-9108
www.centerpointlargeprint.com